I0687299

A DESTINY FORGED BY DANGER & DESIRE

By
Ash Stone

Copyright © in January 2013

ISBN - 978-0-9922076-1-8

By

Ash Stone

Book 1 of 4.

This book is PG rated.

For the Adult version, please consult the Author's website

http://www.ash-stone.com

(ash dash stone)

Contents

Dedication

This book is dedicated to my childhood friend and husband, Iain. Thank you for giving me the inspiration, finances and your patience to write this book. I am grateful that the stars, universe, God, Cupid or whichever divinity or Deity it was, that predetermined you to be my Destiny.

Preface

I wanted a challenge as a reader and challenge you in return. I wanted you to experience their adventure. A story to remember! And characters to inspire and motivate you.

The Capital series is just that. I love realistic books that have a little of everything in it. So I wanted to give you one with mystery, thrills, action, adventure, comedy, drama and a little erotic sizzle. It is not just one genre. It is a mash up of fantastic fiction while you delve into the hearts & minds of Taber and Silka. Are you ready to be challenged as a reader? Go on! Break all the rules with me, you rebel you.

Prologue

Spending summer and winter vacations together was nothing new for the Blake and Fontein families. They had become close friends when their only children were in school together. By the time the kids were in the fifth grade, the parents were the best of friends.

Taber Blake was a year older than Silka Fontein, but they had ended up in the same class, when he was held back a year before starting first Grade. The youngsters, however, merely tolerated each other's company during vacations and holidays like Christmas. They played together predominantly because there were no other kids to play with at the places they went to. Even though they played and fought like adoring siblings on these 'family' excursions, during school they did not give each other the time of day. Long after both children graduated their parents continued what they considered time-honored traditions, without the kids. The friendship had proved both beneficial and rewarding over the years, as the Blakes and Fonteins helped each other with their privileged contacts to further their businesses. By the time the kids were in high school both families had successful businesses and were substantially wealthy.

Don Blake, Taber's handsome father, acquired a massive contract for his distribution company and now had numerous warehouses, trucks, and an equal number of employees to ensure deliveries to all of the large fast food chains on the continent.

Silka's father, Ted Fontein, had started a small insurance firm with the help of an inheritance from his wife's wealthy family, which he grew into one of the most respected insurance and investment firms in the country. While both men had acquired wealth and renown in their careers, their wives reaped the benefits of their success.

Tabitha Blake and Lucelia Fontein were on every school event committee and on the school board. They enjoyed luncheons, charity functions, fashion shows, social engagements, not to mention frequent shopping sprees and spa dates. No one could understand the bond between Lucelia and Tabitha as they were complete opposites.

Tabitha was tall, thin, had long dark hair, and dark eyes. Her pale skin had a natural, healthy glow. She carried her years well and she looked much younger than she actually was. You would never have said that she was a grown woman like Taber's mother. She was always cheerful and positive too.

Lucelia had tanned skin, with platinum blond hair, blue eyes and she was shorter than Tabitha. Her hair was always styled in a long bob and had not changed color or style in decades. She was still a very attractive woman, but her tendency towards the dramatic made her unpleasant to associate with. This was especially true for her poor daughter Silka.

Silka never knew how much the Blake's and Fontein's needed each other, until now.

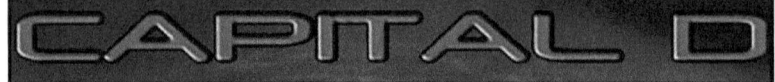

Chapter 1

Silka was not looking forward to going home after a six
year break from her mother. They had phoned each
other on a monthly basis. The conversations consisted of
Lucelia bemoaning and sulking over her lot in life, while
Silka made the right noises and asked the right questions.
Once she had hung up the phone, after eventually
reassuring her mother with some affirmations and
consolations, it took days to lift her own spirits again.
Her mother was an emotional refugee. Always a victim -
ever such a saint - she was never wrong - always
innocent. She was negativity on a stick. Drama Queen
was the understatement of the century!

Now, after all these years, circumstances had led her
back to the city she had grown up in. Being in the same
city as her mother did not make her feel all warm and
fuzzy inside. Thankfully she had already acquired a loft
near town. She would move there after a night at the

family home, to escape her mother's 'poor me' echoes in the suburbs.

The taxi driver that had been waiting outside blew the cab's horn. With a last glance at her empty room she closed the door and soon after, was headed towards the airport.

Her job had taken her away from her home, but it had become a dangerous and emotional occupation she no longer enjoyed. She was happy that this was the last Saturday she'd ever have to spend in *this* country. She had yet to discover whether moving back home was for the better.

More so, she hoped that the five hour and forty six minute flight back to South Africa would brace her for the natural disaster that was her mother. After arriving at the O.R Thambo International Airport's pickup zone, however, all her hopes went up in smoke. She wished it would become smoke signals to send reinforcements for help. Her mother had sent her trusted driver Sam, but he had grave news. Once she settled in the back seat of the car, en route to 'la mansion despair' in Parkhurst, he warned her of the impending cold homecoming.

"Your mother's had a falling out with a friend. She is also exceptionally upset with Don Blake about something." Sam did not know the details, but he knew her mother had been stewing over it for the past few weeks.

Silka was in for a moan session of note.

"You have also been instructed by your mother to be available tonight to attend a party at the Blake's estate." He looked in the rear-view mirror to see her reaction.

Oh butter! Just what I need! As it was, she was already physically tired from packing and the flight, she would be emotionally drained by her mother shortly and now she had to attend a party at the home of an obnoxious little boy. *Just peachy!* At the age of thirty four, she was almost tempted to throw a teenage tantrum of monumental proportions, but opted to take the high road instead and said nothing. Where her mother was concerned, the high road was the only way, unless you were prepared for her 'why do you hate me' routine.

The beautiful summer's day outside could not have brightened the darkness filling her inside. Even the familiar sight of her childhood neighbourhood, with massive properties and their awe-inspiring architecture could not lift her spirit.

As they drove through the gates of 'la mansion', she realized that nothing had changed. The long driveway with immaculately sculptured conifers on either side set the scene of regal, landscaped and lush green gardens complete with ponds, statues and fountains everywhere.

The massive stone-clad, double story U-shaped building was partially covered in creeping ivy and made it seem intimidating but comforting at the same time. The taxi came to a stop. Silka took a deep breath as she got out and inspected the house.

Huge double doors were nestled under an arched roof by the front entrance. She paid the cab fare and entered the awaiting doom.

"Yep, still a museum," Silka stood in the middle of the foyer, and took in the familiar scent of pine furniture polish. Colossal crystal chandeliers hung in the centre of each room.

The natural white walls offset what her mother dubbed a 'smidge and dash' of contrasting colors in the rugs and the paintings.

From the foyer she could see her father's large library, complete with a cigar lounge and a bar that was situated directly opposite the massive formal lounge to her left. Directly in front of her, two staircases on either side of the foyer were separated by a large double door in the middle which opened into a reception room.

Sam came downstairs after dropping off her luggage in her room and led her into the reception room. *Even her own daughter had to be announced to her 'ladyship'.*

Silka glanced around while she and Sam waited for her mother to finish a phone conversation.

Every room in the house, including this one, was elegantly decorated with antique French furniture in neutral colors. *Yeah! It still looks like something out of a 1940's French, glossy magazine.*

A large set of sliding doors ahead, opened onto an outdoor entertainment area with a spectacular view of the back gardens. It was something they only used when they had guests, much like her mother's hospitality.

The reception room flowed easily into the twenty-seater dining room, which flowed into the sophisticated formal lounge that led to the foyer.

These were the entertaining rooms in the house, which Silka had been banned from playing in as a child. *There was a lot of 'flowing' in this house*, Silka contemplated.

The open plan layout that tied the three entertaining rooms together along with the earthy colors would have given an air of openness, peace and relaxation, had it not been for the elephant in the room.

"Sweetie Darling," said the 'elephant' after Sam announced her to her mother.

"How are you dear?" she exclaimed with emphasis on the ARE. Before Silka could answer anything but "fine", her mother launched into full-on 'babble mode' about the neighbors, her hypocritical friends, the Murrays down the road and the general morbid state of the nation.

"Nobody can possibly understand the distress I endured in these adverse conditions. You have been utterly deficient in your solicitude for what I have been through these last decades," her mother snapped bluntly.

As she continued, Silka wondered if she should remind her mother that she had heard all this before over the phone, or request an eighteenth century dictionary. Her mother was loquacious to the extreme, which Silka attributed to her 'old money' breeding. Where Silka was concerned that particular chromosome had gone missing in the gene pool somewhere prior to her birth. Instead she sat down. And sat there... and sat there some more.

Mildred, the very patient housekeeper, had brought her tea and sandwiches during this tirade, unnoticed by her mother. Long after she had finished her lunch, her mother was still looking out through the sliding doors, making huge gestures while babbling on.

Only when her father entered the room an hour later did she dare move. Her father was very attractive for his age. He was a distinguished grey and his kind, blue eyes and genuine smile, could make even a rainy day seem bright. Her father hugged the breath from her and smiled broadly. Even though she was wearing heels, the top of her head only reached his chin.

"Silka, Silks...look at you all grown up," he shook his head in disbelief. "How I have missed you."

"Hi, daddy, I have missed you too. Nobody told me you were here," she said, glancing at her mother. *She could have done with his presence ages ago.*

"I was busy upstairs in my study. Forgive me for not coming down sooner," he immediately interjected and diffused the nuclear missile her mother was about to launch at her.

"How is work?" he asked inquisitively about a subject Silka did not like to talk about.

"Oh! The same old, same old. You look well, Daddy. What have you been up to? "

"I have been splendid, my dear. I have recently won every tournament at the Country Club," he boasted about his golf. When he smiled, his eyes smiled too. It was something Silka never grew tired of. She loved that.

"Oh! For heaven's sake," her mother interrupted. "It is very unbecoming to sing your own praises, dear. People shall think you injudicious," she reprimanded him.

Silka wanted to remind her that he was speaking to his own daughter, but was interrupted.

"Why don't you go get some rest, little one? I shall call you when we need to leave." Her father kindly insinuated that she had better take cover and wait out the enemy until the party.

Right...the party at the Blake estate. Damn! I'm sure my darling mother would undoubtedly remind me of my obligation and inform me of the embarrassment I would cause her if I refused to go. Yep...high road again!

Chapter 2

---*SILKA*---

She spent the afternoon pretending to sleep. Silka only came downstairs again after she had managed to squeeze into one of her old evening gowns and was ready to go to the party.

"I suppose that will do," Lucelia scanned Silka over one last time as they made their way to the car.

"It will have to mother. My only other alternative is a straight jacket." From the moment Silka had stated that, she had wished she had captured the moment on her iPhone. The look on her mother's face was priceless and so was the silence as they squeezed into the back of the chauffer-driven Mercedes. Her victory was short-lived as her thoughts soon turned to the party.

Although she had not thought of the Blakes in a long time, her memory of them was fond and she loved them. Don and Tabitha Blake always referred to her as the daughter they had never had. As for Taber, they called him Tay for short and he was a spoilt brat if there ever was. She endured him, but resented that he had always got his own way, even with *her own* parents. All he had to do was give a long, whiney 'moooooommmmm' and she would have to yield possession of the toy he wanted or accept defeat in the game.

As they grew up and became teenagers, he morphed into a typical obnoxious jock and hung out with the cool crowd. She was always invited to his parties as a courtesy, but no one ever paid any attention to her. She was fine with that. She would go so as not to offend his dear parents. During those parties she sat at the far side of the room watching them graze on food and drink themselves into a new blood group. She always kept her cool and looked in control and relaxed in the circumstances. The Blake estate, after all, was like a second home to her with all the special holidays and family vacations they had spent together.

She was also not intimidated or pressured easily. Any corny one-liner advances from horny jocks or snide remarks from the cool crowd were met with a smile and a quick disarming remark like, "Did you get that line from a bubblegum wrapper?"

Her grace, wit and intellect were something she had inherited from her father.

"Theodore, darling," her mother pronounced almost breathlessly en route to the Blake estate. This was normally the part when Silka wanted to scream that her father's name never had been nor ever would be,

Theodore. His own birth certificate stated his name to be Ted. Just T.E.D!

"Please do not let Mrs. Thomas-Duvall in my presence tonight. My nerves are in no condition for that ostentatious woman. I shall not be made a fool of, Theodore. I absolutely forbid it," she commanded.

Her husband looked into her eyes and with a slight sigh, duly responded, "Lucelia love, you cannot possibly be made a fool of looking the way you do tonight. For whatever Mrs. Thomas-what's-her-face has to say, I assure you, no one will give her much consideration or regard."

His grace and calm 'under fire', made her grin and glow in delight. If Lucelia had been any happier, they'd have to commit her.

The Blake estate was spectacular. The property consisted of the main, double-storey mansion with six bedrooms, three servant's quarters, two guest houses, a boathouse, a helipad and a tree house. The main house from the front boasted tall pillars, bold architecture and big cottage pane windows. It looked like a scene from Gone with the Wind or a modest replica of the White House. The driveway circled around a massive fountain.

The Blakes never did anything by half measure. As they entered the ballroom and stood on the platform by the wide stairs leading down to the ballroom floor, their ears were filled with modern music which played in the background. The laughter and chatter of the guests that packed the hall, along with the clinging of glasses were familiar sounds she had heard so often in her life. There were waiters serving champagne among them on the ground level. Young waitresses carried trays laden with canapés to snack from.

There was a bar along the side of the left wall with a shiny, stainless steel countertop. The barmen served every single drink known to man in every color of the spectrum.

Along the white walls behind the bar, black and white photographs of a male model were elegantly spaced.

At the very back of the room a DJ had set up shop. He didn't have the usual smoke, mirror balls and lights you'd expect. Instead he had only his consol and behind him, a large white screen. A projector suspended from the ceiling, displayed a slide show. Silka barely recognized the pictures of her as a child, taken during family holidays. Every photo was of her doing something at some place she barely remembered. For a moment she was overwhelmed at the gesture by Tay's parents. Her eyes lit up and the happiness she felt made her heart swell.

The right side of the hall revealed double glass Italian doors that led to an equally impressive concrete patio that followed concrete steps to the Lake side of the garden. They had spent many summers swimming and water skiing on the lake.

"Could this be her?" asked Tabitha, as she joined them at the top of the stairs. She was dressed in an elegant cream Chiffon gown with soft flowing sleeves to her elbows. The dress hugged her curves and tapered at the bottom, complimenting her pale skin tone and thin physique. The v-neck elongated her oval face. Her hair was made into an elegant up do and soft curls caressed her cheeks down to her shoulders. She looked like a Greek Goddess. Even for her age, nothing would permit any reference of mutton dressed as lamb. Her makeup was flawless and her teeth pageant ready. She pulled the look off, despite her age and much to all the other older women's dismay, as could be seen on their faces when they passed them.

"Sweetie, darling, hello, but of course this is Silka. Say hello, darling," her mother implored Silka with an icy smile.

"Hello, how are you?" responded Silka, happy to oblige and leaned forward to give Tabitha a generous kiss and hug.

Her mother's blue satin gown looked more like a straight sack, covering her arms, figure and legs, but Silka knew Tabitha could put a positive spin on anything.

"You look stunning!" she complimented Lucelia on her blue evening dress as she kissed Lucelia and Ted to welcome them.

"Thank you for hosting us," Lucelia responded with more kindness this time after that compliment.

"Taber heard of your homecoming and invited a few friends," Tabitha gestured to the masses below, "so you will know some people your own age in town."

Few? Silka smiled at the gesture, knowing his mother had made him do it, but nonetheless she would endeavor to thank him.

"He is here somewhere," Tabitha managed before Lucelia led her away to discuss a matter of grave importance, viz the current disposition of a certain Mrs. Thomas-Duvall. They met up with some other ladies their age to which a competition between air kissing and ass kissing ensued.

---

*T*aber had noticed their entrance immediately and could not contain his curiosity about the lady that escorted the Fonteins. He contemplated going to them, but somehow lost his ability to breathe when he looked at her. She was drop dead gorgeous. Her hair was long, softly curled and brown with lighter shades in some places, the kind of highlights not obtained from foils and chemicals. Her eyes were bright blue and she had long lashes. She had a soft glowing skin in a healthy medium bronze tone. A delicate nose, contoured cheeks and soft red lips completed her stunning face. She wore a red fitted halter neck gown. Her feminine shoulder line was perfectly accentuated by the halter neck. Even with the dress on, he could see she had the perfect figure, unlike the stick figures they considered models on the runways. Her long slim legs and arms were muscular and toned. Her breasts looked as if they had been sculpted by an artist. They contoured down to her small waist, which curved out to her rounded hips.

Hourglass figure was his first impression and it had been a while since he had seen a woman with curves like these. Most women obsessed with their weight ended up with no hips or waistline at all. She had the body of a yummy sex siren, he finally decided. It took a few minutes to gain his composure and go to them.

By the time Lucelia had dragged his mother away, he met Silka and Ted as they reached the bottom of the stairs.

"Good evening," he greeted smoothly.

---Silka---

His hands were behind his back, his stance almost military, but the kind grey eyes that bored into her alluded to something soft and caring. Silka had noticed that his short, dark hair was styled and shiny but not gelled (much to her relief). His dark brows framed his beautiful grey eyes perfectly. Underneath his straight nose, dark stubble made his soft pink lips stand out. They were the most perfect lips she had ever seen. The five o'clock shadow failed to hide his perfect complexion and the dimple on his chin. His cologne teased its way to her nostrils and cast an enchantment, begging her to inhale deeper. His face was slim, but still masculine. Underneath his tux she could see he was well-built. He was as tall as her father. *Yep, I'll tap that.* She looked up into his eyes again. It was then that she realized! The photographs were of him and not some anonymous male model. *Ego anyone!*

"Good evening Taber," she responded coolly, but very pleased with herself to catch him at a disadvantage.

"You remember Silka?" Ted enquired. Very slowly Taber lifted his gaze from her and addressed her father with a firm, but kind two-handed handshake. Her heart pounded progressively faster as he gazed back at her, this time with an excited, wicked glow in his eyes. Fortunately she knew how to keep her heart rate under control, by slowing down her breathing.

"Always a pleasure to have you here, sir, not to mention the company of your lovely daughter." He took a pause as if to catch his breath.

"Please make yourself at home and enjoy the party. Excuse me, but I have to welcome some new guests," he said before he slowly swaggered to other couples.

Just then Don Blake appeared. *What, are they playing relay or are they telepathic? Tag...you're it....it's your turn...no shit.*

"Don, old friend! It is nice to see you again!" Her father greeted him with a warm hug and a firm handshake. Don gave a quizzical look towards Silka.

"Forgive my manners, old pal, but last I checked, you were still with, Luciferia...Un-fairy godmother of my son. Wherever she is, don't let her catch you with the beautiful, future Mrs. Alimony over here."

Both men giggled like naughty school boys. Silka remembered Don well. She always thought something about him was appealing. His good-humored nature, tall physique, green eyes and beautiful smile made him very likable. Remarkably his hair was still mostly brown, although many shades lighter from the bits of grey that shone through.

"This, my dear man, is fortunately my one and only daughter." Ted smiled as he gently nudged Silka. Once Don had learned that it was the beloved Silka that had returned from obscurity, his stance immediately changed. In no uncertain terms had he made it clear to her that she ought never to do that to her mother again!

"Your poor parents were beside themselves when you decided not to return from your trip abroad, young lady. It is a wonder your mother is still a functioning member of society. We almost resorted to slipping her prescription drugs to keep her calm and sane," he admonished.

"Well, look on the bright side, at least now we don't have to do it illegally," her father said, coming to her rescue. Both men laughed heartily and started catching up after a few weeks of enforced 'radio silence', due to some remark Don had made at their last gathering, ultimately upsetting the fragile flower that was Lucelia. As usual, they were all clueless as to what it was he had actually said.

"Excuse me," Silka smiled and went to get a drink.

---

*T*aber watched her intently for hours while circulating between his crowds of friends. She glided from person to person, chatting away, making jokes, even though she didn't know anyone - anymore. Everybody responded to her and lapped up her ability to give them her undivided attention. She could make the homeless feel like they are worth a million bucks.

---

*S*ilka went to the bar eventually and waited patiently to order another drink. She hadn't seen so many people in a long time. Where she had been recently, more than ten people in one place was considered an illegal gathering. Silka noticed that Taber was dancing with a five year old girl in his arms, as her parents stood by laughing about the grin on the little one's face. Silka was not the only one staring. Every eligible woman there had their eyes on him and by the looks of them, wished that they were the little girl.

As the evening progressed Taber and Silka kept their distance, but shared subtle glances and stole slight smiles whenever they could.

Neither could believe that the person they had met was the same kid they had grown up with. There was no way they should not have recognized each other. Neither could comprehend how the other had changed so much.

Neither could begin to understand the immediate attraction.

As Silka stood outside on the concrete patio, relieved that she had finally met the who's who of Taber's friends and that they had left her alone, she pondered on all this. The last time she had seen Taber was during the graduation after party. The fact that fifteen years made such a difference was astounding. She would have recognized the chubby, bulky, blond haired, loud mouthed jock, with a big fat dimple anywhere.

Then again we both grew up in the freaky eighties and grungy nineties.

"The last time I saw you, was here at the graduation after party." Taber's soft voice broke through her thoughts. She was slightly startled, but smiled when he stood beside her.

"That was the very same night I decided to let go and have fun. Tony stole my clothes when we all went skinny dipping in the lake. He refused to give them back and offered me a towel instead...right there," she pointed toward the back of the boathouse in front of them.

"It was the most embarrassing night of my life!" she blushed, but smiled at the memory.

"It was the best night of mine!" he responded with a dashing smile.

"That's because you weren't there," she teased.

"Actually, I was about to get it on with Shelly Anderson in the boathouse. When everyone suddenly went quiet in the water, I thought they were coming to spy on us. Needless to say I got up to check and there you were in the water. Your hair was soaking wet and pulled back from your face and shoulders like a mythical mermaid. You had this wicked smile on your face as you gently rose like a goddess out the water and slowly took the towel from Tony. Every boy's jaw dropped at the sight of you and every girl suddenly covered their body parts in shame, even though they were still very much submerged under the water. Every boy wanted you after that night," he smiled with his eyes dancing and shimmering in the dim light. *I was one of those lustful boys.*

Oh Golly! Taber had front row seats the whole time! She cringed inside.

Before she could snap him out of his wet dream with a witty remark, he suddenly turned to her and gently touched her arms. A concerned gloomy look was in his eyes.

"Where did you go?" he whispered in a serious tone, laced with sadness, *as if* he had missed her.

She would never admit missing him either. He had been the only constant in her life for a long time.

"What's your girlfriend's name, she's about to make an appearance." It was all Silka could do to remove the questioning look he gave her.

After coming to grips with himself and releasing her, he muttered, "Amber."

She gave him a look that donned the inevitable 'seriously?' and with that turned to the superficial, tiny, spray-tanned, bottle blonde in a tight-fitting black mini that now stood by Taber's side. Amber looked highly ticked off and made no effort to hide her jealous rage.

"Hi, you must be *the* Amber I have heard so much about," she smiled broadly, gracefully extending her hand.

Amber shook her hand out of pure reflex and challenged, "Really, like what?"

Game on, Silka accepted her challenge.

"About how energetic, fun and spontaneous you are and that you love sports, fast cars and Xbox. A real guy's gal," she finished off with a wink and smile.

"Yeah! That's so true." Amber gushed.

"I'm game for anything. One in a million, right Baby?" Amber cooed at Taber. Before he could answer, Silka, with all the grace and poise of a lady, excused herself.

"Thank you for the party. It was nice to see you, old friend, and nice to meet you, Amber." She turned away and slowly disappeared into the crowded ballroom. Fortunately her mother had decided that she had endured as much as she could from the inebriated crowd. They said their farewells to Tabitha and Don. Lucelia had finally made peace with Don during the course of the evening.

On the way home Lucelia fell asleep, so they had a very pleasant drive home.

---

*T*aber was too busy being dry humped on the dance floor by Amber to notice that Silka had left. He could've kicked himself. He never had a chance to ask her where she worked or lived. He wanted to offer to help her in case she needed it. At the very least, he wanted her phone number. He had no idea when or if he'll see her again. When he heard about her return to South Africa, he showed no interest in knowing anything about her. The party was a last minute brainstorm he had so she could meet people to spend time with. *Anyone but him!*

Chapter 3

---SILKA---

Monday finally came with much anticipation. Silka had moved into the loft the day before and by Sunday evening she was all settled in. She did not have much, but what she had was earned on her own. Her father would not have given it a second thought. If she had asked him, he would have bought her a mansion, fully furnished and equipped without expecting a single cent in return. Her mother would have let him, but would never have let Silka forget it. For that reason and that alone, she was determined to stand on her own two feet. She had bought a used car which she was paying off monthly. It was not anything fancy, but she was comfortable that it included the basic conveniences like electric windows and an A/C in perfect working order.

On her way to work, she noticed a very glamorous looking coffee place. *How convenient*, she thought as she entered and stood in line. In front of her there was a queue of about seven people. They all looked like young corporate types and portrayed the impatience and self-importance typical of their generation. Part of her was glad to be back in civilization. The last time she had been here, she had spent a night with her parents en route to the new job. There was no time for 'meets and greets' or any reunions back then.

"You're not stalking me, are you?"

Behind her Tay managed to surprise her yet again, but it only took a breath for her to regain her composure.

"Hardly, I work across the street, so that leaves the stalking title to you," she replied slowly and calmly without looking at him.

She could feel the enjoyment emanating from him as his warm, minty breath caressed her cheek. His fragrance turned her on. He was leaning into her making every follicle in her body respond. There was an electric chemistry she felt just by his presence. It delighted her and excited her like nothing before.

"I've gotten my morning coffee here every day before work for the last ten years," he responded way too pleased with himself.

"Good thing we are not dogs, or we'd be marking our territories right now," she quipped back with a smile on her face.
Amused by her response, he offered his solution.

"Or we could start a new tradition and have coffee together every day before work."

"Next!!" A shout came from behind the counter. A young lady with way too much make up on stood there waiting for Silka's order.

"I'll have a regular coffee, please," Silka pointed to the menu.

"And I shall have a Latte along with that," Tay duly informed the clerk and threw a bill of an impressive denomination on the counter as he positioned himself next to Silka.

After she gave them their coffees, he took Silka by the hand. "Please sit and have your coffee with me?" he implored her with a look of anticipation normally seen on a kid about to receive his birthday present.

He wore a dark suit and blue collar shirt with a matching tie. His tidy hair, clean-shaven face and that suit made him look like a million bucks. *Bloody hell he was Godly.* He was by far the most striking man she had ever seen. His looks made her heart contract, let alone her uterus.

"Five minutes!" She raised her eyebrows sternly, but then smiled. She followed him to a table in the far corner.

---

*T*aber pulled out a chair for her. She took a seat and leaned back with her coffee in one hand.

Sitting opposite her around the very small, square table he couldn't help but stare at her. How had he not recognized her? How had he never noticed how stunningly beautiful she was? More importantly where had she been? His mind flooded with questions. What had happened to her in the last fifteen years? Who had happened to her most of all? She had a maturity about her which was way beyond her youthful looks.

She sat looking at him, gently sipping her coffee, smiling slightly and slowly blinking. She had always been confident, but he had never thought of that confidence as being sexy. To him her confidence was arrogance when he was young. Since he had become an adult he realized how wrong he had been. The caliber of women he dated was far from confident, trusting or loyal. They were insecure, jealous, whiney, clingy little girls that loved him only as long as his credit cards were at their disposal.

Which reminded him. "How did you get Amber so spot on? She was highly impressed with you."

Silka gave a huge grin.

"I had my fair share of gold diggers. Amber will be anything and everything you want her to be, until the day you marry her. That is when you will see her true colors." She suddenly realized that this was nothing new to him, although he looked as if he had just discovered a turd in his coffee. He leaned back in his chair.

"What have you been up to all these years?" he asked boldly.

"Why don't you tell me about your side first?" she requested looking as if she could melt a polar ice cap.

"Fine. Graduated high school, obviously, fulfilled other obligations, spent a gap year traveling the world, finished university and then went to work for my dad.

Spill it!" He shot a challenging look back at her as he turned the tables.

"Love to, but I am running late for work," she said, glancing at her watch.

He paused for a second. "Very well," he smiled smoothly. As they stood up, he followed her towards the door. "Same time tomorrow?" he asked.

"Only if I get the next round. Thank you for the coffee."

"Not a problem," he said as they stepped onto the pavement. For a moment they stood there staring at each other.

She smiled suddenly, and turned to cross the road.

"Bye, Tay."

"Bye, Silly," he yelled back. Sure enough he stood there watching her glide into the building across the street.

Climbing into the back of his chauffeur-driven car, Taber wondered if she had taken offense at the mention of the name he used to pull out of the box regularly to rile her up. It got her every time.

Silka used to hate being called Silly. She hadn't heard that name in ages. It used to make her angry, but hearing it out of his gorgeous mouth today made her smile. His mouth was all she could think of as she headed out the elevator, into the parking garage, and drove out to the place she really worked at, on the outskirts of town, in a car that was not really hers, no less.

The following morning, she inadvertently arrived at the coffee shop much earlier than the day before. As she entered, there was no sign of Taber. She stood in the queue waiting. She thought she had arrived way too early. Then she thought he might be running late, so waited patiently again. As the end of the line drew near, she wondered if he had stood her up. In time, she got to the front of the queue and in the hopes that he would show up, ordered him a Latte anyway. She glanced around the shop and saw him at the very table they had sat at the previous day, in the far corner of the shop. She smiled and paid for the drinks and proceeded towards him.

--- *T*aber---

"Thought I'd beat the rush." Taber shrugged and smiled. He had arrived earlier and snuck to the table to see her reaction. She hadn't looked around once to find him, until she had got to the counter. She was so in control and self-assured. He had sat there watching her the whole time. Her hair was in a low ponytail. Her makeup was day-time Emmy Award stuff. She had the kind of lips that weren't puffed up like a blow fish. They were in perfect symmetry and looked delectable. She wore a low cut button-up shirt. The buttons over her breasts were so tight they threatened to pop. He wished he could be there when it happened. *Screw it.* He wished it would happen right then. The pants she wore accentuated her tight ass and slender legs. He could write sonnets about her figure.

"Well, thank you," she smiled sweetly, but sounded pleased.

He leaned back in his chair in a sexy pose, looking very relaxed and confident. He was clean-shaven, wearing a black suit with a light grey shirt and dark grey tie. It made his eyes the color of the ocean on a cloudy day. She could swim in them forever.

She had hardly sat down, when he hit the un-pause button on yesterday's question. She gave an extremely seductive smile, which made him pay attention.

"I went to university. Afterwards I went on holiday overseas and before I knew it, spent my time traveling all over the world for a very nice man, translating meetings and other mundane stuff. Recently, I went into private contracting for the company I worked for, which brought me back here."

---Silka---

Pleased with the answer, they continued for the next few minutes talking about 'old times'. Silka was only too happy to engage in the conversation as she really did not want to divulge either who the 'nice man' was or what the nature of some of the translation that she had done had been.

"Who was that friend that you always hung out with in school? You were inseparable. While the rest of us split into little cliques, you guys stuck together." Taber stroked his bottom lip with his index finger contemplatively.

"Oh, you mean Nicole. She moved away after graduation and I never heard from her again."

---

*T*aber remembered her as a stuck-up, rigid prude. Silka and her Paris Hilton equivalent of a BFF that he called 'Nicole Bitchy' were not popular and never tried to fit in. All the kids experimented with something or the other, even the geeks, but not them. They stuck to their nun routine.

"How did you guys never succumb to peer-pressure like everyone else?" he asked sweetly.

She gave a big chuckle. "Tay, you *were* the peer pressure!"

He laughed genuinely at the remark because he'd never thought about that.

"Who was your high-school crush?" he asked as he briefly jerked his eyebrows up. He had never seen her with a boyfriend in school. All the girls used to swoon over him and his friends, but not her. *Curiosity…meet the cat.*

The way his eyes flickered and his naughty smile winked at her, made her squirm. Silka decided to give him payback.

"I didn't do high school boys," she gave a smile so sexy it required an R rating and parental guidance warning.

His heart rate and his body responded way too willingly. *Whoa boy!* He tried to keep junior from unzipping his pants itself and launching itself at her. His eyes went glittery grey as he looked at her with his lips slightly parted. His gaze flowed from her eyes to her breasts. He smiled lazily and slowly leaned forward.

Silka could have jumped his bones right there, her body craved him so much.

"It's fair to say then, that you also didn't have any favorite high-school moments," he made a statement in the guise of a question. He remembered his well. *Graduation after party!*

He looked as if he had just got laid or something. His gaze was much too distant and self satisfied.

"High school wasn't really my thing," she slowly licked her lips. *There you are!* He was spellbound and speechless. She took pity on the poor thing.

"Although I remember some kids and the trouble they got into," she offered as a consolation prize.

He glued himself back together again. The conversation gently flowed to the safety of 'do you remember so and so' and 'the time the lab burned down'? All too soon their time was up.

By the time the next Wednesday came, they had their morning routine down to a tee.

They took turns buying coffee and always sat at the same table. Instinctively people got to know it was 'their' table.

They talked about the holidays they had spent together and their favorite holiday moments. His was the time they went to the mountains.

"We had been hiking and came across the most beautiful cave with drawings on the walls."

She remembered that hike too. "Yes, we did. We were about ten years old and you had taken my hand to help me down the steep side of a cliff afterwards to get to a waterfall. We swam in our underwear!" They hadn't had cares back then. The whole sex thing had still been a mystery to them. Their eyes had not opened yet to the marvels of the opposite sex and their bodies.

Silka told Tay, "I love waterfalls! I had looked for them in every country I had ever been to, to find one that was more beautiful than the one before. I am yet to see a waterfall that disappointed me or that I felt was average."

"I love waterfalls too." He had always promised himself that his home would have a lot of waterfalls when he grew up. Once more their time was up.

Tay walked her to her building and went back to his car to go to work. The half an hour they spent drinking coffee and talking every morning became the highlight of his day. He liked the way she teased and excited him.

Silka spent every night at home, wishing for time to fly by. She looked forward to her morning coffee with Tay. Her day would not be the same without it. Every day they rekindled childhood memories. He remembered things that she had already forgotten. It was nice to have so much in common with a person and relive those simpler times. She loved how they reacted to each other's chemistry and how he turned her on.

The next morning at coffee time, they sat down and chatted away as always.

"It's hard to believe I didn't recognize you at first," Silka admitted to him later on in the conversation.

"I didn't recognize you either," he confessed. "You have grown into a beautiful woman, Silka." He nodded his head and looked at her with sincerity and honesty.

Her smile was genuine and she was pleased to hear him call her beautiful.

"Thank you." She smiled. "You have surprised me by going from an immature blond jock, to a very handsome, kind man," she flattered him. "A bit egotistical, but handsome none-the-less," Silka threw in to keep him in check.

"Egotistical? What makes you say that?" he exclaimed, almost hurt.

"The photos of yourself plastered all over the walls at your party," she smiled.

"Ah!" he said, as he followed where she was going with this. "Those photographs are permanent fixtures placed there by my mom. She would kill me if I removed her first attempts at being a professional photographer." He grinned as his face gave her a gotcha glare.

"And for the record," he leaned forward. "I decided to throw *you* a welcome home party and invited all those people." He drove the nail right in there to establish it was not 'his' party, just to shut her up.

"Perhaps it's not ego then, but munificence," she said imitating her mother, not fazed by his small attempt to outdo her. "Maybe one day I shall return the favour." She gave a wicked sexy smile.

"I look forward to it." He challenged her with a look that made muscles she forgotten she had, clench.

---

*T*aber became unequivocally fascinated by Silka's cool demeanor, intelligence and sex appeal. He felt the chemistry daily, when he looked in her eyes or at her mouth or when he sometimes touched her accidentally. Her work attire was a mix between naughty secretary and kinky librarian. Much was left to the imagination, apart from a little leg showing here one day or a bit of cleavage showing there the next. Her hair was always tied up or held in place with a head band or clip. She had that something about her that made her like honey to a bear. She was hot, sexy and everything he had always wanted in a woman.

---*S*ilka---

He was being the perfect gentleman, opening doors, pulling out chairs and conversing in polite small talk with enthusiasm. Something Silka never thought she would experience from him. Her attraction for him was growing stronger by the day, and not just physically, but emotionally too.

"Why don't I also have a second little brain like most men to sort this shit out?" she muttered to herself when she left him in the street on the Friday. She headed for her office on the tenth floor, across the road from the coffee shop. She worked there doing admin work for the company she was contracted to, when she wasn't doing her other job. She sat there looking out onto the street. Next week she would have to distance herself permanently from Tay. The last thing she could afford right now was a relationship. Her life was complicated enough. Tay was a Distraction with a capital D.

Chapter 4

---SILKA---

The next evening, Silka had to accompany her mother to an art show in town. An up and coming artist was being showcased, courtesy of a friend in the field. Her mother's spirits had lifted some, but as always her mood was very much dependent on others. Silka opted to wear a figure-hugging blue dress that ended just below her knees, with two of her favorite diamond accessories - a bracelet and matching necklace. As she was slipping on her red heels, there was a knock at the door and her mother's voice rang out.

"We are here, darling. I hope you are ready? Goodness knows I shall be very vexed to be late on your account!"

Silka opened the door to her loft. "Hello mother, prompt as usual, I see?" Silka could not hide the irritation in her voice.

Her mother pushed past Silka to inspect her loft for the first time. It was a sizable loft, all open plan, with a small cherry wood kitchen right in front of the room where she stood.

Behind a small granite counter was a small dining room set with magazines, newspapers and junk mail strewn all over it. Beyond that was a very colorful living room, with a coffee table in front of a flat screen TV against a brick wall.

"Dear lordie, do you not know a decorator, child?" Lucelia asked in a very condescending tone as she scanned the rest of the room. There was a door on the left side of the brick wall, which she deduced was obviously the bedroom.

"Perhaps I shall meet such a person tonight at the gallery," Silka said calmly, as she grabbed her clutch by the front door in hopes that her mother would catch the hint.

"Let us not dawdle any longer, dear ... you know how I detest dawdling!" Lucelia uttered as she followed Silka out the door.

They drove in perfect silence.

Inside the 'gallery', people were chatting together and the drinks were flowing in a turmoil of excitement. Everyone clearly had their opinions on everything, from the venue to the sculptures of mutilated women and children, and finally, on the paintings of men with no faces.

"Good Golly, who would buy these disturbing, tasteless pieces?" exclaimed Lucelia under her breath, in exasperation.

"I personally think they are authentic representations of the era in which we live," said one of her mother's friends.

"Of course you do, dear," snapped her mother sarcastically.

Silka decided to go the farthest point at the back of the room to escape the looming, never ending criticism her mother continually unleashed.

Thankfully, Tabitha had joined them and was trying to stifle a giggle, while instilling some form of peace.

The undercover parking lot, adjacent to a shopping mall, had been converted into a mobile studio slash gallery and had a large section cordoned off with white partitioning, turning it into a large white and grey room. There were massive pillars every few feet between the clearly visible parking bays painted on the grey concrete floor.

The art work stood on huge white columns with brackets designed to hold either a sculpture or a painting in place. Silka was not as familiar, nor did she have any appreciation of the arts as she ought to have had. When it came to food, wine, art, music, theatre and history, she was pretty much clueless. Despite her affluent upbringing, she opted to reject it, so she never really paid attention.

"This will have to stop!" Taber laughed as he and a young woman strolled towards her. He had been standing with his back to her, engrossed in a conversation with this woman, when he was made aware of her presence.

"What exactly are you referring to, Taber?" Silka teased, with a smile and batted her eyelids playfully at him.

"Us pleasing our mothers," he smiled back, looking dashing in a suit and tie, obviously aware that this was not their idea of fun. He pointed his glass towards their mothers. Silka smiled and just shook her head.

"I should like to introduce you to the artist, Madison," he cordially introduced her to the young woman next to him.

After the usual pleasantries were dispensed with, she learned that Madison had showcased her art in galleries all around the world.

She was fascinated to learn that due to some uproar over some art at the gallery she had reserved, she was prohibited from showing her artwork there. Until such time as the controversy around the gallery had died down, she was forced to make last minute arrangements, ergo the parking lot studio. Her artwork was meant to highlight the plight of cancer victims, for whom she was raising money.

What pleased Silka even more, was that she had learnt that Taber and Amber were no longer *sitting in a tree*. It bore no reason or consequence, but she was ecstatic about his new single status.

Suddenly, there was a roar of automatic gunfire. Everyone screamed and dove to the floor. Silka took cover behind a pillar. She knelt behind it, hiding herself from the attackers that had burst into the gallery space. She listened as the crowd's screams slowly died down.

In this country where the usual MO was to shoot first and ask questions later, something seemed off. Instead of demanding money or jewels, the four attackers just walked among the crowd. Two Caucasian men with short, black spiky hair and body builder physiques surveyed the people on the left. They could have been twins had it not been for the fact that one was shorter than the other. Their eyes were dark, their noses crooked and their beards untamed. One dark-skinned African man scanned the people on the right hand side of the gallery. He was taller than the other three, with a lean, muscular body. His shaven head glowed under the lights. The fourth man was a young Wesley Snipes look alike. He stood guarding the entrance. They all looked like hardened war veterans. Silka realized in that instant the motive behind their attack.

---

*T*aber was lying out in the open a few feet away watching Silka. At first Silka had looked scared, but as if a light bulb had gone off in her head, she suddenly started scrabbling inside her clutch. *Stupid woman, what are you going to do?* he wondered in a panic.

He saw her undo her hair, loosening it and combing it into her face with her fingers. From her clutch she drew out a large pair of oversized glasses with dark frames and put them on. The lenses were so thick they looked like prescription diving goggles or the bottom of antique Coca Cola bottles. They made her eyes look big and distorted. He thought for a second that she merely needed them to see better, but then she took something else out of her clutch.

As soon as she had set the mouth guard on her lower teeth and dropped her jaw, the shape of her mouth and all her facial features immediately changed. Taber started to crawl to her to ascertain the reason for her instant facelift. He gained a few feet when he found himself staring at a pair of black boots.

"Where are you going, Twinkle Toes?" the shorter twin demanded.

"Just checking that I'm still as agile as I was when I was six months old." Taber got a boot to the back of his head for his troubles. The man's weight forced Taber's head right to the floor. With his boot holding him in place, he cocked his weapon. Taber rolled his eyes. *Here we go!* He was about to go Chuck Norris on the guy's ass when they were interrupted.

"Jeez, this is not what we came for, find the USAID woman!" big brother twin screamed at the gun-yielding asshole.

He lifted his foot, spat at Taber and turned to move towards Silka. He stared at her for a moment, before continuing his search among the remainder of the guests.

After a heated discussion, dissatisfied, but out of options, the gunmen eventually left. The African men spoke in an accent Silka knew all too well. They were Nigerians.

Taber quickly made his way towards her when the coast was clear. "Why were they looking for you?" he snarled at Silka in a whisper so no one could hear.

She had restored herself to her former glory and stood looking around for her mother. "None of your business," she hissed back equally softly.

"If you are in trouble I can help you!" he exclaimed in an undertone. Deep furrows appeared between his eyebrows as he frowned.

"This is not something a credit card can fix, sweetheart, so back off. I can take care of myself!" she snapped back in a low voice.

"Then start by getting better looking disguises, you freaking scared me more than they did!" he responded, trying to sound serious, but failing hopelessly. He looked away and smiled.

She tried to hide a smile. Then, she tried to hold back a giggle. She, too, hopelessly failed, and both burst out laughing much to the disdain of everyone else who thought this attack had been anything but funny.

Seeing the confused faces of the crowd, made them laugh even harder. When they finally managed to regain control, she turned to him wiping tears from her eyes.

"I don't know why they are looking for me, but I am going to find out. Perhaps by Monday morning when I meet you for coffee, I shall have more answers for you. Right now I have to get my traumatized mother sedated."

Taber escorted them to their car and then walked to his own. They were too busy thinking of each other to have noticed the tails they grew on their way home.

Chapter 5

---*T*ABER---

Monday morning Taber waited at the coffee shop with their two hot beverages on the table. He had no idea that Silka was not going to show up. He looked around, wondering where she could be. He didn't know that Silka wasn't even in the country.

---*S*ilka---

She had made sure that her mother received proper care and hopped straight onto her flight. Then she had taken another flight until she was smack bang in the only place she was sure to get answers.

After checking into a hotel during the afternoon, she spent the rest of the day planning her next move, and thought of Taber. She was still awestruck by how he had kept his cool during the 'search and destroy' fiasco. What was it about that man that captivated her now more than ever? Normal men cowered on the floor during the attack and some wept that night. Not him. He was as cool as a cucumber in a day Spa. How was that possible? Perhaps the time he had spent overseas during his gap year, had taught him to handle himself in these situations.

Yeah right! Surely he must have been involved in lots of attempted kidnappings and dangerous situations while partying with the A-List, she teased herself.

She had yet to meet a man that she felt was worthy - a man in control with the power and means to make problems go away. Rich girls don't want men with money. Money is nothing to them. Rich girls want power. She was one of them. That was the secret to her confidence all these years. She deemed no man or woman worthy of a second thought, because they had nothing that interested her. She wanted a man who was not just physically strong, but powerful as well. Men with power always had connections. Those connections assisted in sorting out delicate issues and everything else in between. Her ultimate fantasy guy was a tall, intelligent, good looking, well-built man who became aware of a problem and without so much as a word or a look, just pressed a speed dial button and made the problem disappear. *Poof!!!* Like a fairy godmother, except this man had a magical wand better suited to her 'other' needs. She was dying to play abracadabra with him. Taber Blake suddenly fitted that fantasy description. How the hell had that happened? This discovery was a whole new different enchilada. One she could not afford. She vowed again to stop this thing, whatever it was, as soon as she returned home. Distraction with a Capital D, she reminded herself.

--- Taber ---

He had waited at the coffee shop for hours. The worst scenarios went through his mind about those men at the art show. How had they found Silka? Why did they want her? Had they gotten to her? He was about to lose his mind. He phoned Silka's mother to find out if she had heard anything from her.

"Hello Mrs. Fontein," he said as soon as she answered the phone. He almost expected her to say something along the lines of 'Lady of the Manor speaking', but fortunately she was not that far gone yet.

"What an unexpected surprise, Taber. I hope all is well with your mother?" She could not imagine why else he would phone.

"Not to worry, Mrs. Fontein. My mother is in excellent health," he assured her.

"What can I do for you, dear child?" She always spoke very plainly in his presence. No big words to fly over his precious little head.

He cut to the chase. "I was wondering if you could tell me where Silka is?" The less he had to endure her brusqueness the better.

"I believe she had to leave town on some work related business. She phoned an hour ago to say she was fine." She hung up the phone. She was intrigued that Taber had a sudden interest in Silka's whereabouts after he had not once shown any in the past fifteen years Silka was abroad. They seemed to be on better terms since she had moved back, yet their relationship was conciliatory.

"Clueless," Taber said dryly when he realized she had cut him off. At least he knew she was out of danger and 'fine'. He put his phone on the table and remained at their corner table to think about his next move.

Two men came and sat by the coffee table in front him. Taber thought it odd that they had no coffee in front of them. Another man sat at the table opposite him. He also didn't have any coffee. He was fiddling with a device in his hands. Feeling slightly boxed in the corner, Taber decided to leave.

"Excuse me, Sir," said one of the two men party. "My friend and I are here on business from overseas. We are looking for interesting places to visit for the day, before we continue our business meetings tomorrow. Could you suggest anything?"

"Try the Cradle of Mankind." Taber tried to cut the conversation short. He got a bad vibe from these guys.

"Where about is that?" the other man tried to extend the conversation.

"Google it." Taber stood up to leave.

The two men looked at the guy playing with his toy. He gave them a slight nod and left.

"Thank you, we will ask our taxi driver to take us there." The guys bid him a good day and left as well. Taber was glad that they left. He needed to get info on Silka.

There was only one thing left to do. He had to go and see a friend called Geo. He had protected and saved Geo once, so he owed him big time. Taber made a few calls to get his ducks in a row, arranged for the company jet and flew to see Geo. He arrived on the Tuesday. Geo had a very big apartment in an up-market side of Moscow. He had taken Taber there once after he had rescued Geo from a sticky situation in the UK of all places. Taber hadn't been sure of all the details back then, but he was not in the business of asking questions. The man had needed to get out the country and he had made it happen. Taber arrived at his house the late afternoon. Geo had more security systems and locks than a state penitentiary.

"Geo!" Taber greeted him warmly when he finally opened his door.

"Taber Blake! Good to see you," Geo smiled. He offered Taber some tea or coffee but in the end they drank the national pastime - Vodka. They sat talking about their past, present and future for a while.

"I have a friend. I think she is in trouble." Taber explained the whole story to Geo when he finally decided to change subjects.

"I'll see what I can dig up." Geo never made promises. He had learnt that the hard way, which is how he had met Taber. The man was a legend and he felt lucky that they were friends.

"What's her name?" Geo asked.

"Silka Fontein," Taber responded and could not understand why Geo found her name funny. Silka was a weird name, but not that weird!

"Meet me tonight at 9pm," he said when he managed to rub the amusement off his face. He wrote the name of the restaurant on a piece of paper and pushed it into Taber's hand. "By then I should have some answers for you, Taber."

--- **S**ilka---

That same Tuesday, she was in Moscow and set out to find her old friend, a man she knew would help her discover the reason for that little party of five almost held in her honor. She searched all his favorite haunts in the city, but came up empty. She had known Geo from dealings through her company. They had become close friends and chatted via Skype regularly. Whenever she had been in Moscow, however, he had never invited her to his house. She had a feeling he was a private person. Needless to say she did not know where he lived and no one else seemed to know either. By late afternoon, she struck gold at a bar frequented by Geo.

A barman leaned in close and whispered in her ear, "He is going to be at a restaurant in a part of town popular for its nightlife." He passed her a napkin with the address on.

"Thank you," she tipped him generously and after finishing her drink, pretended to wipe her mouth with the napkin. She placed it inside her handbag and left.

She went back to the hotel, grabbed a shower, ate some dinner and waited for time to pass.

It was cold in Moscow this time of year, so she decided to wear her black 'winter underwear', thick black fish net stockings, long black boots, black woolen pencil skirt and white long sleeved collared shirt. She grabbed her ankle-length leather coat and handbag then headed out the door.

As soon as she got to the restaurant, she sat at the bar near the entrance and waited for Geo to arrive. She was careful not to look around too much and attract attention to herself.

---

*T*aber noticed the minute Silka walked into the restaurant where he was to meet Geo. He was about to go to her when he spotted the four men from the gallery standing outside. They seemed to be looking for someone. They saw Silka sitting near the front door at the bar. He could tell they were concocting a plan. He stopped two waiters and offered to pay them to play a prank on his friends. They were to take a bill to them, and claim that they hadn't paid for their dinner. While the one waiter would argue with them, the other would use his iPad to take photos of their 'confused' faces, while pretending to look up their reservation. As the waiters went outside, Taber immediately went out the back door and around the building to wait for the waiters.

Silka smiled broadly as Geo approached her. He was a short, podgy man, with grey hair. A thin moustache curved over his lips. No one knew his real name. They called him Geo, because he was the National Geographic of the real world and underworld. He was the master of finding and hiding people anywhere in the world. The same applied to 'some things'. He could have located the late Sadam Hussein's hidden treasure stash had he been given the opportunity back then. He had more high tech gadgets at his disposal than most first world countries. The reason being he had worked for all of them and then some.

You could have made an entire alphabet out of the letters from the acronyms of the organizations which had at one time or another used his services - for a generous fee of course. He always made sure they provided him with the necessary equipment, if he did not have it already. Oddly enough he managed to hold onto those things after he finished the job. Boil it down to unsolved mysteries, but this man had clout and guts.

He greeted her warmly. "Silka, love! To what do I owe this unexpected pleasure?"

"I had an urge to see a very old friend and here I am," she explained. She hugged him tightly and smiled.

"As much as I do believe that, I also happen to know better," he squeezed out trying to catch his breath from her hug. "Old friends don't extract bone marrow when they hug," he added by way of an explanation.

"I'm so sorry, Geo. Did I hurt you?" she asked, her voice showing concern.

"I'm almost as big as the globe, dear. It would take more than that to hurt me." He laughed off the guilty look on her face.

"Now tell uncle Geo what dragged you half way across the world to come see an old fart like me?"

"I was hoping an old fart could tell me why my life suddenly went down the crapper?"

He smiled at her choice of words.

"A few nights ago, four men armed with enough automatic machine guns and hand guns to sustain a small guerrilla war came looking for me. Now I am not normally one to play hide and seek, but I got the distinct impression they were not interested in my collection of Barbie dolls," she said coolly.

"The word on the street is that you have gone rogue or AWOL, but," he added, "I have no idea who those men are or why they want you. They could be working for anyone you ever crossed paths with." He looked at her intently.

"That's a lot of paths and for the record, I could never go rogue after everything that the company has done for me," she said with a sigh. Her shoulders dropped and she looked around in dismay.

He could not bear the look of defeat she had.

"Now don't go advertising this, but I am going to help you. Yes, yes, totally out of my 'self serving' character, but I believe you. Come back tomorrow and I will have some answers for you. Right now, get some rest," he softly assured her.

"How do I prove my innocence?" she asked softly.

"One thing at a time ladybug. All in good time." He smiled compassionately.

"Thank you very much, Geo. Bye." She smiled and gave him another hug before she left the restaurant.

--- Taber---

The four men had managed to reach an agreement on their course of action by the time the waiters met up with Taber around the back. The waiters gave Taber his iPad back in exchange for their hefty tips.

Taber decided to wait for Silka in the front, but as he reached the corner, baby twin went past him. They'd obviously decided to surround the building and keep in touch via Bluetooth. This Taber discovered when he turned around to follow the guy who was speaking to someone on his device.

Taber snuck up behind him. He wrapped his arm around the man's neck and held him tighter than a Boa Constrictor. With his other hand he administered the Military version of the Vulcan Neck Pinch. The man could not breathe and struggled aimlessly in pain.

"How did you find her?" Taber said in a low, but clear voice.

"Her…cell phone," he struggled to say in a last-ditch effort to stay alive.

Taber's fingers deftly squeezed the man's subclavian artery. Blood flow to his brain was slowly constricted. He pinched harder.

"Tell me how you managed that!" Taber grimaced with a strained voice as he applied more pressure.

"It doesn't…matter," he struggled out the words, "she's going to be dead soon."

With that Taber realized that he had left Silka alone. His heart almost stopped beating and he could feel the blood drain from his face. He struggled to breathe until the man tried to pull his hand away from his neck. The brazenness of his victim and the threat he had made against Silka suddenly infuriated Taber. He pursed his lips as a fiery frown darkened his face. Taber saw red and lost all train of thought. In his anger he managed to squeeze the man's veins so hard that he fell unconscious. Taber decided not to leave him alive. He grabbed the man's head with his two hands and snapped his neck.

It didn't take a brain surgeon to figure out that they were using GPS tracking on her mobile phone. After disposing of the guy's body, he ran as quickly as he could to see if Silka had left the restaurant. If he'd known then that the guy had lied, he would've displayed a bit more patience. They had inside help. Someone close to her had given them her whereabouts. This person probably had no idea they were helping them.

---

*S*ilka was unaware that they could trace her anywhere in the world. As she entered the street and walked towards her hotel, a sudden urge to run overcame her. The little sixth sense she relied on screamed for her to run. She slung her handbag over her head, and hung it across her chest. Everything she knew told her to stay calm, but that damn voice in her gut screamed again. She turned left at the street corner and had broken into a brisk walk when she heard, "Run!!!"

She looked behind her, because she sure as hell hadn't said that out loud. A tall man was running towards her. She ran as fast as her tight pencil skirt would allow. Behind her, at least half a block away, she heard three of the voices from the art show yelling orders at each other.

The fourth man was right behind her. Her hotel was three blocks away in the other direction. She needed to find a hide-out and quick. He gained on her faster than a cat on water. His hand suddenly grabbed her arm from behind and dragged her into the entrance of a building. When she resisted, both his arms encircled her from behind and dragged her through a push door into the hallway of the building. Resisting the urge to scream, she tried to fight the arms holding her. She lifted her arms up and away from her, then dropped like a sack of potatoes, her dead weight releasing her from his grip. Before he leaned down and tried to grab her again, she turned and kicked hard.

"Jeez!" the man screamed grabbing his chin.

"Tay! What the hell?" she screamed.

"Sshhh!!" Tay silenced her while rubbing his chin. Listening for sounds and satisfied that they were still ahead, he turned to her.

"Come with me if you want to live!"

"Now is not the time to quote movie lines, Tay!" she hissed.

"Baby, you have no idea!" He held his hand out to her and helped her off the floor. She had torn her pencil skirt at the seam, almost all the way to her crotch, so she turned the skirt towards her side. The torn skirt was hidden underneath her long leather coat.

While she was doing that he rifled through her bag and tossed her mobile phone on the floor. It shattered into pieces.

Silka looked at him as if he had just killed her child.

"Time to audition for a marathon right now... And we'll discuss the how and why the first chance we get. Now run!!!" he yelled again and they flew down the long hallway.

By the time they had reached the back door, the front door had pushed open and deafening shots rang out. Bullets ricocheted off the walls around them. Tay and Silka raced up the alleyway behind the building and screeched around the corner to find the most populated part of the street. The gunmen were going to catch up with them at any minute.

Silka saw a nightclub and pulled Taber's arm in that direction.

"In here," she forced their way to the front of the queue, paid their entrance fee and led him down a dark hallway towards the loud music. Inside, was big and dark apart from the strobe lights and green laser lights that flashed and flowed over a massive crowd from the DJ booth in front.

Rave music...great! Torture me more why don't you, she thought.

The massive rectangular space was filled with people, so a quick escape out the other side without being spotted was a problem. She quickly dragged him through some dancing zombies to the corner closest to them in the dark club. She faced herself away from the doorway.

---

*T*aber positioned himself in the corner in front of her to keep a look out for their new trigger-happy friends. She immediately pulled out two hair bands from her bag and made high pigtails on either side of her head.

"Take off your jacket and put these on!" she yelled in his ear over the music and handed him the infamous Coca Cola glasses she fished out of her bag.

He slowly removed his leather jacket while watching her intently.

As quickly as she could, she tossed her jacket over her bag, kicked it into the corner and made him lean against the wall. She shimmied out of her torn pencil skirt, tossed it on the floor between his legs and unbuttoned her white shirt. She lifted it up and tied it tightly beneath her breasts.

She looked the part of a rave girl with two ponytails. Her chest heaved rapidly inside of her shirt with every quick breath. Sweat glistened from her neck to her cleavage. The cropped up tight shirt was showing off her perfect cleavage, and her full breasts supported by the cups of her black bra. The area underneath her shirt to her fishnet stockings exposed her soft, glowing torso, her thin waist, rounded hips and well-defined stomach. A perfect round, indented belly button moved with every breath. She wore what looked like very short black hot pants over her black fishnet stockings. The fishnets wrapped like a second skin around her well-toned legs. Her knee-length stiletto boots curved along the contours of her calves. Never had he seen any woman look as naughty hot as she did right then.

---**S**ilka---

He didn't put the glasses on and instead put them in his jacket and tossed it to the floor. He rolled up the sleeves of his blue open collared shirt to his elbows. As part of his 'disguise', he spread his legs wider and lowered himself against the wall to her level. Taber gave a drop dead gorgeous smile and pulled her into his arms where she stood between his legs.

She could feel his hard leg muscles underneath his blue jeans. She smiled, put her arms around his neck and leaned into him.

Still breathless from the run and the sight of her, he held her closer until practically every part of their upper bodies touched. They stood there staring at each other, breathing heavily, still spinning from their chance encounter and unwelcome guests. Their heart beats matched the *boom, boom, boom* of the music. The tingle and electricity sparking from the touch of their bodies tightened and contracted every muscle they had. The combination of their scents weaved a sensual spell. They stopped smiling as they looked at each other's mouths.

The fast, deafening beat faded slowly as an electric guitar strummed out a hypnotic solo. All the flashing lights were replaced by smoke. In complete darkness a green laser light slowly shone from the ceiling and fanned down to the crowd in rhythm to the slow strums of the electric guitar. Like good little zombies the doped-up dancers all raised their hands and swayed from side to side touching the light. The light reached the corner where they stood and drifted away, leaving darkness.

At exactly that moment Taber kissed Silka softly. Their lips gently touched at first. He pulled away slightly and kissed her top lip. Then took her bottom lip between his lips and gently pulled it. With the next kiss, their lips touched and the tip of his tongue gently ran over her lips. Encouraged by the chemistry and the adrenalin rush,

69

their tongues found each other. They pressed together in a slow, soft passionate rhythm. Their caress and sensual kiss only slowed down for a moment, when they heard a zombie behind them swearing at someone. Their lips still touched slightly, when Taber glanced over her shoulder.

He could see that the men who had chased them were in the club. They pushed rudely through the crowd. One headed their way. For some reason he didn't give a hoot about that.

---

*T*aber kissed Silka with a vengeance this time. His hands explored her body. He palmed her rear, stroked her half naked back, and slid his hands up and down her sides and hips. His tongue explored deep into her mouth as his hands roamed freely and touched her with purpose.

She in turn, stroked his hair. She ran her hands up his arms, down his chest and up his back. The deliberate motions of her hands flowed in a sequence, but not once repeating her touch before. She opened her mouth wide to give him access to explore her mouth with his tongue. They looked every bit like a couple in the throes of a passionate kiss so intense, it seemed reserved for only people high on ecstasy or love. The man gave them a cursory glance and walked away. Out of the corner of his eye, Taber saw the men eventually leave, but could not bear to separate himself from her kiss and her touch.

The last few weeks' sexual tension and attraction had finally caught up with them. All those smiles and looks.

All the clenches, twitches and aches. It all was released right there in the corner of the dance floor. They hadn't even held hands yet and there they were publicly devouring each other like two bears in a fight.

---

*S*ilka was pressing herself hard against his body, turned on by his scent, taste and touch. Only when things got heated to the point where she was about to touch his manhood and he her breasts, did Silka stop the kiss. She rested her forehead against his. Slowly she waited for her beating heart and breathing to slow down. It was a while before they braced for the inevitable separation of their aching, pulsating bodies.

She couldn't let him go further. She knew that once they started touching *those* sensitive, aching and hungry parts that there would be no stopping. She was not into public displays of affection, let alone sex in public places. She had confidence, not stupidity. She achingly, slowly pulled away from him.

---

*T*aber had never felt that kind of need in his life. He couldn't get enough of touching and kissing her. If they had continued a little longer, he would've needed a twelve-step program to stop him. Even though he was not a fan of being arrested for public indecency, he would have done very indecent things to her in that club. Thank heavens she had stopped him. He let her go.

Shocked at what had taken place but certain that now they were safe, they reluctantly put on their jackets, collected their things and left. They walked holding hands and slowly made their way through the zombies and out the club. The streets were busy, but the further they walked, the less crowded it became.

Taber was distressed by what had happened in the club. He couldn't grasp what had made him lose control like that. He needed to shake it off.

As they walked along the streets, he finally broke the silence, "I see you took my advice."

"Advice?" she questioned.

"You changed your disguise and may I say it was a huge improvement."

"Thank you, glad to hear it," she said with a shy smile as she looked away.

"My pleasure. I certainly would have to give you my stamp of approval for your quick thinking in there," he stated sweetly.

"Is that what they call it these days?" she laughed. "You forget who you are talking to, I have known many girls you stamped your approval all over," she teased.

"Those were seals of approval. Stamps are reserved for ladies of exquisite beauty and intellect." He looked at her askew with a sinful smile on his face.

Silka didn't know if she should feel revolted or flattered by that remark. The old Taber she would have blown off, shot down and double-dropped on that one. The new Taber, she was not sure about. Had he grown standards and a moral compass for his 'stamps' during this time and had become more discerning in his taste? Was he genuinely impressed?

When she did not reply, he decided the moment was over and addressed the issue that had brought them to Moscow.

"What brings you to Mother Russia and don't tell me it's because you ran out of Vodka?" he asked solemnly.

"You should Google the concept of time and place," Silka casually informed him. After a pause she sighed and added, "To see a friend. And you?"

He answered carefully, "to see a friend." This came out half-heartedly.

"Does your friend have a name?" she asked softly.

"No, but we call him Geo," he confirmed her worst fears. He could tell she knew Geo as well. He was about to ask how she knew Geo when she interrupted him.

"Are you with the company?" she asked suspiciously. She was also curious as to how he knew Geo, but this was by far the most important question to her.

"Depends on which company you are referring to?" He was beginning to think they had more in common than a childhood.

"Let's get some coffee. We need to talk," he said grimly.

"I think this conversation is better suited to the privacy of my room." She wondered how Taber had got to her before they had.

Chapter 6

Once they entered the hotel room, she gestured for him to make himself at home on the couch in front of the TV. He looked as if he was expecting a killer ninja to jump through the window at any minute. The frowns on his forehead suggested that something had rattled his calm demeanor. For the first time in his life, he seemed suddenly very scared. The thought made her heart drop to her knees. She had grown utterly fond of him. More recently, after the way he had floored her in the club with his gentleness and then his fiery passion, she was hooked.

---

*T*aber had a very bad feeling about her suddenly. The woman he thought she was had rapidly become a stranger. He had no idea why she was concerned about some company or why men were trying to kill her. She was Dangerous with a Capital D.

"Let's start with my details seeing as you're in ankle deep now," she offered in the hope of making him feel more comfortable and sat next to him on the couch.

"I spent several years at University studying political Science, law and many languages. The holiday I took after that, started off in Ibiza and finished in New York... loooong story! I was in front of this restaurant near Time Square, when a man ran into me. At the same time another man in a suit came out of the restaurant with some colleagues. The crazy man stormed at him and started rambling away in a foreign language that the suit clearly didn't understand. I jumped in and translated for him and soon the whole issue was cleared. The suit, impressed with my conflict resolution and communication skills, offered me a job. In a matter of weeks he had sorted out all the necessary paperwork and accommodation issues and started me off as his assistant. His name was Joshua Stonewall and he was the Mission Director for the U.S Agency of International Development at the time. The USAID organization provides assistance after natural disasters and epidemics and also assists with economic growth, promotes political stability and ...."

Taber interrupted her, "I know who they are. I deal with them too."

Her obvious shock matched his and for a moment they sat in silence.

Eventually she dared ask a lingering question that nagged like her mother on a bad day. "Did they send you after me?"

He realized that she had gone as white as a sheet.

"Heaven, no. No, they did not," he re-iterated before continuing. He looked deeply into her eyes. "I just knew you were in trouble and flew here in the company jet to see Geo to fish for information. You had me worried sick when you did not show up for coffee. Thankfully your mom told me you had left town. She didn't mention you had left the freaking country!" he scolded her and immediately took a deep breath.

Silka shook her head and then looked apologetically at him. "Yeah, about that…I am sorry I didn't tell you where I was going, but I couldn't risk you getting involved," she explained.

"Sorry to say, but your plan back-fired." He smiled in acceptance of her apology. Truth be told, had he been in her shoes, he would have done exactly the same thing.

Silka smiled and calmed down. All of a sudden she looked like someone who had just come out of a day spa. Her entire posture relaxed. She fell back onto the couch.

"What did you do in the company?" he asked in a soothing tone.

"I did the PA thing. I became an Administration Operations Specialist, doing things like analyzing and reviewing financial reports, monitoring office communications, and so forth. Then I ended up going on missions once I received the correct training and cleared the correct GS levels... and you?" She cocked an eyebrow at him and listened carefully to his reply.

"My company is in partnership with them to supply logistical and other support in case they need it."

Hmmmm, it was 'the other' that she was more interested in, but she let it go for the moment.

"What did Geo tell you?" he asked staring into the distance.

"Not anything useful. There's a rumor that I had betrayed the company," she said softly. After a while she added the explanation she owed him. "At the gallery... I thought those men were looking for a rich girl to abduct for ransom. I tried to make myself as unattractive as possible. I didn't know until the one mentioned USAID that they were looking for me. I did not betray the company and I still don't know what's going on." She spoke softly but with sadness in her voice. Her eyes were closed in defeat.

Pleased with her answers he felt better now that she had divulged the details she had been so secretive about in the beginning. He leaned back on the couch next to her. He could understand why she was rattled by the mere mention of the word company. His heart ached for her. She was in deep trouble. The situation seemed unnatural. Beautiful women like her were meant to *be* trouble, not be neck deep in it.

"You still don't know who those guys are?" He looked at her as he softly confirmed, more than directed the question at her.

"Oh! The four nice 'gentlemen' with their impressive set of toys?" she asked sweetly, to lift his mood.

"Three," he interrupted her, and by the look in his eyes she knew exactly how four had become three.

"How and what do you know about self-defense and attack techniques?" She seemed visibly upset at the thought of him taking on an armed assailant.

"Battlefield Bad Company," he said smugly.

"You insult my intelligence," she giggled at his platform game response, but stared him down to break his silence. Before she could push him for answers, he pulled one of her own stunts on her.

"I have to go, it's late. I shall see you here tomorrow morning at 8 am. We'll go to see if Geo has lost his mojo."

She smiled at the word as if she had never heard it before. Mojo was by far the one thing Taber didn't lack. He oozed it in abundance - so much so, that she still hid the evidence from their heated exchange at the club.

"Well, if he has, I know a guy who can easily teach him the meaning of mojo." Her eyes lit up as memories of the club played again in her mind. She did not want him to go. They had just learned more about each other. Despite the danger, she felt closer to him. She was still rocked from that kiss. It was the most intense experience she had ever had. It scared her, but she wanted it again. She didn't care that it was wrong.

---

*T*aber felt her desire and hell…he did not want to leave! All he wanted was to take her and make love to her on that couch..

She sat there silently while her beautiful blue eyes looked deep into his soul.

He knew that if he stayed she would eventually have pushed him for answers about his skills and probably not want to touch him afterwards. He stood up and when he reached the door, looked back at her again. She was looking half amused and yet somehow hurt. She wanted him, and he wanted her, but without the lingering questions right now. He'd tell her in his own good time, maybe, when this was all over.

He dragged his hand through his hair before giving an almighty sigh. "Someday… someday soon, you will see the extent of my mojo," he promised. "Good night," he said quietly and closed the door behind him.

The next morning, Silka was drying her hair after her shower when there was a knock at the door. She looked through the peep hole and saw Taber standing there. It was not even seven o'clock yet. She fastened her robe and opened the door.

"He's dead!!!" Taber blurted out, as he walked into the room, taking his coat off and closing the door behind him.

"Geo was killed last night." He rubbed his hand over his freshly shaved jaw.

Shocked, Silka went and sat down on the bed in stunned silence. Her eyes welled up with tears and a wild, bewildered look questioning the whys and hows, appeared on her face. She started shuddering and looked away.

"Shhh, hey, baby, no, please. Do not do this to yourself. It's not your fault, Silks. That kind of thinking is just useless. Shhh," he said tenderly, while he sat next to her and pulled her into his arms and gently stroked her.

Taber had heartfelt, deep compassion and empathy for her. She was so strong and composed, but everything about her suddenly seemed so fragile. He knew all about loss and fear. He could understand what she was going through. Empathy. To the self-entitled brat he used to be, this sort of thing was as foreign as wireless internet to a WWII vet. He was also very afraid for her. It seemed no matter where they went, danger followed. He needed her. She had something about her no other woman could compete with - that special something that turned him into a weak, ankle humping Chihuahua one minute and a strong, fierce Doberman the next.

He wanted her more than anything in the world, but that was not in the immediate future. The need to get his head in the game was paramount. He was not going to think about last night. First, get her somewhere safe or die trying.

81

*S*ilka held him around his waist. His muscles were hard, but she could also feel the softness and warmth of his skin. The soft, clean smelling fabric of his grey Cashmere jersey caressed her cheek. His black jeans against her thigh concealed the muscles she had felt the night before.

Alas the sense of loss, guilt and sadness she felt could not be replaced by those thoughts. She cried for some time, while he held her close to him and gently shushed her, stroking her hair and back. When she finally regained her composure, he gave her a peck on her forehead.

"We should leave before they start asking questions," she finally managed.

"Way ahead of you baby girl, grab your stuff. I have a taxi waiting to take us to my jet."

She stood up, slipped on a warm dress in the bathroom and packed as quickly as possible. Once they had climbed into the taxi, they sat in silence all the way to the airport. *Freaking fabulous!* she pondered. The company thought she had betrayed them, she had people who wanted her dead, a good man had been killed and Taber had officially become a co-worker. Silka could not help feeling utterly depressed. Since discovering he also worked for the USAID, despite all the chemistry, the sparks and the electricity they had, they could never be more than friends because of company policy. She wanted him like a desert needed water after last night.

Hopeless was not a word she had thought possible in her vocabulary, until that day.

At the airport, Silka decided the best option was to go to see her old boss in Washington DC.

---

*T*aber wanted to hear nothing of it.

"I am going with or without you. I cannot run for the rest of my life. I need to sort this mess out and clear my name," Silka said forcefully.

"Fine! Where you go, I go. If anything happens to you, there is no way I am explaining it to your mother." He shook his head to bring home that statement.

"Roger that, sergeant major," she mock saluted him and turned to walk. "Let's go, bodyguard." She teased looking back at him over her shoulder.

He playfully scowled at her first, but then bit his lip as he smiled.

They had to wait for a while in his company jet, because the pilot wasn't ready as they had arrived too soon. The jet had seats along the side with tables, rotating swivel chairs, and sleeper couches at the back, all covered in soft cream leather.

"What are you hoping to achieve by going to your old boss in DC?" Taber asked, as they sat opposite each other in swivel chairs.

"I worked for him until my contract expired recently and I started a new contract with another division. He might be able to shed some light on why the company thinks I have gone all ape shit." She smiled. "If nothing else, he could at least help me to clear my name, because he knows about every one of my missions and will know exactly where this might have stemmed from," she continued.

"I am sure we'll have this sorted out quickly," he reassured her.

"Well, perhaps it's one of those company politics issues where some bitchy woman has spread a rumor. Wouldn't that be great!" She sighed and knew somehow that was wishful thinking.

"I don't think bitchy women send guys with guns after people," Taber laughed.

"I would," she joked.

Taber let go of her hand and sat back. "You are a frustrating woman, you know that?" He gazed into her eyes, folded his arms and shook his head. This woman oozed sex appeal, looked sexy no matter what. Sex personified. For her to joke like that scared him!

"You are a very, very frustrating man," she winked. He knew she was referring to the way he turned cold on her.

"Guess that makes us two very frustrating people." He wasn't smiling, so there was no way for her to take it as a joke. He didn't need the distraction. He needed her to be safe.

Silka was depressed enough as it was. His coldness towards her made matters worse. It didn't matter that nothing could ever happen between them. She needed the distraction.

"No, only frustrated." She shook her head slowly as a soft seductive smile played on her lips. She tried to lighten the mood. With everything that had happened, she preferred to think of what had happened in the club. Not death.

Taber blew out a deep breath.

" You are unbelievable Silka!" he said out of the blue. He leaned forward and rested his elbows on his knees while rubbing his face.

"Mind telling me why you are so upset?" she asked.

"You have a wanted sign on your back with a small posse after you and you make jokes and sexual innuendos as if you don't care!" he reprimanded her.

"What would you have me do, Tay?" she asked surprised. "I'm not going to fall apart or stop feeling and living. It's not going to change the fact that those men are after me. It's not going to change the fact that I need to clear my name. It's not going to bring Geo back. It's not going to change the fact that I want you when …." she stopped in mid sentence. She was crying. She had no idea why. The whole situation was such a mess. She stood up and walked away.

Taber ran after her. He grabbed her and turned her round to face him.

"I'm sorry," he said softly. "I'm scared for you, Silka, and you seem so unaffected, you scare me." He wiped the tears away.

"I'm sorry if my priorities seem out of whack. But what happened in the club last night frightened me but also excited me unlike anything I have ever felt. So I prefer to think of that to keep me sane," she explained.

He grinned. The pilot came on-board and made them take their seats again and buckle up.

"So what's the longest relationship you've ever had?" asked Silka in a bid to make small talk.

"Three months," Taber thought that honesty would at least serve as a warning.

"Two months," she stated, as if she had just won a competition.

"Commitment phobe or stalker crazy?" he probed for a reason.

"You met my mother? Commitment phobe!" she stated the obvious.

"Me too!" he smiled.

"Because of my mother?" she smiled and shot him a look.

"No, because of mine," he laughed.

They spent the rest of the ten hour flight to Washington DC chatting about their interfering mothers, commitment issues, stories about Geo and everything else under the sun, until they fell asleep peacefully.

If only they had known.

Chapter 7

They arrived in Washington DC in the evening and went to a hotel and checked into separate rooms. They both subconsciously thought it best to avoid temptation. After a pleasant dinner, they both decided to get some well deserved sleep.

The next morning Silka showered, dressed in a pair of white fitted slacks and matched them with a red, tight-fitting, long-sleeved top which showed off a lot of cleavage.

She went to Taber's room to wake him up. As she sat waiting on the bed for him to get ready, she set up a lunch appointment for later with her former boss.

Taber showered and dressed in a black pair of trousers and a black collared, long sleeve sports shirt. He was towel drying his hair when she looked up.

"Didn't know we were going golfing?" she joked. He winked at her and smiled, looking at her with pure lust.

"I have many urges right now, might need a game or two soon to distract me," he joked back in a low sexy voice and tossed the towel on the bed next to her.

Her heart skipped a beat.

Since their brutal honesty on the jet, he had allowed himself to relax a little more. Now they both enjoyed and welcomed the distraction together. It was almost a game to see who could push the other over the cliff first.

---

*S*ilka smiled seductively and slowly ran her eyes over the length of his body. Yep, she sat on the bed and openly perved like a teenager over a pop star. He looked like the poster child of pro sports, yet at the same time very business-like. She always had a thing for a man in a suit and tie, but this look made her turn into a Slush Puppy. The temporary distraction he gave her was very welcome.

Until she remembered. Overcome with the loss and sadness that they could never be together in any way, shape or form, she snapped out of her schoolgirl mentality.

"Right now my urges require the bathroom." Her voice was husky as she dashed past him. *WTF?* It was not that she had planned a future for them. It was not that she wanted a future with him. Last week she was going to nip this in the bud. Until the club in Moscow! All she knew was that she absolutely wanted to bed that man and then discover where it went. Now it was not possible anymore. The disappointment she felt was unbearable.

---

*T*aber waited for Silka to finish. He was on the couch, bewildered by thoughts of her in there. She seemed tormented - as was he. Her touch, her scent, hell! Everything about her drove him closer to the edge. Right now he needed to keep it together and pull himself toward himself if he was going to help her get out of this.

After she had composed herself in the bathroom and assured him she was alright, they went shopping for a new mobile phone. Afterwards they headed for the restaurant where they were to meet with Joshua.

While they waited they sat at the table and made small talk.

"Silka!" a man greeted her in a friendly voice.

"Josh, nice to see you again! Thank you for meeting with me," she said, before introducing him to Tay.

"Taber Blake, this is Joshua Stonewall."

"Pleased to make your acquaintance," Taber said kindly and confidently as he shook his hand.

"As am I," said Josh with a smile. He was an attractive man. He reminded Taber of replica of Robert Downey Jr.

"What brings you two to my neck of the woods?" he asked after placing his order.

"Rumor has it that I have gone rogue or AWOL and now I have some men with guns after me," said Silka, showing the confusion she felt in her expression.

"Oh-me-oh-my!" replied Josh, clearly perturbed by the news.

"Everyone knows you are doing contract work for us. I don't understand the connection. People leave the company all the time, some remain in our employ like you, and others do not. There are no possible scenarios that would deem the words rogue or AWOL remotely applicable in the company. There is no reason why anyone in the USAID would want to harm you. That is not what we do." The seriousness of his conviction demanded the harshness in his tone.

"Tell me about your last mission in Nigeria?" he continued.

"For the last six years I was running missions to curb the polio epidemic and religious conflicts, with the assistance of other organizations. We had our hands full brokering peace in both the political and religious arena," she answered.

"What is your role in this?" Josh asked Taber.

"My company is in partnership with the USAID to provide assistance where they need it. I was not directly involved in any missions. Silka is a dear friend and I'm trying to help her," Taber smiled, leaned back in his chair and folded his arms.

"Did you make any enemies during these missions?" He directed his attention back to Silka.

"Enemies are a kind word for them. Where politics and religion are concerned, everybody hates what they consider the clueless foreign intruder preaching!" She grinned.

They sat in silence as their food was served and started eating. As they ate in deafening silence it became clear to Silka that the only way out was to be completely honest and forthcoming with the two men at her side. They both looked as if they had lost a puppy. She waited until their plates had been cleared by the waiter.

"I was trained by members of some other US organizations to defend myself and helped them do negotiations and translations of the more persuasive kind," she confessed.

As soon as Silka had said that, both men looked like they could kick a puppy.

"Well that explains a lot!" Josh gasped.

"You went along with other organizations to instil peace and prosperity, but ended up interrogating and engaging in hostile activities. Damn it, Silka! Do you have any idea what you've done?" he blasted under his breath, trying to contain his anger and the volume of his voice.

"I did what was necessary. Our lives were in danger on a daily basis. We needed Intel before setting up missions and needed to protect the people during those missions as well as the locals we were helping. We had to know what we were up against, defend ourselves and protect innocent lives," she insisted. Taber shook his head in disbelief.

"No wonder the word spread that you had gone rogue. You not only disregarded the policy and procedure of the USAID, but broke several international laws as well. You have pissed off a lot of people." Taber lectured her while he nodded his head and raised his eyebrows.

"Those actions were sanctioned by Uncle Sam, I assure you of that!" Silka hissed as she tried to maintain the '*I'm not stupid*' façade.

"You know this how?" Taber cocked his head to one side and gave a perplexed glare.

"Special Forces," she uttered in a tone that screamed *DUH*.

"You need to go to see this guy," Josh handed her a business card from his wallet, very certain that the conversation between Taber and Silka was about to disintegrate to the level of that between two five year olds.

"He is an old friend of mine in the intelligence community. He might be able to dig up something about what happened in Nigeria to warrant hired guns. With any luck you can find the person responsible for this, clear up any misunderstandings and get back to your life." He looked at both of them sternly.

"I am certain there is no need to tell you two that you not only have to be careful in your search, but also of each other. We don't let people in the agency become involved, for a reason." He smiled and stood up. "It's bad for business when lovers become enemies. We like our employees and partners in one piece," he said, smiled and glanced playfully at the two faces that stared at him in utter shock and left.

Silka narrowed her eyes at Taber. "No problem here," she said coolly and, with her lips pouted confidently, she walked out.

Taber called the waiter for the bill. While he sat there and waited, Silka's words haunted him. She didn't want him for anything but a distraction. She could never be in love with him or want him in that way, because of company policy. She knew it, which is why she played the game so easily. Or did she? That is why she had locked herself in the bathroom that morning. He felt a sense of despair. After everything they had said, did and felt they could never be together. She was upset about that. It made him feel good to know she felt the same way he did now, except his feeling ran deeper. *What the hell, Tay?* He thought about it. He had never spoken so openly and honestly to anyone before. He had never shared such chemistry and sparks with any woman like that before either. In fact, he had never used his company jet to gallivant with a woman on a mission half way around the world!

"Shit!" he exclaimed and paid the bill.

---**S**ilka---

As Taber settled the bill she waited outside, deep in thought while studying the business card. *Who was she kidding?* She was in love with Taber. After everything they had been through and he had done for her, how could she not be? She would not have been so overwhelmed by the thought of them not being together, if she wasn't in love with him. Josh could tell. He had known before she had. There was only one thing to do.

When Taber joined her outside, she informed him that the man that Josh had referred them to was Bill Miller in New York.

"I'm going to New York on my own. Josh might not know that we are not involved, but he was right. We should not be together. Every moment you spend with me puts you in danger," she said in a quiet, calm tone.

"In danger of what? Falling in love with you or being killed by armed men?" he asked intently.

She said nothing.

"If it's the first, then let me tell you now, it is already too late. If it's the latter, then let me reassure you I can take care of myself," he continued.

"Tay, please, you should go back home," she said softly and looked away. "We cannot be together, personally or professionally. The company's policy forbids it. I do not want it," she stated bluntly, in a bid to make him accept it.

It was the last thing she wanted. It broke her heart to say that to him, but she needed him safe. They couldn't get more involved than they were already. It was the wrong time, the wrong place, the wrong everything.

He looked devastated as he glanced around, trying to find words to say.

He shook his head. Eventually all he could say was, "fine."

She gave him a sad smile.

"Come, I'll take you back to the hotel so we can pick up our things and arrange a flight for you," he said, as he turned to hail a cab.

Once at the hotel, they reluctantly and awkwardly packed and after she had given him her new mobile number they went down to the lobby. When they reached the street, an ominous silence fell. They turned to each other for the imminent farewell. There was absolute dead silence as they stared into each other's eyes. In the middle of town on a week day, they could not see or hear anything or anyone around them. It was as if the whole world had stopped. He pulled her into an embrace, but she flung herself at him and kissed him passionately.

She kissed him as if it was the last kiss she'd ever experience. She kissed him as if her life depended on it. That was a kiss of a promise to be kept and a dream to be fulfilled. Her heart and soul was poured into that kiss for eternity, to be set in stone and remembered for all time.

--- *T*aber---

Relieved that she felt his longing, his frustration and his loss too, he returned her kiss with as much fervor as hers. In that moment he knew she wanted him and was in love with him too. When their cabs pulled up, he pulled away slightly.

"Promise me, beautiful. Promise me you will be careful," he begged her softly and then hugged her again.

"I will. You too," she whispered. They broke their embrace.

"Phone me if you need anything, okay, baby?" he said and handed her his business card.

"Thank you for everything, Tay. Goodbye." And so they climbed into their separate cabs and went their separate ways.

"Airport please," he said to his driver.

Every minute he was away from Silka, pained him. He thought of her in the cab, on his jet on the way to New York, in the Plaza hotel and every moment in between. He was staying in New York, as there was no way in hell he was going to leave her until this mess was sorted out, even if it turned him into a stalker.

He wanted to ask her to run away with him where no one would find her. He wanted to stay with her and was willing to beg her. In the end, he realized that for all that he wanted to, she would not have it. She had told him she didn't want to be involved with him. At the time it had almost knocked him on his ass. How could she not want him after the way she had passionately consumed him in the Moscow club? It almost killed him when he had to let her go.

Now he knew. The very thought of love used to scare him, but somehow being the object of Silka's love made him happy.

When he had realized that he was in love for the first time in his life in that DC restaurant, he had been shocked. Admitting that he was in love with Silka of all people, on top of it all, wasn't as hard as he thought it would be. It made him strangely happy.

But for now, he could not be with her. He could do nothing. All he could do was make a call.

"Check your email," he said, as the person on the other side picked up. "You know what to do."

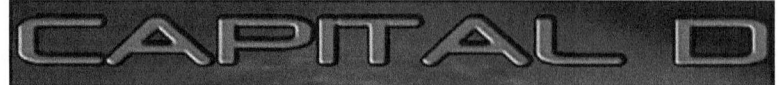

Chapter 8

*S*ilka had a short and eventless flight from Washington DC to New York. When she arrived in New York she took a taxi and then booked into a small hotel in Upper Manhattan. She managed to get an appointment with Bill Miller the next morning. As it was already early evening, she settled in for the night in the empty hotel room. Silka felt devastated as she thought about Taber. She had enjoyed getting to know him better. Most of all she had enjoyed the club in Moscow and the street in DC. Somehow she had suddenly become a fan of rave music and public affection. Now he was thousands of miles away, going back home. Taber Blake, she thought. Who knew? Love was a funny thing. *Tay, Tay, Tay!*

She loved New York. Much like other big cities, Tokyo and Hong Kong, it was always busy, but held an energy and atmosphere like no other place in the world. That morning she had dressed in a pair of black trousers and long-sleeved, pink, button up blouse. She finished her look off with a black handbag and her trusty black stiletto boots. After she had breakfast, she headed to

Harlem where she was going to meet Bill in a shop she had never heard of. Fortunately Josh had given his friend a head's up, so she knew he might have information for her. Not just any information, hopefully blow-this-case-wide-open information.

On the subway, however, the little voice came back. It was telling her to run again. She looked around. The place was packed. She could see people from all walks of life and all professions minding their own business waiting on the platform for the train, like her. No one looked out of the ordinary. She looked behind her. Two men were standing behind her. She faced the front again.

Not just any men. She didn't have to hear their voices to know it was the same men from the gallery and Moscow. She recognized the big twin, the bald guy and the Wesley snipes wannabe. She felt her heart stop. She had to draw on all her strength to keep her pose and her breathing under control. She was between the Nigerians and the Grand Central Station tracks. There was no way out.

The 6 train pulled to a stop. As people boarded, Silka was pushed along through the doors. She climbed on and proceeded to the other side of the car. The train filled up quickly and pretty soon she ran out of room. As the train pulled away, she turned around and pretended to look outside. She saw the three men walking in awkward silence through the packed car. They maneuvered their way through the passengers, ignoring their remarks and displeasure. As they drew closer, Silka made her way towards the other exit door. The train stopped at the next station. Silka ran for the door and bolted off as fast as she could, bumping into people boarding and disembarking the train. She had no idea where she was going, but she would figure it out when she got to the street.

Running up the long set of stairs, two steps at a time, had her breathless when she reached the street. Over and above that, her stiletto boots were not Nikes, which made balancing and running as difficult as licking your elbows. She kept on running regardless, in the direction that had people. There was no telling if the three men had made it off the train as quickly as she had, given the crowds.

The traffic was bumper to bumper. The sidewalks bustled with pedestrians. The noise levels were sky high. All her senses were kicked into high gear.

When she reached the most populated pedestrian section she started walking at the same pace as the crowd. She loosened her hair into her face and fished in her handbag as she dropped the hair clip inside. She couldn't find her glasses and realized that Taber still had them in his leather jacket.

"Bloody hell!" she blurted out loud. Her mouth guard was in there and she quickly proceeded to place it on her lower teeth. She needed to improve her disguise if she was going to lose the men tailing her. There was a boutique further ahead, which hopefully had a change of clothes and shoes.

As she entered the store, two hands grabbed her arm. For a moment she had a flashback to Taber rescuing her in Moscow. When another pair of hands grabbed her other arm, she knew it was not him.

"Not going to work this time!" a voice from the gallery hissed.

"Bring the car!" he shouted at the third member.

Silka had been in many different situations. She knew that she handled fear and adrenalin very well. Her confidence had never let her or her team down. Until she realized right then, that for the first time in her life, there was no one there. During school she had the gutsy Nicole for back up. All missions, all situations, all dangerous work she had ever done, was done with her boss or the team. Even in Moscow, she was not alone because she had had Taber. For the first time, she faced danger alone. Fear and adrenalin suddenly became an enemy. She was frozen and all ability to think or scheme abandoned her in her hour of need. Her legs shook and her hands trembled. She hoped they wouldn't notice.

"Now be a good girl. If you scream we will kill you. Let's take a nice little drive and we can straighten this mess out," one of the men barked in her ear.

She spat out her mouth guard onto the street as they pulled her to the sidewalk. Apart from Josh and Bill, no one would know she would not make it to the meeting.

No one would find her, she thought, as they pushed her into the back of a black SUV, with dark tinted windows. As soon as they covered her head with a black hood, it sealed her fate and she was as good as dead.

At first, they sat in traffic like everyone else but eventually they were driving fast. Her sense of direction was dismal, even more so now that she could not see anything with the hood on. She had no idea where they were, let alone where they were headed. All sense of time became distorted. Was it minutes, hours or days they had been driving? After what felt like an eternity of speeding up and slowing down again and again, they came to a stop.

The two men yanked and pushed her out of the car. She fell and could feel her knees chafe on the ground. They picked her up brutally and forced her into a building. From the click of her heels on the floor she estimated it to be concrete. Many more voices from other men came closer. They all spoke English in Nigerian accents.

"Put her in there," one of the voices ordered. She heard a metal door open while they stood and waited. As soon as the entrance way was cleared, they led her into a larger room. She could hear from the echoes in their voices, that this was a large empty space.

A warehouse! How original, she thought sarcastically. They sat her down and one of the men proceeded to tie her hands together behind the back of the chair. Another man tied her feet together and then secured them to the legs of the chair.

Cable ties… kinky bastards! What happened to good old rope? Then they left her there in absolute silence, darkness and solitude.

What no goodbye kiss or empty promise to call me later? She wanted to giggle at her own expense and over her lousy sense of humor during this extremely dire time.

The chair was highly uncomfortable and started to hurt her delicate derriere. She tried shuffling her weight, but the wooden back of her chair dug into her shoulder blades. Her armpits started aching from the pressure of the chair on them. Sometime later her neck felt stiff.

Like a rising sun, the gravity of her situation dawned on her with every passing moment. She knew that in order to stay alive, she had to be strong… no matter what. The fear inside her slowly grew more pronounced. It hadn't occurred to her who she was dealing with until she had really thought about it. Her sense of humor evaporated.

Her mind replayed memories of the methods and modus operandi of guys like them. They were strong believers in the motivational powers of pain. She would have to fight the pain. Fight with everything she had. If she showed one ounce of weakness, they would increase their efforts to break her. She could not give them that kind of power over her. In her mind she had already decided that it would take a lot to break her. She was all alone and no one knew where she was. It would take anybody days, even weeks, to find her. She had no idea what they had in store for her. Her best defence was fight or flight.

Since she could not see, she decided to use her other senses. She could not hear anything. There was no traffic, no people and no birds outside. This area was as remote as they came. She tried wriggling her arms and stretching the cable ties. They must have been made out of industrial strength plastic, because they would not budge. The binds around her legs would not move either. She was stuck. Flight was out of the question. She would have to fight. The pain in her arms, butt and legs increased as time ticked slowly by.

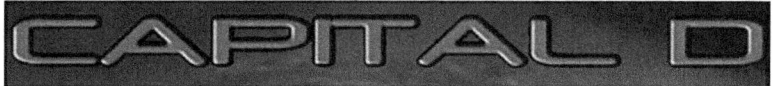

Chapter 9

--- *T*ABER ---

The day before, Taber called Joshua to find out where and when the meeting was going to be held. He was pleased to learn that Silka had arrived safely at her hotel a few blocks away from his. Josh informed him that she had a 9am meeting, but he didn't know where. All Bill had told him was that she had agreed to meet him and would go by train. The next day he received grave news.

"What! Are you kidding me? How the hell did she not make the meeting?" Taber flew into a rage.

Josh had flown to New York as soon as he had heard. He tried his best to get as much information as possible, before he phoned Taber to relay the news. He had his connections trace her movements that day. She had gone from the Park Avenue Viaduct into Grand Central Station and later ran into 125th Street, but after that, all trace of her had vanished. The combined efforts from various departments, with enough facial recognition software and surveillance equipment to find the proverbial needle, had come up empty. He was beside himself. He should never have let her go alone.

"How long has she been missing?" he asked, after he managed to calm himself down.

"Only a few hours. Whoever took her could not be far away. We have set up road blocks and have transport authorities on alert. They all have her picture," Josh replied.

"Please keep me posted. I'm going to 125th Street," Taber decided.

"See you there ... we'll combine efforts on this one." Joshua's support was reassuring.

"Thank you, goodbye," Taber replied and hung up the phone. He dialed another number.

"Is it done?" He asked. The person on the other end hesitated to reply. "I sent you the profiles of the three men to take care of days ago. *IF*, as a result of your incompetence, they are now in possession of someone dear to me, you can consider my retribution to be swift and decisive." He laced each word with an icy promise which left no room for interpretation.

It was time to call in the cavalry.

"Paul! Hi. It's Taber. How's it going, my man?" he asked when Paul answered. Paul trained Navy Seals for a living in Fort Lauderdale.

"Howzit, Taber, well and you?" Paul answered.

"Could be better, buddy. I'm in New York and I need a favor. Some men kidnapped a friend of mine and I need help to rescue her," he said, right off the bat.

"Sure thing! I have a few friends in New York busy doing a training exercise as we speak. I'll catch a flight and meet you at my aunt's place this afternoon."

"Thank you. I really appreciate it. SMS me a list of things you need and I shall see you later. Bye," Taber said. He was grateful he had such connections in the Navy Seals. He had never thought he would have needed them in his lifetime, but he was glad he had them now.

As soon as he had hung up, he arranged for a car. His thoughts raced between Silka and the men that had taken her. All her sexy, seductive confidence would do, is either piss them off or turn them on. She needed to play ball and as he knew Silka, she was not into team sports.

For the first time in ages he prayed. He prayed hard. Do not let anything happen to her? Keep her safe? Please let him find her? Please do not let it be too late? His prayers continued and so did the calls to her mobile phone… voicemail.

They met at the street where Silka was last seen. Taber filled Josh in on the arrangements he had been able to make. Paul could hook him up with a few guys so they could help him get Silka. Weapons would not be a problem, as Taber had a criminal mastermind that was about to repay a debt. He just didn't know it yet.

Josh agreed and promised all intelligence and communications at his disposal. He wanted to go on the rescue mission too, but Taber refused. He needed eyes and ears if the shit hit the fan, so somebody could run a backup plan. They searched the street. The two men made their way through every store. Finally a young, cheeky Goth-looking salesclerk inside a shop described a lady entering the store with two men.

'The lady just stood there looking as if she was spastic and then left with them." She was quite irritated that the retarded lady with the drooping mouth had not answered her when she had spoken to her.

"That's like, so rude, and I was like, whatever. If those two dudes hadn't taken her away, I would have called the cops to take her back to whatever Looney bin she had escaped from." She gestured little circles around her temple with her forefinger.

The concern was etched on Taber's face and evident in his voice. "Can you describe these men?"

"No, one was white and the other black, but you can ask my boss if she saw anything, or, whatever," she motioned to her boss.

An attractive woman in her mid thirties floated over, obviously wanting to impress the two gorgeous men in her store.

"Gentlemen. I am the manager. How may I be of assistance?" She flicked back a lock of blonde hair from her face in a flirty motion.

"We were hoping to look at your security footage from this morning, amongst other things," Josh flirted back openly and checked her up and down.

"Oh, that is against policy, I am sorry to say," she apologized. "You get all sorts of crazies in New York and we cannot just show anything to anybody," she continued, in an effort to appease the hunky man.

Josh put a hand in his pocket, cocked his head to the side and stepped closer to her.

"Really? Not even if we ask pretty please?" he growled in a low, sexy voice against her ear.

She visibly blushed as she stared up into his dark eyes.

"Perhaps, I can repay you for your kindness over dinner tonight?" he said slowly, tracing his lips with his index finger and giving her a drop-dead gorgeous smile. Her breath hitched and her resistance began to crumble.

"I would be very grateful and generous if you could help my friend and I out," he whispered, while rubbing his long middle finger down her cheek to her neck and playing with her necklace.

"What time?" She gasped. *SCORE!!!*

As they looked at the footage in her small office, Josh could not hide his concern.

"Do you think they drugged her? The clerk said she looked like a retard."

Taber mulled it over in his head. For a moment he almost considered it. He had wondered what had made Silka go into a store, with no exit other than the front. *What was she thinking?* Taber thought back to all the dangerous situations they had encountered together. First there was the gallery, and then there was Moscow. He chuckled and turned to Josh.

"No, Silka had a mouth guard in an attempt to disguise herself. She was probably wearing it at the time and decided to purchase a change of clothes in this store to escape from the bad guys."

While Josh and the female manager whispered in the background, the thought of the bad guys brought Taber out of his nostalgia. A flood of emotions - anger, fear and frustration combined washed over him. If only he had flown there with her. If only he had been with her. If only he had taken her away as he had wanted to. If only - famous last words.

They stood there watching people enter the store and exit again. These people were oblivious to everything, living in their own little worlds. It had been excruciating watching as nothing gave them any indication of Silka. As all hope failed, the screen suddenly exploded as he recognized Silka.

"Pause! That's her!" he yelled excitedly.

They saw her walk in and suddenly freeze when the men grabbed her arms. They were standing behind her and one of them was talking in her ear.

"Zoom in!" he instructed.

"Our equipment is not that state of the art, sorry," the manager apologized again.

"Can you give us a copy...?" asked Josh.

"No need," Taber interrupted.

"I remember them from Moscow," he said and pulled out his iPad. He flicked over the screen and showed Josh close-ups of the kidnappers.

"How did you get these?" Josh sounded astounded and impressed.

"I paid people to distract them while their pictures were being taken," he said mildly, as if it was no big deal.

They continued watching the footage and could make out that Silka had been taken to a black Ford SUV, before a large group of teenagers entered the store and blocked their view.

"Come with me, I can help you identify them," Josh demanded more than requested by his tone.

Before they left, Taber politely thanked the manageress and gave her a kiss on the cheek.

Josh turned to her. "I'll see you later, Jessie," he said, as he bit his lower lip and slowly pushed his business card down her blouse and into her bra. Beet red came close to describing the shade her face turned, but could not quite do it justice. She fell back onto her desk and braced herself on her arms as the two men left.

"Are you taking one for the team or are you really interested?" Taber lifted an eyebrow and smiled at Josh, on the way to Bill's office.

In a non-committal way, Josh pouted his lips, "I'll tell you tomorrow," he answered, pulling a face in pseudo-fright.

As soon as they reached Bill's office, Josh immediately uploaded the pictures on the computer and started emailing them to various people. Bill and Taber introduced themselves.

"One track mind," Bill smiled as he apologized for Josh's rudeness.

"Yeah, I noticed," Taber smiled back.

Bill was close to retirement. He had a full head of white hair, combed back like a 1950's Elvis. He was tall and slightly on the podgy side. Nevertheless he had a demanding air about him. It was clear that he didn't take nonsense from anyone.

The emails were soon followed up with phone calls and urgent requests issued to the party on the other end. Taber used this time to call in his chips with the criminal mastermind who owed him one. This guy had a CV that read like a jail inmate list. Nothing was beneath him. Taber had helped him 'move' some stolen goods using his dad's company back in the day when he had been more interested in making a quick buck.

Luck was on his side. Criminal Mastermind could hook him up and deliver that afternoon. This guy ran a few gangs in New York. They would drop off the guns, ammo and equipment Paul needed.

"So now what?" Taber asked when Josh had depleted his pool of resources able to identify the men.

"Now we do like the Italians and eat," he said with a smile.

Bill excused himself as he had a meeting to attend.

Josh and Taber headed for a small Italian Bistro down the street.

"What information did Bill have for Silka?" Taber inquired after they sat down.

"Not much. Looks like Nigeria just became the new Las Vegas. Bill was going to meet with her to get more specifics on her definition of translation and negotiation."

By the time they had eaten and paid the bill, Josh received a call.

"Joshua Stonewall." He listened for a while.

"Send it to my phone. Thanks Pete," he said and hung up.

"We got ID's on those guys. Both are Nigerians. They work for a large crime syndicate with fingers in every pie, weapons, Internet scams, precious metals, minerals, cars, trafficking...hell, even medical supplies. Whatever can be stolen or screwed over, they do it!" He shook his head and pulled his lips in disgust.

"Any idea if they have a base of operations in New York?" Taber's thoughts were in overdrive.

"Still searching known aliases pal," Josh said, giving a sympathetic smile. Of course, what were the odds they could actually catch a break, he thought.

Every minute they wasted, Silka's life was in danger. They had to find her and quickly. After he received the

Intel on the kidnappers on his phone, they headed back to Bill's office.

They spent a long time going through the Intel on them. Dennis Cromwell was an unemployed former soldier and had been recruited a few years before by an unknown syndicate in Nigeria. Alaji Omar belonged to a Muslim organization known as Basel Hakim (meaning brave brothers). He was still associated with them and it was believed that the syndicate was run by some of the big boys in the terrorist organization.

"They both had a criminal record that made Satan himself seem like a freaking amateur." Joshua relayed the bad news.

"Yeah, and the fact that a terrorist organization and the crime syndicate are involved is really bad news." Taber could not play out any scenario in which Silka got out of this alive. For all intents and purposes, she was a goner. This was a Disaster with a capital D.

As Josh reached out to his contacts to find out if the two men had been spotted somewhere, Taber left to meet up with Paul and his friends.

It was still afternoon when he arrived at Paul's aunt's apartment in Queens, aka, the new base of operations. He had arranged for criminal mastermind to supply the whole wish list that Paul wanted, to be waiting by the service elevator of Paul's building. Along with Paul, there were two other men.

Paul was nicknamed Bulldog, because of his tenacity. He was excellent at recon, tracking and shooting. Taber had seen him once when he had tracked a guy and shot him into a tree. The guy was literally stuck standing against the tree.

Paul's best friend and brother in arms was Riley O'Conner aka Eagle Eye. He was the sniper of the outfit. He needed one shot to take someone out, rather than the two short bursts they were normally trained to take. Naturally, he could also shoot from great distances.

Herman Schultz specialized in making things go Kaboom! His friends referred to him as Flash, because that was normally the last thing his enemies saw. He was quick, quiet and ruthless.

Taber was introduced to them by Paul shortly after he had arrived and they established that everything was supplied to Paul's satisfaction. He told them that he had met Taber shortly after finishing school in South Africa. Paul merely hinted that Taber had a specific skill set they required for the op. The exact extent of their relationship was kept secret from the other guys. For the time being, how they had met was on a need to know basis. Roughly translated in the real world as never! As soon as the initial pleasantries were dispensed with, they sat down and made small talk while they waited for a call from Joshua.

Eventually, Bulldog paced up and down, impatient for some action. Eagle Eye and Flash went through the weapons and explosives to make sure they were 'clean'.

Taber grabbed a shower and changed into black Military Ripstop BDU pants along with a tight, long-sleeved, black v-neck shirt. It clung to his bulging chest muscles and well defined abs. It complemented his athletic V-frame upper body. His pants that sculptured his lower body looked like cargo pants, but the pockets were less visible. He was soon pacing around like an expectant father in a delivery room.

Paul's aunt had cooked them dinner which they ate because they were hungry - the woman could not cook.

Meanwhile, Josh had been on his phone so much, it had become a second appendage. Taber kept going back and forth between Bill's office and Paul's base of operations. He was in constant contact with Josh and Bill. The waiting was killing him.

That night he kept his clothes on to be battle ready when Josh called. The other guys were dressed in their Navy Seal pants but plain black shirts. The time seemed to drag forever.

"Better get some rest, Bud," Bulldog urged Taber.

"Damn straight. Can't show up all puffy and ugly when we rescue a babe," Eagle Eye smirked.

"Doesn't matter," Flash said. "One look at you and she'll run in the other direction," Flash teased him. The mood lifted in the room as they all laughed at Eagle Eye's 'make believe' mortified expression.

"I should have gotten some curling irons and facial masks instead of weapons for you lot," Taber joked.

They settled into various corners of the lounge in the one bedroom apartment. No one was going to get a lot of sleep, but some would at least help.

It had been twenty-four hours since Silka had been kidnapped. They were running out of time.

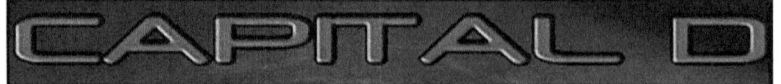

Chapter 10

Silka's hands and butt were finally numb and the heat was unbearable. It felt like she had been subjected to solar flares for the last few hours. She had no concept of how long she had sat there. It seemed like days, but was in fact only hours. The door flung open and became stuck on the cement, making a nail-on-chalkboard irritating sound. She heard voices nearing her, along with footsteps that drew closer. The men seemed to drag something along with them. She heard a lot of clanging noises and thumping. Just when she thought they were done, they poured a foul smelling substance over her hood and her entire body. She had never felt or smelt anything like that in her life. It was unexpected, unfamiliar and subzero cold. She wanted to throw up from the stench. It was an oily substance, but smelled like ammonia, vinegar, olive oil and urine all at once. As the oily substance clung to her face, she could hardly breathe from the stench, let alone swear at them like she wanted to. As she sat there freezing and almost asphyxiated from the lack of oxygen, they laughed and started beating her with something from all directions. The pain from the blows combined with the pain from the cold was almost unbearable.

"You think that was fun. That was just a warm-up. Wait for our boss to land tomorrow," one man threatened as they left. She deduced that he was the reason she was still alive and that he was probably coming to the States from somewhere far away. She hoped it wasn't all the way from hell.

One consolation was that the men were leaving her alone for the night until the boss man arrived the next day. If only they knew her ultimate torture was a big hairy spider. She had a chronic case of arachnophobia!

Sore, gagging and shivering from the cold, she sat there for what seemed like an eternity.

She had no idea what time it was, but she woke up when she heard the door scream open again and then heard the footsteps. A hand pulled her hood off, and with it a chunk of her hair.

"Ow!!!" she screamed, as she tried to look up and adjust her eyes to the light. It was daylight again outside, not that she could tell much at that point. She was exhausted, sore, hungry, tired and still very scared. The two men that had abducted her were standing in front of her in a bouncer pose. *Boy! She'd like to bounce them!*

"Miss Fontein. I am General Stan Shuman," a voice sneered behind her, as if he expected her to recognize his name and fear him.

She tried to turn to see him, but her neck was too stiff.

"So glad we finally caught you!" he almost sang the words, he was so pleased with himself.

"What the hell do you want?" she hissed through clenched teeth. Her hands and knees were shaking again. It felt like a giant fist was squeezing her heart and stomach together. It clenched them tightly to the point of implosion.

"What do I want? I want my damn shipment!" he yelled at the top of his voice into her ear.

"I don't know what you are talking about," the uncertainty of said shipment and fear both evident in her voice, but her tone screamed disdain.

"You know," he said softly, as he approached her from the front. "I really tried to make this easy for you," he said calmly, shaking his head.

This man was the new kid on the block. Silka did not recognize him, but she knew he was the one with all the Lego blocks.

He was old, dirty, tallish and morbidly obese. He looked like a T-Rex with fat lips. He had a huge fat grey moustache that hung over his fat purple lips. His eyes were dead glass beads. *The big honcho*, she thought.

"But you leave me no choice!" The pitch of his voice went almost soprano from his excitement.

"I told you the truth," Silka tried to hide the terror she felt, but her voice was shaky.

He smacked her across the face. Clearly not satisfied he smacked her again, but this time across the other side of her face. *OK he was pissed, she got it, thanks.*

"I will not accept that!" he screamed in her face. "You know where my shipment is and by golly, by the time I am through with you, I will have it back!"

He pushed his one hand onto her left shoulder and gave her a right hook punch across her jaw so hard even her grandchildren would feel it one day. Her hair slapped her face on the one side from the knock.

She tasted blood from her lip and tried to blow the hair off her face, but it was too heavy and oily. Silka remained quiet.

He reached behind her neck and grappled a hand full of hair. He pulled it hard as he forced her to look at him.

"I can't hear you sing little birdie," he crooned. He was very passionate about this job. Very few people enjoyed what they did, but he seemed to enjoy taunting and hurting her.

When she refused to answer, he gave her a left hook. Her hair flung into her face again like she was in a shampoo ad, except for the fact that it hurt.

She was going to be swollen and bruised tomorrow - if she made it through this day, she thought.

He gave the two men a nod.

Her eyes welled up with tears as the hopelessness of her situation just hit defcon 5. They were going to go

Fight Club on her. It did not matter in how many different ways she told them the truth.

Twit One and Twit Two went to a table a few feet away from her. With all the excitement surrounding her new best enemy, she had never noticed it. She did not need to look at what was on the table to recognize the torture devices. They had brought a selection of items to the man.

He looked at his endless choices in their hands. She could almost tell he was playing eenie, meenie, mynie... but his first choice stopped her heart right there. She shook her head but refused to cry. She could not bring herself to speak.

"Let us try this again." The sadism in his voice would make Satan quiver.

"Please, I told you I don't know what you are talking about. I know nothing about a shipment." She was beginning to think they were ignoring her on purpose.

"You're telling me you were not in Nigeria two weeks ago!" His level of rage hit nuclear proportions and sweat dripped down his face.

"I was there, but I did not take anything," Silka's irritation was beginning to sprout branches let alone grow.

"Save it! Your team told me about your whole little scheme. Unlike you, they still believed in right and wrong. They told me you took my shipment, before I even knew it was gone. Now where is it?" He sprayed spittle into her face as he spoke.

"What scheme? How would I have pulled something like that off?" she said, as she tried to get more information and convince him of her innocence.

"I'm getting tired of your games. You want to play freaking dumb?" he screamed.

"You followed the car and stole my case, while the driver and guard were still unconscious after the accident you caused!" he yelled. His voice suddenly became strained.

"That reminds me, you also owe me a freaking vehicle!" A renewed fury hit his voice, and without warning he ripped her shirt open.

Silka saw buttons fly all over the place. He took the box cutter, stabbed her chest and ran the blade down her cleavage, cutting her flesh and bra off with it.

Silka grimaced in agony as the knife cut and stabbed into her all the way down to below her breasts. She cried out at first but muffled the sounds by tightening her lips.

"Next, I will use this to remove your nipples," he threatened.

The cut quickly became distorted as blood oozed out everywhere. She closed her eyes and breathed in harshly to fight the pain.

The man was breathing heavily as if he was about to faint from the exertion and stormed off with the two bouncers in tow. He needed a break from the heat and get a drink while he fetched plan B.

---

*T*aber and the guys had spent the whole day planning and he had even got his new 'team' to do dry runs of possible scenarios just in case they were up against a small army. By the end of this they would know each other and their roles. It was better than sitting around waiting.

That afternoon they got lucky. Some traffic cameras caught that Black Ford SUV speeding down the I-495 Long Island Expressway and then again on the NY-25 to Greenport. It was a drive of over two hours. Taber immediately jumped into action. He did a search on all the possible locations where kidnappers would be able to interrogate and keep a hostage. There were a few possibilities.

Greenport had a lot of abandoned houses, but they were still in busy, built-up areas. The only possible locations were some abandoned warehouses in industrial areas just outside town. There were four of them. These guys needed to have her somewhere far away from possible escape routes for her and far away from any nosy people who might get authorities to check out the buzz surrounding the place. They would have to kick their search into light-speed gear if they hoped to find her alive. They did more research before agreeing on the best location where Silka could be.

Taber strapped the ammo belt that holstered his guns around his waist. He strapped holsters that secured his knives on either thigh. He looked kick-ass ready like in a scene from The Expendables. It was go time.

Taber, Bulldog, Eagle Eye and Flash drove off to Greenport. They drove slowly past the first warehouse. Through the perimeter fence, they could see the front of the property. There were no cars outside and inside the building they could see no movement. They decided to drive around the corner to scope out the back of the warehouse. There was only the entrance in the front and loading docks at the back. Taber and Bulldog decided to take the front. Eagle Eye and Flash were delegated to take the back.

"Let's see if there's a party we can crash," Taber joked.

"Watch your six!" Bulldog warned the band of merry men. They seemed way too pleased to be here.

"Okey Dokey," Flash said.

"Glad I can count that high," Eagle Eye joked.

With their gear locked and loaded, they split up.

This building might have been abandoned, but someone still saw fit to keep trespassers out. Taber and Bulldog cut through the padlocks of the front gates with bolt cutters. They manoeuvred through some barrels and drums that gave them cover outside. A short run to the reception area left Taber and Bulldog slightly exposed until they reached the door. They picked the lock and went inside.

In the meantime, Eagle Eye and Flash had cut a hole through the back fence and made it past some empty crates to the loading bays at the back. The loading bay doors were locked. They made quick work of the padlocks and lifted the door. It made a horrendous noise. They squeezed through the narrow opening they had made.

---**S**ilka---

As Silka sat there, she thought about her mom and dad. She wondered if they would bury or cremate her. She thought about Taber and the passion they would never share. Her depression hit a new low at the thought that she would never see, hear, smell or taste him again.

These overly prepared mother truckers had all the torture devices available to demon-kind on the table. They were going to cut out her nipples, mutilate her and start slicing, stabbing and burning everything that was left of her. Her torture was going to be excruciatingly slow and was going to take all night. Her face and body would be beyond recognition by the time they eventually decided to put her out of her misery. *With a bullet*, she hoped.

---

*T*aber and his team searched every inch of the warehouse. She was not there. In fact the whole building was empty. They had to regroup and find out where they had gone wrong. They were running out of time.

---

*S*ilka felt hopeless. How in the hell was she going to get out of this? She did not steal a shipment or a case. What was in it that was so important? There was no way she had done it. Her team would not make up lies like that. Why would her team tell him that? Her mind flashed back to the years she had spent with them. The four men were not interested in her for the first five years she was working in Nigeria.

These four were members of the most prestigious organizations in the US there in Nigeria. Their skills were far beyond what she had to offer. She was the youngest there and was nobody compared to them and had been treated as such. They had never bothered to learn her name and had just called her 'Tadpole'. She had continued with her work, made friends with the others and ignored them as the years went by. It was only last year, when they had learnt that she was a South African that their interest in her had peaked. The guys had taken her under their wing and taught her how to kick ass in hand to hand combat and how to shoot. One guy had even taught her tracking tactics, disguise techniques and survival skills.

Pretty soon she had been considered one of the boys and had joined them when they had gone to the villages looking for some General and his troops. They had been always gathering Intel. It hit her like a bomb. They had not been looking for soldiers and troops of the terrorist organization to pre-empt a possible attack and defend innocent lives. What she had thought was safeguarding the mission to complete the work of their organizations, were actually fishing expeditions. Every person they questioned, every combat situation had been in a bid to find 'this' General here.

They had been looking for the location of the crime syndicate boss the whole time. *Holy Cow!!* How could she have been so stupid? They had used her in a plan to be the fall guy. In a few hours she would be dead because of a bunch of pricks who had framed her. Why?

Just then the General came waltzing in. He was alone this time. He looked at her bruised and battered face and smiled.

"Have you decided to cooperate yet?"

"I would tell you to go F yourself, but I see it is impossible for your short little arms to even reach there!" Silka said, not wanting him to see how scared she really was.

He kicked her in the stomach forcing her to fall backwards. Her head hit the concrete floor hard but she couldn't feel the pain as much from her head injury, because he had started kicking the shit out of her. She cried out from pain a couple of times. Luckily his fat tree trunks for legs couldn't continue long. He stopped to catch his breath as she laid there in agony on the floor. She mentally tried to focus on a part of her body that did not hurt. Sadly there was no part left. Even her back and behind that were protected by the chair, hurt from the long sit.

Stan called his men. Exhausted and sweating still from the physical exertion he was obviously not used to, he ordered them to sit her up.

"Bring the cables!" he ordered breathlessly.

Silka watched them carefully. They brought a battery and cables.

"I have made more plans for your nipples," Stan pronounced.

Silka thought he seemed proud of his ability to think let alone plan something.

The two men stood there as Stan reached for her bra cups and flipped them aside. Tweedle Dee and Tweedle Dumb stood there staring at her naked breasts for a while. Even Stan's head moved from one to the other like he was watching a tennis game.

Silka wished her hair wasn't oily and stiff so she could obscure their view somehow.

"These will do just fine," Stan reached out and pinched her nipples hard.

Silka's eyes watered from the pain.

"Just do it already!" she screamed, so that he would stop ogling and touching.

---

*T*aber and the brave company arrived at their next location. It was another abandoned warehouse. In the cover of darkness they could easily sneak in undetected.

129

All four of them pushed through the gap in the front gate like they were made out of butter.

"Time to cowboy-up boys. Time is running out," Taber informed them, as they made their way to the nearest door.

"Yee-haw on that," Eagle Eye responded as they broke through the door.

"Let's make like a PC virus and crash this place," Flash chirped in as they walked in.

They were in a long corridor with a series of doors what looked like offices on one side and a long solid wall on the other where the production facility must have been. At the end of the corridor there was a T-junction that met a hallway.

"Enough with the one-liners boys, we have company." Bulldog was not one to make light of a situation. He had that quiet cool about him and was always very alert. Someone with a torch was coming from the hallway ahead of them. Bulldog and the guys took cover behind the closest doors, all of them apart from Taber.

He flew like a silent arrow to the T-Junction and waited behind the wall. When the torch light reached the corridor, Taber grabbed the man's arm and punched him in the neck. The man fell down to his knees and grabbed his throat. Taber was about to finish him off with his knife when he realized it was a security guard. As soon as he had knocked him out with the back of the blade, they pulled him into one of the offices and locked him in. In no time they had split up and searched the building, giving more guards a little nap along the way.

Taber almost lost his cool. They were in the wrong place again. Besides the guards, the place was empty. He was not going to stop until he found Silka.

---**S**ilka---

Stan waited for Silka to stop convulsing from the last shock.

She had endured three shocks so far. Each one was worse and longer than the other. Silka's whole body shook violently as she made garbled noises through her clenched teeth. Her nipples that were clamped by the chargers felt the worst. That sort of pain on the sensitive flesh felt like she was being burned with thunder conjured by Thor himself.

"More or will you talk now?" he spoke loudly, as if she was deaf.

"D… don't… know," was all Silka could manage.

"Again!" Stan ordered his men.

She was finished after the last two rounds. It was now dark outside. She had no idea how much longer she could endure the electric shock therapy. Her whole body was buzzing from pain and the currents that still shot through her. She slumped her head down.

"What have you done with it?" Stan screamed again about his precious cargo.

Silka did not respond. Even when he shocked her again, she did not lift her head.

Stan made his two henchmen fetch and set up a bright light right in front of her. He decided that she was not going to go to sleep on him and would stew under the heat of the light. He also made them set up a portable radio. Instead of playing a soothing tune, they played something that sounded like a puppy constantly yelping in pain.

This is not the music I specifically requested from the DJ, Silka thought.

When the men left Silka squinting and squirming under the intense light and loud noise, she almost felt relieved about it.

It was much later that evening and pitch black. The two men entered the room after she had been alone for several hours. They switched off the annoying puppy sound. One carried a rolled up plastic tarp. He laid the large 6x6 plastic tarp on the floor next to her. The other carried a fold up table. He set the table in the centre of the large plastic tarp.

"When your friends told me about the spy that came from South Africa to steal back the diamonds I got, I never imagined it would be someone as beautiful as you," Stan calmly slurred as he walked in through the door.

Shit, shit, shit. They had been drinking. That was not good.

"I'm not a spy ... I work for the USAID organization. Neither my country nor I have an interest in your diamonds. My country has lots of them ... they wouldn't send a spy to get some back." She spoke calmly and in very Basic English so he could understand her in his current state.

"The Nigerian crime syndicates are rife all over the world, including South Africa. Those who worked for my *special* syndicate would send their spoils across the borders. They would be paid generously for their contribution to the company coffers," Stan boasted as he signaled his men to move.

The two men dragged her out the chair. The one carried her by her feet and the other by her armpits. They laid her on the portable table. They positioned her so that her lower back lay on the edge of the table.

The one smiled as he cut the ties that bound her feet together.

Silka knew then exactly what they wanted to do.

Holy mother of all things good. No, no. "Noooo!" she screamed angrily. She tried kicking and wriggling, but then Stan came and stood behind her and held her down as well. His one hand pressed her upper body down, on the long cut he had given her, while the other held her bound hands above her head. The two men each took a leg and struggled to tie her feet to the table legs at each side.

"This is not what I signed up for!" Silka screamed louder.

"We might as well have some fun before we make you confess, don't you agree?" Stan slurred.

With her legs spread and tied, the two men went to the torture table. They were going to rip off her clothes and brutally force themselves on her.

Panic set in, but she controlled her breathing. They were going to inhumanely and violently use her body to pleasure themselves no matter how hard she fought against it. She could not live with their disgusting germs and vile semen and STD's inside her.

"Give me a gun and I'll show you fun!" she spat at him even though her jaw felt like it was about to break off after his punches. They would decimate her body, in every way possible with whatever they had brought back from the table, once they had raped her. She wasn't a human being to them. She wasn't a person. She was nothing. It would hurt physically and she knew she would end up wrecked, damaged and disfigured. The inhumanity and cruelty of forcing her body to satisfy them was not sexual but sadistic. It almost made bile rise to her throat. They would take the essence of her womanhood and a part of her soul before they left her to die as a beast not as a human being. She would not live through this night. *Don't let these dirty, disgusting animals rape and mutilate me*, she prayed over and over again.

Stan started touching her breasts with the hand that was on her chest earlier. Her blood smeared all over her in the process. He squeezed and pulled her breast very hard while he touched her flaming nipples. She lost her breath for a minute from the pain. He leaned his fat

134

stomach over her face as his bloody hand slid down to undo her pants.

"NO!" Silka screamed trying to sound commanding and threatening at the same time. She wriggled and struggled to free herself. Words came to her like powerless, helpless, alone, scared, hopeless, small. So very, very small.

The two men reached the table with scissors and a variety of knives. They stood there and waited for orders from Stan. They must have received a signal from him, because they put the weapons down next to her body on the table. The one man tried ripping her pants down. While Stan held her down, the other secured her tied up hands to the table with rope. Minion Two went to help Minion One take off her pants when he was done. They could do anything but that to her. She was not about to allow them to rape her. She would rather die.

---

*T*aber, Bulldog and the other men of steel drove around to the third location. This place was closer to town, but also matched the criteria they would need, if they were to keep a kidnapped victim somewhere for an extended period of time. It was still in a remote area. Again there were no signs of life anywhere in the front. Flash contemplated that they turn around and search another warehouse they researched, but Taber wasn't prepared to leave any stones unturned. After they drove around the building they noted three possible entrances. Three of

135

them decided to split up and each take an entrance while Flash would serve as back up. Nothing indicated that there were hostile forces and that Silka was in there. Taber knew this was a possible dead end, but at least he was doing something.

Eagle Eye had reached the front of the warehouse unscathed and unseen. As he opened the door, he saw three men sitting around the table playing cards. Only when the one noticed him and tried to reach for his AK-47 leaning against the wall, did Eagle Eye start shooting. The muffled sound of his silencer was concealed by someone screaming. He turned around and followed the noise.

Bulldog had reached the back door safely. He was about to enter when two men came out for a smoke break. He grabbed the one and used him as cover while he shot the smoker. As soon as he dropped, Paul turned his gun on the man he had grabbed. The guy had balls, because he fought back and managed to free himself from Bulldog's grip. He yelled for reinforcements as he fought with Bulldog. He managed to disarm Bulldog with some impressive moves, but then again, so did Bulldog. Their armed combat was impressive.

Bulldog delivered a precise kick, which was met with a perfect arm block by the man. The man launched at him, but Bulldog grabbed his one arm, pulled him close and elbowed his face. Out of pure reflex the man fought back and Bulldog received an uppercut punch to his face. This caused him to move back slightly, before he launched and punched into the man's chest with force. The man stumbled back, but composed himself just enough to deliver a kick to the side of Bulldog's head. Bulldog snapped right back and returned with a kick to his groin. Bulldog followed with an arm block, right before the man could deliver another blow.

The man hunched over and turned his back on Bulldog. He recovered before Bulldog could make his next move and delivered a spinning kick right into his abdomen, but Bulldog turned his body to the side at that exact moment. He turned away from the punch exposing his back to his opponent. Before the man could make a move, he leaned forward and back kicked the man in the face. The man shook his head as they both returned to position again. Quickly the man jump kicked Bulldog right in the heart. The force knocked Bulldog a few paces back. Bulldog regained his balance and then ran up to the man and flew into the air, at the same time raising his knee. He connected his face perfectly. As Bulldog's feet touched the ground, the man moved forward, raised his leg and pushed kicked with force into Bulldog's upper leg. Bulldog used his uninjured leg to swipe his attacker's feet underneath him. He was about deliver the crucial final blow, when more men came outside.

Then Eagle Eye made an appearance. Together they finished off the menacing men.

Flash had been in the front. He saw Eagle Eye's signal as he came out the front door and then ran to the back of the warehouse. Flash gave him a flicker of his torch, to roger his response.

Taber found no obstructions when he came through the side door. There were no guards and no offices or corridors. With his luck so far this empty place didn't have even a ghost that haunted the place.

That was when Taber heard the sound of screaming too. He hoped it wasn't a ghost messing with him.

---**S**ilka---

The two men were struggling to get her pants past her hips. Twenty/twenty hind sight, they should have removed her pants before they had spread and tied her legs. Stan looked down at her. He forced his exposed hard-on in her hand and made her grip him tight while he waited. She gave a blood curdling, heart wrenching scream as she tried to fight in a last ditch effort.

"I will rip it off!" She tried to fight for her dignity, her body and her life with whatever her painful, sore and tortured body could muster.

The two men had an 'A-Ha' moment as they grabbed scissors to cut her pants off. Stan yelled to be heard over her screaming.

"While I F you, think of where you put my diamonds! If you tell me the truth, my men won't finish you with scissors and slice off your tits, once they fin..."

Pew-Pew!!! Two shots, one on top of the other, fired from a gun with a silencer somewhere in the background. As quickly as the bullets hit the two men by her legs, another sound caught her attention. Silka didn't know what it was. She arched her back and looked behind her. Stan had blood gushing from his throat. He almost fell unto her, but somehow was pushed to the side and fell to the floor.

Chapter 11

There. Right there stood Taber, with bloody knife in one
hand and a gun in the other. He effortlessly cut the rope
and cable ties and quickly moved to cut her legs from
their bounds. She laid there in shock, still gripped by
terror. Everything had happened in a blink of an eye -
she had no idea if it was real.

He leaned over her and looked to see if she was hurt.

"Hi, you OK?" he asked softly as he folded her shirt
over her exposed breasts and wound.

He restored her pants to where they belonged. His
touches made her flinch, but shook her out of her
traumatized trance.

"Yes...how..." she started but couldn't finish her
questions. Even if she had been able to speak, she was in
too much shock. She wouldn't know what to ask first.
How did you find me, how did you do that, how...

"We have to stop bumping into each other like this,
people will talk," he interrupted her thoughts and smiled.
He picked her up and carried her in his arms out the side
exit.

---

*S*ilka could hear more gunshots in the warehouse. She flinched, shook and shuddered with every sound. She was hoping the bad guys weren't going to win this fight and finish what they started. She never showed Stan and the others how afraid she really was, but for the first time in her life she had been through something really harrowing. She had always been the one in control and had never been on the receiving end. This was a very new and all too realistic experience for her. She would be traumatized for a while.

"Shh, it's OK baby. You are safe now. Those are my friends," he cajoled softly and smiled. He placed her gently into the back of a car parked at the side of the warehouse. He pulled a small bag from underneath the seat. The car door was left open for light. Out of the small first Aid kit, he fished some antiseptic lotion, safety pins, some medical suture strips and gauze.

---

*T*aber tried not to notice her flinching and jerking every time he touched her when he cleaned her wound. She was shaking and trembling from the adrenalin and fear.

---

*S*ilka tried to show Taber how strong she was, but she was still very frightened. She was afraid that things would take a turn for the worse and she'd end up back on that table with the bad guys.

After he dressed her wound and pinned up her shirt and pants with safety pins, he proceeded to gently clean her face with his sleeve.

"There we go, beautiful," he lulled her in a calm tone when he was done.

Taber closed the car door, slung his arm around her neck and rested his arm on the seat behind her. She looked at him intently.

"You," her mind struggled to find words and she shook her head. The driver's side car door opened making her jump. Taber took her in his arms, gently stroked her arm and introduced her.

"Paul this is Silka. Silka this is my friend, Paul Hubert." Paul gave her a smile, closed the door and he started the car. "Please call me Bulldog" he said softly.

"Thank you," Silka muttered softly. Paul was everything you'd envision by the phrase tall, dark and handsome. He was clean-shaven and tidy. Remarkably tidy! Considering he had just been in a combat situation. He had not even broken a sweat in all that time.

She, on the other hand, looked like hell. Her face was swollen, bruised and battered. Her hair was oily and hard. Her clothes were torn, bloody and smelled like a sewage farm. She still had some form of pride, which was hanging on a thread. Most of all, she was mortified that Taber had seen her like this too.

The front passenger door opened. Silka gasped for air in fright and clawed Taber's knee. Another guy climbed into the passenger seat.

"Greetings Earthlings," he joked from the front.

"This is Riley O'Conner. Riley, please meet Silka."

He was slightly shorter than the other two, his nose had the evidence of a few bar fights, but with his brown hair, green eyes and dashing smile, he was still very attractive.

"Eagle Eye at your service, ma'm," he turned and said softly in his southern drawl.

"Thank you," she mustered.

Almost immediately, the door next to Silka opened. She gave a shrill shriek until she realized it was not one of the dead guys. Taber held her closer and calmed her again.

"Sorry, love, didn't mean to frighten you." A tall blond-haired man smiled in a friendly way.

"I'm Herman Shultz, but you can call me Flash if you want," he said softly, as if he was speaking to a frightened little girl.

At that moment she realized that was exactly the way she had been acting. She took a deep breath. "Oh, Gosh. I'm sorry. Thank you for saving me - nice to meet you all."

They all told her 'it's okay' in unison. Even their calming, non-threatening tones matched - as if they were trying to calm down a startled wild kitten.

"Better step on it, Bulldog, unless you want to stick around for the encore," Flash patted Paul's shoulder.

The car pulled away in a skid and the building soon disappeared from view.

Her relief at the knowledge that she was safe after the trauma she had been through overwhelmed her.

"Thank you for saving me," she repeated as if she wasn't sure she had said it before.

"Glad you are in one piece," Flash said, until he saw the blood on her shirt.

Silka smiled but turned away from him, embarrassed and uncomfortable. She was clinging to Taber like a lifeline. Taber kissed her on her forehead. A tremor rocked the car and an explosion was heard in the distance. Flash looked like he was about to burst with joy.

"Lady and Gentlemen, welcome to the sound of shattered dreams," he smiled. Eagle Eye gave him a high five.

---

*T*aber looked at Silka. She seemed calmer in his arms, but she was visibly traumatized. They spent the rest of the drive back to the city in absolute silence.

The guys dropped them off at the hotel where Silka was staying. After she thanked them all again, Taber walked her to her room like a big brother with his arm around her shoulder.

Once inside, Taber sat down next to her on the bed. They couldn't afford all the questioning that would come from taking her to a hospital.

"Are you hungry?" he asked in a soft gentle manner. She smiled and shook her head. "Do you want to bathe?" It looked like he was about to cry.

He had heard the last conversation with the men in the warehouse. Her screams he would take with him to his grave. Never had he heard screams like those. It had ripped his heart out. The thoughts of what they were going to do to her disturbed him to the core and almost destroyed him. He had no idea what or how the hell it made her feel after experiencing it firsthand. When she nodded, he stood up and filled the bath for her.

"I shall be right here if you need me," he said as he coaxed her inside the bathroom.

"Thank you," she smiled and closed the door.

While she bathed, he ordered room service and sat on the couch by the bed. He called Josh, on his date with Jessica, and told him the good news. Everything she had been through was finally over.

He felt relieved but his main concern was Silka's mental health. That wound would be a scar she would carry with her for the rest of her life to remind her of this day. He wished there was something he could do to make it all go away. She had been traumatized by Satan's spawn and there was no telling how she felt about him or mankind in general right now. He feared the repercussions this would have on her.

Silka took so long in the bathroom that he was tempted to check that she had not drowned herself accidently. Instead he waited patiently for several hours more.

---*S*lka---

"Better," her confident voice broke the silence. She was wearing a robe and stood there smiling.

"Are you OK?" He was surprised that his voice emanated confusion rather than concern.

"Yes, actually I am," she said with conviction.

Now that she'd had a bath and straightened out her thoughts, she was almost back to normal. Taber had saved her. She wasn't hurt... much. Things could have gone much worse and she could have gone the way of the Dodo. Instead she was here and Tay was here. She was safe. Those men were dead. It was okay. Taber was there.

During her bath she had found a new sense of purpose. It brought her very welcomed consolation but not closure. That would come when she cut off her team's balls. Silka poured herself some wine from the mini bar and sat down to eat. She did everything in super slow motion as her whole body felt broken.

While she ate, Taber watched her nervously. The woman
who had gone into the bathroom and the one who had
come out were equally scary. The one who had gone in
was a traumatized nervous wreck. This woman here - she
looked like a woman who had faced the worst hell and
whose scorn now gave her determination. *Crap!!!*

He knew that look. It was similar to the look his
mother gave his father when he messed up. It was similar
to the look Silka used to give him when he had gotten
her into trouble as a kid. The universal look men got
from women that said...*you are so screwed!!*

The look that Silka had, however, was more than that.
She was going for the jugular. He just hoped it wasn't his.

He sat there nervously as she smiled at him between
taking bites and drinking sips. Her eyes were dark, empty
and dangerous. The undercurrent in the room reached,
'Mr. and Mrs. Smith' proportions. Unlike the movie,
however the male character he was playing had done
nothing wrong. Or HAD he?

Chapter 12

---SILKA---

The positive spin on the whole drama was that now Silka knew why they had wanted her dead. She also knew who had started this. She was going to find them and repay the debt. They were going to feel....everything.

Right now she had some questions for Taber Blake, playboy millionaire and GI Joe extraordinaire. He had surprised her at every turn since the day they had 'met' at the welcome home party he had thrown for her. Her ultimate fantasy guy had showed up when she had needed him the most. He was her knight in shining armor. She couldn't be more in love with him than at that very moment. She put down her fork when she'd had enough to eat.

"How come you're here?" Her head was cocked to one side and her eyebrows furrowed.

Taber visibly relaxed.

He leaned back into the couch, crossed his leg over his knee and held his hands behind his head. In a nonchalant manner he proceeded.

"I followed you to New York. I wasn't going to leave you in this alone, no matter how much you rejected me," Taber said, with kindness rather than resentment in his voice.

"How did you find me?" she asked, almost concerned, but more surprised that they had found her at all.

"I had some help from Joshua and Bill." He smiled. She looked at him with awe in her eyes.

"Tell me. How did you kill them so fast? The one minute they were about to...you know… the next, they were dead." She shook her head in astonishment.

"I have ninja moves, baby." He widened his eyes briefly and smiled. Clearly he didn't want to talk, but that was fine because he looked adorable right then.

"Tell me something I don't know! You have snuck up on me a few times already," she joked back, waving her finger at him as a warning signal.

"Not my intention, I swear. I'm completely unaware of my moves." He held his hands up in surrender and lifted his eyebrows to declare his innocence.

Silka smiled as she thought, *Yeah Right!* He had many moves and he was pulling one now.

Taber stood up to leave. He walked slowly towards her. His eyes were shining and his smile was comforting and sincere.

"I am glad you are safe, Silka," he whispered.

Silka looked up at him from where she sat. She slowly stood up and stepped closer to him. She put her hands

on his chest. The look in her eyes was of love and
wonder.

"I thought I'd never see you again," she whispered.

"Me too, you had me scared there for a minute," there
was pain in his voice but relief in his expression. She
kissed him good night and then he left.

--- *T*aber---

For two weeks Taber took care of Silka during the day
and went to his own hotel room at night. Her ribs were
broken and her jaw was fractured. She stayed in bed
most of the time, because moving hurt too much. Her
nipples, face, arms and legs were every colour of the
spectrum and swollen. She looked like a multi-coloured
balloon animal. The only part that did not hurt was
between her legs. Despite the fact that they were all alone
in a hotel room, Silka did not feel sexy. Her self esteem
was at an all time low.

Every day Taber sat next to her on the bed as they
chatted away and watched television. He refrained from
making any advances or touching her. Occasionally they
would read or do crosswords. They decided to lay low
for a while until she had recovered. In no time at all, her
wounds started to heal. She still had taped stitches and
gauze on her cut. Her face and body weren't swollen
anymore and the bruises were almost gone and didn't
hurt anymore. All in all she looked normal with make-up
and lots of clothes on. She was getting better by the day

in every way, apart from her lust for revenge. Each day she became more and more hell-bent on payback.

On the Sunday night, they'd had room service as usual and after she'd had a bath, she stood there in her silk robe. Taber prepared to leave. He had decided they were going home the next day now that she looked well enough to face her mother.

---*S*ilka---

"Stay with me tonight?" Silka pleaded softly. After the whole experience, she needed a man. She needed Taber. She did not want to be alone. She needed him to make love to her and give her the re-assurance she craved. She wanted to know that everything was going to be alright. For a moment he looked tortured. He didn't touch her.

--- *T*aber---

"Silk, I can't. It's not right. You have been through so much," Taber said with his eyes closed to hide the torment and conflict brewing inside him. At that moment, she was irresistible on every level and he wanted nothing more than to comfort, reassure and indulge her. He wanted to stay to make sure she was OK and give into her every command. The fact remained that she was emotional and vulnerable. She wasn't thinking straight. If she had been, she would have remembered that they were not allowed to be lovers, not even for one night.

"You need to pack and rest for the trip home tomorrow, okay, baby," he said before he prepared to leave.

"Oh, I am not going home. I have a score to settle with some dumb ducks who thought they could F with me." The ice cool, deep calm in her voice and innocence in which she relayed the information had Taber step back. Way back.

"What? Do you have a death-wish, Silka!" he screamed. "Hell, I'd almost lost you for goodness sake, now you want to go all Kill Bill on me?" he yelled at her. The thought of losing her made his heart pulse like a blender. Now she wanted to endanger her life even more by going after some more bad guys.

---*S*ilka---

Wow, pissed off was not even close to what he'd just become. His face went blood red and his nostrils flared like a bull during the San Fermin Festival. He looked like he could breast feed a crocodile or punch one into a handbag, either one of the two.

"I was framed by guys who stole from the syndicate. I need to clear my name and give them some payback, Taber. Is that so difficult to understand?" she yelled back.

"Why Silka? It's over! Those guys will never hurt you again!" he roared.

"Because of this!" Silka shouted and ripped open the top part of her robe, careful not to expose her breasts.

She had taken off the gauze and the taped stitches came off in the bath. The beginnings of a scar began to form - dead centre where most women's breasts started. She could never again wear low cut tops, cleavage exposing outfits or even swimwear.

Taber stared at it and then looked down. He rubbed his forehead with his thumb and fingers while the other hand rested on his hip.

"Come here, let me fix that," he said softly. He retrieved the first aid kit and sat on the bed. When she stood there vacantly staring at him, he whispered hoarsely, "Silka, please? I won't hurt you." Taber looked into her eyes hoping she trusted him still.

She reluctantly stepped to the bed and sat down. She trusted him. The look in his eyes when he had seen her wound - *that*, now that made her scared. While he was re-stitching and dressing the wound, Silka stared at the ceiling.

Silka wondered if he would ever look at her the same again. He used to look at her with desire. She had often found him staring at her. Lately he hardly looked at her, let alone touched her. He hadn't once kissed her or even held her hand since they had come to the hotel that night two weeks ago.

She had been spread-eagled on that table, half naked, beaten up, messy, smelly and bloody. The sight must have repelled him. He must have heard the conversation with the men. He must have pictured what she'd look like afterwards. Those thoughts of her that way must have repulsed him. Seeing her damaged and mutilated like this now, must surely revolt him. That was why he didn't want to stay with her. She tried to hold back. She tried to fight it, but in the end the unstoppable tears rolled down her face. Whatever they'd had in the beginning was over.

---

*T*aber patched her up and closed her robe again. It was then that he noticed her tears.

"Silka?" he questioned. "Don't cry, please?" he pleaded, as if it broke his heart to see her cry. He wasn't sure why she was crying. All he knew was that she looked hurt. It wasn't a physical pain kind of hurt she must be feeling.

---

*S*ilka looked around the room, unable to stop the silent tears. She was unable to speak. She wanted this man, just tonight. Just for that one moment in time. It didn't matter that it was wrong. But he didn't want her. He did not need her. He could not bring himself to look at her in any other way but with pity. He wasn't attracted to her anymore. Her head sank in utter desolation to match the dejection she felt.

"Talk to me?" His faint voice tried to get her to look up at him.

Still she could not bring herself to look at him or say anything. She held the collar of her robe against her neck with her shaky hands. Her soundless tears fell down onto her hands.

--- *T*aber---

The look on her face told him everything. It almost killed him to see this confident sexy woman reduced to feeling like she was worthless and damaged.

He made her look at him. She looked into his grey eyes that blazed with intensity.

He wanted to tell her that he needed her, but didn't want to take advantage of her. He knew she'd convince him that he wasn't. He wanted to tell her that she was emotional and vulnerable. He knew she would hit the roof hearing those words. He wanted to tell her she was still attractive and beautiful. She would have asked him to prove it.

After everything he had been through and when he almost thought he would not find her, he could not think of enough words to convince her of how he felt. He could not explain to her how he felt about her still and how much more he felt for her then. Now, more than ever, the fear of losing her and the joy of finding her had brought about feelings he'd never had for any other woman.

The last two weeks they'd spent together, where he had taken care of someone for the first time in his life, was indescribable. He'd enjoyed every minute of it. He loved the connection it had brought them. He loved the need it fulfilled in both of them. It was inconceivable that he of all people was capable of any *lovey-dovey* crap.

Up to now he had been a playboy. He didn't do the love and commitment thing. That was the reason he was 35 years old and not married. He had never pursued a woman. Especially one he wasn't allowed to be with. He made her look at him. When he was sure that she would maintain eye contact, he summed up what he felt.

"I love you, Silka."

Chapter 13

---SILKA---

Overwhelmed, she fell into his arms and cried. As she sobbed, he held her tenderly. She had never felt this insecure in her life. She had lived a sheltered life for the most part. The torture and true traumatic fear she had gone through was nothing compared to the thought that Tay didn't want her.

This man had become her everything. She had felt like he couldn't stand her or her mutilated body.

Now he claimed he loved her. She was overcome with it all. Part of her could not believe it. How could he love this insecure, damaged wreck?

"Gosh, I love you, no matter what," his voice was husky and his breathing erratic. He picked her up and straddled her onto his lap. He hugged her and held her tight, not thinking that he might be harming her wound. His love for her almost hurt, it was so strong.

"I love you with the scar ... I love you for trying to clear your name, even though it scares the living daylights out of me. I love you for everything that you are right now, right here," he managed through his stunted,

157

staggered breathing. He had never felt this way before. He loved her so much it scared him and her resolve scared him too. It was foreign and disconcerting to him to feel fear.

She stopped crying and looked at him in astonishment.

---

*T*aber had tears in his eyes. He was heartbroken for her and overcome by emotions he had never felt before. He had a lump in his throat from the intensity of emotions he felt for the first time in his life. He wasn't sure that he even loved his parents compared to the love he felt for her. That kind of love made him wonder if he even loved anything at all besides her.

"I love you too, Taber Blake," she said in all earnestness to him.

He leaned forward and kissed every tear on her face. Starting at her eyes he managed to plant gentle kisses all the way down to her mouth.

Her lips were parted. Her eyes were still closed. Her breathing was as erratic as his.

"Goodness, you are breathtaking," Taber muttered, as he leaned forward and kissed her. His tongue parted her lips further and madly searched hers. He ran his hands over her body and robe.

Silka pulled herself closer until she was right on top of him. Desire with a capital D, flooded over her.

Taber kissed her hard, but his touch was gentle on her breasts. His hands moved to the bottom of her breasts and then over to the sides, relishing their softness and fullness under the fabric. He wanted to squeeze them and push them hard against his hands, but resisted so as not to hurt her. Her touch, her scent, her beauty and the way she felt underneath his hands, drove him insane. The intensity of the love and longing he felt was too overwhelming for him. He wanted her, ferociously hard and fast. He was about to lose control and possibly scare Silka. She'd had enough of that for a lifetime.

He stopped to catch his breath. Right now he wanted her so much he might manhandle and hurt her. She had bruises and bad dreams already - he wasn't going to make it worse.

"We shouldn't do this right now," he whispered.

Silka leaned her forehead against his. "No one will know," she whispered out of breath.

"There's plenty of time for this, baby, I'm not going anywhere," he whispered, trying to soften the blow.

Silka took a deep breath and looked at him.

"You are killing me here, you know that." She laughed out of frustration.

"Do you even want me, Taber?" she asked genuinely shocked at the turn of events.

"I want you badly, Silka. I want you too badly right now, to be any good to you. A woman as beautiful as you deserves to be savored and enjoyed inch by inch. I want my first time with you to be slow, gentle and perfect." He touched her face and sighed heavily.

"I can't do that right now. I'm way over my threshold of self control in that department, but I want to stay the night and be beside you. I don't want to be alone tonight." He lowered his head and closed his eyes.

---*S*ilka---

Boom! That did it. The manner in which he had said it broke her heart. All desire wasted away and was replaced by a feeling much deeper and more powerful. A feeling of incredible compassion and nurturing filled her. Beneath all his self control, his calmness and his abilities, was a scared boy who didn't want to hurt her. It almost broke her to tears again.

"I'd like that. I don't want to be alone tonight either," she said truthfully and kissed the top of his head. She raised herself and re-adjusted her robe.

Taber still sat there with his head bowed down. He raised his hands to his forehead, lifted his head and ran his hands down to his neck in a deep breath.

"I'm going to have a shower, why don't you get into bed," he said, giving her a reassuring smile.

Silka lay there wide awake while Taber showered. She was fascinated by this man and still thought about his words.

When Taber came out of the bathroom in his boxers, all evidence of their passion had done a one-eighty. He was calm, relaxed and smiled when he climbed into bed next to her.

"Are you OK?" he asked her.

Silka rolled over to face him. "Yes, I'm OK," she smiled.

"I meant every word I said about taking it slowly, Silks. It will be worth it, I promise," he said.

"Come here," he softly commanded.

She snuggled into his arms. "I know, because I'm going to make damn sure you won't stand a chance to resist me next time," she said and secretly smiled.

"Let's sort out one vendetta at a time, OK, babes," he chuckled.

"Tomorrow we'll track down the assholes responsible for getting my baby upset," he mocked.

"Thank you, Tay. Thank you for everything," she said and vowed to make another important decision tomorrow.

The next day they met with Josh at Bill's office. Silka wore a black suit and shirt that covered her fading bruises and dressing.

Taber wore a suit and tie, which he had arranged with the hotel Concierge to obtain and deliver to him.

Though she had never met Bill, Silka received an affectionate reception from him. They had known that she was okay and safe but Taber had insisted that she have no contact with them or anyone else during her recovery.

Josh informed Taber that his date had gone exceptionally well. Nudge-nudge, wink-wink implied he'd already gotten lucky that night and was now involved with Jessica. When he greeted Silka, the level of his happiness was evident in the mother of all bear hugs he gave her. The four of them stood there for a while chatting. When all the small talk was out of the way, Silka told them everything about her discovery.

"Here's what we know," Joshua started the next discussion. "The team of guys Silka had worked with in Nigeria had essentially consisted of four men. The most senior was Brett Sheffield, the team leader."

Silka remembered Brett well. He was in his early forties, tall, dark and hideous. The kind of looks that could break cutlery let alone a mirror. His deep set eyes, almost disappeared when he became angry. Every aspect of his face screamed for a razor, tweezers or Botox. He looked much older than what he was because of his unkempt black beard. Years of combat had turned him into a hard, fur ball of testosterone, but he could be kind and caring at times.

"The next was Ferdy Kowalski," Joshua said. He was in his late thirties and had served with Brett for a long time. These two men were the masterminds of the operation. Ferdy was fair skinned, but also rugged. His light blond hair was always short. He had a nose like Owen Wilson's, but that was about the only remarkable thing about his features. He was very funny and helpful.

"Then there was a younger man in his early thirties, Ricardo Rodriguez," Joshua continued. Although more pleasing to look at than Ferdy or Brett, he was very short.

Like almost circus midget short. He looked like a Latino gangster, but he had been kind to her.

"Last but not least was Alex Willis," Joshua said.

He was in his late twenties. She remembered him as kind of a sweetheart. He wasn't very attractive but he had a nice smile, deep black hair and black eyes. His hair and eyes complimented his dark skin tone. He was nevertheless very effective at his job.

"These guys had joined her and the other organizations during very difficult and dangerous times. They were former Special Forces, recruited by the Special Operations Group (SOG) and Special Activities Division (SAD) of the CIA to gather Intel. Their goal was to gather information on the Muslim extremists belonging to the Basel Hakims terrorist organization, and protect the lives of the USAID, UN, Red Cross and members of other organizations. The Basel Hakims terrorists were responsible for a lot of destruction and bombings in a religious war with very tense political consequences," Joshua concluded. They were also linked to a crime syndicate, which Taber and Josh knew already.

Apart from Bill and Josh, there was no one else to help her trace them. She needed to get these guys caught and execute her revenge. Neither the CIA, SOG nor SAD would ever condone their actions, but they would deny their involvement. These guys never wore uniforms or anything to identify them, so that the CIA and US government would have deniability if they ever got compromised. The same stood to reason that the CIA and the US government could deny any knowledge of Silka and her team. The four men needed to be exposed and pay for what they had done to her. *Boy! Am I going to find them and make them pay! They would shit diamonds by the time I'm finished with them.*

From what Silka had gathered, the theft had taken place three weeks ago, the night before she had left Nigeria to return to South Africa. The assholes she dubbed Team BARF (Brett, Alex, Ricardo and Ferdy) probably had had all the Intel they'd needed. They must have set up the accident and also framed her to take the fall after she had left. *Her revenge would be served - hot and spicy!*

So far, one thing was not clear. What the hell did they want with the General's diamonds? Josh and Bill decided to make a few calls. With no genius like Geo around anymore, they needed to find someone else who was equally equipped to help. Just thinking about them made her blood run cold enough to freeze hell over. She would give them her own version of Russian roulette. *All chambers would have bullets!*

---

*T*aber watched as Silka sat in silence behind Bill's desk. She had taken off her suit jacket. Her black shirt and black pants echoed the look on her face. She had gone over to the dark side. He didn't know if this was going to be permanent, but right now he did not like it. He wanted the sexy, seductive, confident goddess not the vindictive, princess of darkness. The look did not become a face like hers. She had the face of an angel. Many people used the saying, 'lights up my world' when they referred to someone's smile. Her smile was the world to him. Right now, her whole demeanor screamed pissed-off Ice Queen for life. She was out for revenge and once she achieved it, she'd never be the same again. Taber walked out the door.

Silka couldn't let Josh or Bill see that she was surprised and upset at his departure. As far as everyone was concerned, Taber and she were just friends. They were not in love and she did not just feel like her heart was ripped out of her chest. Silka sat there in silence, wondering where he was. She smiled at Josh when he came over to her.

"How are you doing there, kiddo?" he asked.

Silka looked him in the eyes. "Great! Any luck with the search for a new mortal god with eyes and ears everywhere?" she joked.

"Not yet," he laughed.

"Where did Taber go?" he asked.

"Um, can't say, but I am sure he will be back shortly," she squeezed her nose up in a reassuring gesture.

"While I have your attention," she said to Josh. "I made a decision today. I'm resigning from the USAID," she said bluntly.

"You have my support no matter what, Silka," he promised her sweetly.

They were all waiting to find a person anywhere in the world able to locate someone with high tech gadgets without counting on governments. Silka missed Geo a lot during times like these. She was more determined than ever to avenge his death as well. They had not needed to kill him. *All those pricks would pay for that too.*

Silka was beginning to feel as useful as an artificial indoor tree, just sitting there while Bill and Josh made phone calls and exchanged emails with the world. She stood up, put on her jacket and decided to take a walk. As soon as she had walked from behind Bill's desk, Tay walked back in.

"Gentlemen, I'm sure there is nothing more Silka and I can do here. We are going to leave the search in your capable hands and check in with you later. Right now, I think she needs some lunch and rest," Taber duly informed them as if no one else had a say in the matter, not even her.

"Of course. We will phone you if anything comes up," Josh agreed and Bill nodded his approval.

Silka gave them each a hug and kiss goodbye. She stormed off with Taber closely on her heels. Once inside the elevator she wanted to take him on about arranging her life for her. She turned to open her mouth, only to be interrupted.

"Remember what I said in Moscow?" Flaming eyes, wild and excited stared into hers.

"No, not exactly," she said. He had disarmed her completely with the way he looked at that moment. She could barely think with those distracting eyes of his and the way he looked in a suit.

"I said that one day you'd see the extent of my mojo," he said as he nodded and bit the corner his lip.

"And that means…?" she questioned hesitantly. *Let it involve you in my bed,* she willed him to say, as if she had mind control powers.

"You'll have to wait and see." He turned with a wicked smile and faced the elevator door.

She could not hide her excitement. Her eyes glistened and she smiled so much her face hurt.

Finally, all she wanted was that man. She loved him. No, she adored him more than life itself. Whatever he had in store, she was up for it. The naughty, wicked gleam in his eyes and the sex-on-steroids smile he had, was intoxicating. She couldn't help but feel like she had just won Miss World or something. Her smile was as big as that of a Cheshire cat.

---

*T*aber saw it too. *Phase 1 complete,* he mentally ticked off in his head.

They headed out the elevator and outside. There was a black town car waiting for them. Taber opened the door for her and sat beside her in the back seat. If there was any more suspense and anticipation inside her at that moment, she'd howl at the moon in broad daylight from pure over exposure. Taber's mojo was all she could think of the entire trip.

Chapter 14

---SILKA---

He opened the car door for her at an upscale restaurant called Daniel. There was a table waiting for them, even though there were queues and waiting lists for eternity to get into this place. They placed their orders, had some wine and chatted away about the magic that was New York City and other places they had been to in the world. They shared stories of funny people they had met, experiences and attractions they had seen. Both were equally impressed by the number of places they had in common. This new place as of now, they both had in common too. She'd never been in a restaurant with perfection of this magnitude. The opulence was staggering. The level of service was outstanding. Each table had waiters that gave them undivided attention and ensured that they wanted for nothing.

"What's the occasion?" Silka asked after lunch when he ordered champagne and had it poured for them.

"Mmm, let's see," Taber was pretending to think hard about his answer. "It's a number of things really," he smiled.

"Your stunning beauty, mind blowing wit, all out drop-dead gorgeous body and intimidating intelligence for starters…" He gave her a shy smile, but naughtiness flickered in his eyes. He raised his glass and they toasted.

--*T*aber--

"You didn't mention my heart," she mocked him with that seductive smile that made his legs weak. She took a long, slow sip from her glass. She closed her eyes and licked her lips.

The sound she made after that made him twitch. He leaned forward as to whisper a naughty secret.

"I'm working on that," his silky smooth voice teased her.

---*S*ilka---

"You're working on my nerves at the moment," she reprimanded him playfully. He was full-throttle sexy. She wanted him so desperately, yet he was up to something entirely different.

"Am I now?" he grinned knowingly and took a sip from his glass. "I can fix that you know," he said.

She cocked her head, leaned forward, rested her arms on the table and smiled. He had sparked her interest and she was hoping this sexy hunk could read her mind - *Moscow, DC streets, hotel room last night.*

"How exactly do you intend on doing that?" she asked coyly.

He motioned for the bill. The waiter brought it immediately. "I have a butter knife," he joked.

She was not amused.

He handed a folded wad of cash to the waiter and stood up. He held out his hand for her and smiled.

"Follow me!" he whispered loud enough for her to hear.

"Very well," her eyes lit up when she smiled back. She took the hand he held out for her. In full composure mode, despite feeling slightly tipsy, she glided between the tables after him. In the car she glanced at him.

--- *T*aber---

He looked her up and down, and then smiled at her. The sexy smile she gave him made his heart do a fire drill. *Stop, drop and roll.* She held his hand like a naughty teenager.

They drove until they arrived at Central Park. Waiting for them was a white carriage with two black horses.

---

*S*ilka could have been disappointed that he brought her here and not his hotel room, but the romantic gesture was heart-warming and swept her off her feet. She had to give it to Taber… *the man had mojo*! She shook her head and smiled.

"I'd like you to meet our carriage driver, Mohammed," Taber introduced them and led her in front of the horses.

"Silka, meet Serenity and Destiny," he gestured to them and began to stroke Destiny.

Silka reached out and touched Serenity. She had grown up with horses and loved them. Her parents had several Caspian and Arabian geldings at their stable.

"Did I ever tell you why I was held back a year before starting first grade?" Taber asked out of the blue.

"No, I just figured back then that you were slow or something," she mocked him. He squinted his eyes and pulled a funny face, which made her laugh.

"When I was five, we went on a holiday to the coast. I was sitting on the beach playing near the water, when a freak wave knocked me over. It dragged me out to sea and under the water. I was rescued by two guys but I wasn't breathing. They tried to resuscitate me for over five minutes. I eventually came to but ended up with some brain damage," he said quietly.

"My parents heard of Equine therapy that was used to help Autistic children. They sent me there and eventually bought me a horse, because the therapy healed me completely. Horses helped everything from my motor skills, balance, to my speech and PTSD." He looked at Silka as he strolled towards her and stood next to her.

Wow, that explained a lot. No wonder his mother was always so protective and crazy over him and gave him everything he wanted. Her only son had almost died and then had miraculously recovered. Silka felt a sense of guilt for being mean to him at times as a child.

"Look at this majestic creature," he shook his head and touched her horse too. Serenity was a beautiful horse. Her name suited her well.

Her big, black beautiful eyes looked at Silka. She blinked slowly as Silka stroked her in a therapeutic trance. The tranquillity and peace Silka found in that moment was indescribable. She was more relaxed than she had been in weeks. If they could bottle the calm she felt, there would be world peace. Taber took her hand and helped her get into the carriage.

He put his arms around her as she relaxed her head on his shoulder and held him around his waist.

"When we were kids you always gave in to me when I wanted something," he said with such kindness.

"It didn't matter how angry you were or how much you resented me, your kindness and generosity always prevailed." His voice was soft and deep.

"You always had a goodness inside you that blew me away," he kissed her head. "You are one of the kindest, most generous and loving people I have ever known."

Silka was smiling at the memories of all those times she had thought him insufferable and had given in to him. She knew he was right.

"I know," was all she could say.

Phase 2 complete, he mentally checked off in his head.

They drove through Central Park on one of the most beautiful afternoons she had ever seen. The soft gallop of the horses with the sound of their hooves on the road was hypnotizing. The view of Central Park was spectacular and awe-inspiring. When the ride ended, Taber helped her down from the carriage.

He took her back to the car where they drove to the next place. Inside the car she leaned into him and closed her eyes. She was still under Serenity's spell.

They arrived at the American Museum of Natural History. Taber held his hand out as they made their exit out the car. They walked inside holding hands.

"I thought you didn't like arty things," Silka asked.

"Some, not all, but that's not why we are here," he winked and smiled. They went into the museum but headed for the Hayden Planetarium.

Silka was smiling like a schoolgirl on her first date. Come to think of it, this was the first date she and Taber had been on. They walked hand in hand, smiling and chatting. When they reached the inside of the enormous sphere, they sat down and looked up. The state of the art projector showed them what the night sky would look like in a few hours. As they sat there, Taber held her close.

"Beautiful isn't it?" Taber whispered.

Silka was mesmerized. "Beautiful," she agreed.

"There are billions of stars and planets, some a hundred times bigger than Earth," he said softly.

"It makes you think about how insignificant we really are," he spoke slowly and softly.

Silka sat there in quiet contemplation for a while. For all the good and bad in this world, no matter how it affected us, we were all very insignificant in the greater scheme of things. She thought about her vendetta against the men who were responsible for Geo's death and what they had put her through. She couldn't change what they did, but she could bring them to justice. What they did mattered, but brutal revenge was an inappropriate and an unnecessary action. They were all small in this universe. Looking at that sky, she decided to still expose them, but she would leave the consequences of what they did to others. This new prospective, feeling the way she did right then and being with Taber became her new priority.

"It is humbling," Silka agreed. She looked at Taber. His eyes were reflecting the stars above them.

"I think we should get the authorities involved to catch the men responsible for what happened to Geo and me," she said softly.

Taber smiled at her. "If you say so. I think that it is a very good idea." He leaned forward and kissed her.

--- Taber---

Phase 3 - Mission completed, he mentally gave himself a high five.

He pulled away. With their lips mere inches away from each other, he said softly, "I have been meaning to do something since the night I saw you at your welcome home party."

He smiled as he kissed her.

175

Silka pulled away slightly and smiled against his lips.

"What would that be?" She smiled seductively and kissed him again.

"It will require you to dress up," he said, not able to hide his joy as he nodded slowly and kissed her again. With a last gentle kiss Silka looked up into his eyes.

"What are we waiting for?" Silka's sultry voice matched the lust in her eyes.

He grinned from ear to ear and took her hand.

---*S*ilka---

They went to his hotel suite. She was turned on as hell. They stepped inside. On the bed was a large black box with a silver bow.

"Open it," Taber implored her.

She lifted the lid, and dug underneath the paper. She lifted out a black evening gown.

"This is your idea of dress up?" This was not remotely close to what she had in mind.

"For now." His promise was so hot and sexy, her body compressed in anticipation.

"You certainly know how to drag out the suspense," she said, giving him a scornful look, but winked at him playfully.

"All part of my mojo beautiful," he consented.

Taber insisted that she dress in the bathroom.

When she came out he was in a tux. He looked like a movie star on Oscar night. He smiled a dashing smile when she looked at him. His smile was soon replaced by something darker, deeper and sexier when he looked at her body.

--- *T*aber---

The dress was tight fitting. It had a high round neck with a deep slit in front. The back of her dress had a low cut back that completely exposed her from the shoulders down to her sensual hips and lower back. She looked like a glamorous Victoria Secret model. She had curves, the likes of Cleopatra, Aphrodite and Athena combined could not compete with. *God help me!* He thought as she turned around for him. He did not dare go near her. His self control was halfway out the window about to commit suicide.

"You look stunning," he swallowed and gave a slight smile.

He went to the door and opened it for her. She blinked slowly, nodded, smiled and walked out. Her scent made him go dizzy from the blood rush to his groin. Taber could feel his excitement soar as he walked behind her. Her swaying hips, naked back and graceful glide, had him throbbing so hard, even the Lohans would think ill of him. *Think, Tay, think of dirty baby diapers, shopping or golf. Just anything, think of anything but her.*

---

*S*ilka felt sexier than a roofied Playboy bunny. She knew she had him. Revenge for the other men, might not be on the cards anymore, but her promise to him was. He would not be able to resist her after she was through with him tonight.

She had been so insecure when he had left that afternoon. It took him mere minutes to pull off the whole afternoon and whatever he was planning next. In one afternoon he managed to drag her from hell into the light. He held *that* much power. He was the tall, good looking and powerful man she had always fantasized about. After what he had done today, she wanted him more than air.

Night had fallen over New York City. Millions of little lights in the buildings illuminated the night sky. A little light shone out of every one of the windows of tall buildings in every direction. It was staggering to think that each little light represented an office or home with people in it. The city was on fire with energy.

They reached Chelsea Piers. Taber stepped out and help Silka out the car.

"Madam," he bowed as she stood next to him.

She could've eaten him up on the spot. Taber directed her to Pier 61 and on board a Spirit yacht. There was a bunch of red roses and a bottle of champagne on the table inside. Taber pulled out her chair for her and Silka sat down. She wondered if now would be a good time to tell him of her propensity for sea sickness.

"And now?" Taber was curious about her secret smile.

"Just planning ahead honey," she lied, not relinquishing that smile.

---

*T*aber caught his breath. *Damn this woman is sexy.*

He had booked the entire boat. It was just them. They were poured champagne and they made another toast. Afterwards, they walked around before they were to set sail. Among the many amenities there was a dance floor as well. The entire place was sleek and chic. They went out onto the open deck and stood side by side, looking at the Manhattan skyline as they drifted off into the sunset.

After they ate and were entertained in pure Broadway style, Taber led Silka to the dance floor. They melted together in perfect rhythm. His one hand was on her bare back.

His touch sent small thrilling tingles up and down Silka's spine. His scent inebriated her and had her breathless with pheromones and lust.

The music changed to something sensual and Latino.

---

*S*ilka turned around. *Playtime Mr. Blake*! With her back pressed against him, she lifted her arms in the air and slid down his body in a long sensual move. He grabbed her one hand, lifted her up and swung her around into his arms. He guided her backwards as they stepped into full on tango mode. They twisted and moved in a sexual tango like they were born to do it. They turned, twirled, stepped and touched to the seductive beat of the music. When she turned to face him once more, she lifted her leg to his hip and flung her arm around his neck. The look on her face was burning desire and flaming lust.

He grabbed her leg with his free hand and resisted the urge to take her right there on the dance floor. They were both breathless from the need and desire they felt.

The music turned to another track. The staff that had stood there mesmerized until the music switched woke from their spell. They looked confused for a split second before they continued doing what they were busy with before the distraction.

"All Mighty," Tay breathed out as he released her.

"Yes?" Silka answered in a naughty as hell voice. He grinned, turned her towards their table and gently smacked her bottom. Silka giggled. After she sat down, she leaned back in her chair and played with the rim of the champagne flute.

"So this is what you've wanted to do since the party?" her silky voice teased.

"In a word," he tilted his head to one side and gave her the kind of smile that could dissolve panties.

Silka licked her top lip and gave him a lusty look. "Only this?" She asked again.

---

*T*aber was about to explode. *Call him roast beef and stick a fork in him, because he was done as in Capital D - Done.*

"Come with me," he whispered hoarsely. He needed fresh air. He pulled Silka's chair out for her.

When they reached the outer deck again, she realized that they were almost back at the Pier. He led her to the edge and stood behind her.

---*S*ilka---

Please God, not that overrated Titanic shit, she almost blurted out loud.

"I have one more surprise for you and then I'm taking you off this boat." He snaked his one arm around her waist and pulled her against him hard, "and into my bed," he whispered deeply in her ear.

Holy Mojo!! His words and his voice right then yielded the ultimate aphrodisiac which fuelled her desire even more. Her entire body screamed for his touch and clenched in anticipation.

He held out his other arm in front of her. In his hand was a long Tiffany box.

"Open it," he gently instructed.

Dumb-struck, she took it and opened it. Inside was a beautiful diamond necklace. She stared at it as he planted gentle kisses along her neck.

"It's exquisite. Thank you," she said softly.

"You are welcome," he whispered against her neck while continuing his gentle kisses.

--- *T*aber---

She turned around and kissed him. Her lips and tongue fondled his mouth in a manner so sensual *his* legs went weak.

All too soon their cruise came to an end. Taber put the necklace around her neck. He took her hand and dragged her so fast behind him, she almost became airborne like a kite. They headed back to the town car. Just then his phone rang.

"Hello, Taber Blake," he sounded annoyed at the interruption.

"Josh, yes, what's up?" His tone became friendly and more relaxed.

Silka was happy that Josh and Taber had become good friends.

"Of course! Not a problem. We'll meet you there now, bye." Taber frowned and put his phone back into his pocket.

Silka immediately felt frustrated. The last thing she wanted was to meet up somewhere or go anywhere. She did not want to be anywhere but with Taber in his hotel room.

"Sorry, baby. We're needed urgently." He seemed just as upset as she was.

In the end she knew Josh would not have called if it hadn't been important. She hoped that they had found someone who could help them trace the team. Taber dropped her off at her hotel room to change.

Taber was going out of his mind. He should've taken her last night or on the dance floor. The things he did for this woman! He changed in his hotel room and left to pick up Silka. *What now?* He wondered.

Chapter 15

---*SILKA*---

They met at Otello, the same Italian restaurant Taber and Josh had had lunch the one day. Bill and Josh looked exceedingly worried. There was a nail-biting suspense in the air.

"Thank you for coming here so late," Joshua said grimly.

"Not a problem. What is this about?" Taber asked concerned.

"The cleanup crew found some things in the debris the day after you turned the warehouse into a parking lot," he looked disturbed but his voice was calm.

When nobody said anything he continued.

"The one stiff had this on him." Joshua took a device out of his pocket and placed it on the table. Taber and Silka looked at the black plastic thing like confused doggies. It was squashed like a pancake and some buttons were missing, but apart from that it looked like a basic 1990's cell phone.

"It is a cloning device for a cell phone. It took some time to find someone technical enough to crack this damaged baby and find out what was on it. We received the result a few hours ago. It seems that your phone was used to locate Silka," he looked at Taber as he spoke.

Silka looked at Taber. He was in shock. She was confused. "How did they do that?" she asked, astounded.

"I sure as hell didn't give my phone to anyone!" Taber sounded almost defensive, but his demeanor remained calm.

"That's the thing," Josh added, "They don't need to have your phone to clone it. This device just needs to be in close proximity to your phone," he explained.

"This high tech gadget can clone your phone from three feet away, trace your phone and record every call you make or receive."

Wow! To Silka this was straight out of Star Trek. She had no idea technology like that existed.

It took a minute, but Taber put two and two together. It was not four.

"There were three men at the coffee shop the Monday after the art show. Two kept me company while the other one seemed to be playing with a gadget," he said, looking at the device. "Seems like we found his little gizmo."

"That explains a lot, but you should also know," Bill hesitated a little but continued, "The terrorist organization used it to track Stan."

"You lost me," Silka chirped.

"Way over my head," Taber chimed.

"We did some digging. The three men at the coffee shop belonged to Basel Hakims. They were friends of Alaji Omar (or Twit Two), and offered to help him search for Silka," Bill stated.

"Somehow the Syndicate management must have heard about what happened and what Stan did in Nigeria. Since we all know the terrorist organization runs them, it became involved. The bosses of the terrorist organization wanted their diamonds back and decided to send help to the criminals. Except the help reported everything back to their bosses," Josh proclaimed.

"Based on what you told us and what we discovered, it seems that while the criminals focused their energy on Silka, the terrorists followed them. They probably saw you walk Silka and her mother to their car. When Silka vanished after taking her mother to the hospital, the criminals kept searching fruitlessly, but the terries only had eyes for you," Bill joked, but looked at Taber intently.

"So the terrorist buddies helped the criminals. All the while the terrorist bosses used the terrie buddies to trace said criminals to get to Stan?" Taber nut shelled the gist of it in his question.

"Yes. That's the short and curly version," Josh added and then paused. He took a deep breath.

"The terries followed you to the warehouse in time for front row seats to the Crash Boom Bang concert. They managed to get word out to their bosses before they were baptized with fire. The terries know Stan is dead and have now expanded their crew since then. The whole terrorist organization knows Silka is alive and are searching for you guys in New York as we speak," he said.

Silka and Taber sat there looking like wax dolls in a Madam Tussauds' exhibition.

"We think that you guys should lay low for a while. Maybe go back home, since the terries can't trace you anymore," Bill completed the whole story.

"But what about the guys who are responsible for this? We can't just go into hiding and stop looking for them!" Silka was appalled at the suggestion.

"We will continue the search for someone to help and include the NSA, CIA and whoever else we can to help catch them," Bill reassured her.

"They have a point, Silka. We should not be out there chasing bad guys with rabid hounds on our trail," Taber agreed and cocked his head to the side. *Please God let this woman see the light!*

"Fine, but you will call us if you find them." Her words were more like instructions than a request.

"Of course. You will be the first to know," Joshua assured her.

They finished their drinks and left. Taber and Silka packed and headed for the airport. They flew back to South Africa that night in his jet and slept the whole way. They were exhausted from their emotional yo-yo day.

"What are you going to do now?" he asked when they finally made it through customs and the terminal gates. He was hoping her plans included him.

"Work and play," she smiled. She wasn't going to lay low. She had a life to live and Taber to nail! She would get some other friends involved to help out with her predicament. She trusted Josh and Bill to find those team mates of hers and catch them. Their day would come, but for now it was Taber's day she was more interested in.

--- *T*aber---

Tay was relieved that she wasn't going to try and find the guys herself. The Silka he knew would probably be out on the next flight to some ungodly place to find help.

"You should go see your folks first," he commanded her kindly like some father figure. His dazzling smile remained as he also made the same plans.

"I shall meet you tomorrow morning for coffee at our usual spot, okay?" He stepped forward and gave her a kiss goodbye.

He had some swift and decisive retribution to make. He drove to the house of the man he had contracted to kill the Nigerians. The guy was a local he had met many years ago. Taber had saved the cocky assassin slash party animal from certain death when he had been too drunk and too outnumbered one evening at a drug deal gone wrong. It had been mere coincidence that Taber was hired to take down the drug lord and his drug dealing mignons at the very same time the unarmed assassin's score went south and they had tried to kill him. The guy had been out of his mind, threatening armed drug dealers! He had been over his head and had promised to do anything Taber wanted, if he would save him that night. Needless to say his promise had been as empty as his sobriety pledge.

He waited in the dark shadows. When the guy struggled out of the car, he was as high as a kite. He hovered over to his front door and felt a sharp pain in his side.

"Let this be a reminder never to break your promises to me again," Taber said as clearly and calmly as a President at a press conference. As quickly as Taber had appeared, he vanished into thin air without a trace. The guy would either bleed to death or find help. Taber didn't give a shit.

Silka was glad to see her parents after everything she had been through. Even her mother was somehow bearable. When she arrived back to her own place that night, she had a stack of things to do. It made the time fly at the very least.

--- *T*aber---

The next morning Taber met Silka for coffee. Their affectionate display made everyone around them uncomfortable, but they did not care. Afterwards they sat chatting until it was time to leave for work. After coffee he walked Silka to her building entrance like he used to and set off to leave.

"Don't work too hard, because you are going to need all your energy tonight," he said seductively, in a low voice and gave her a look that could make crass Viking Wenches weak-kneed.

"Aw, poor thing. You have no idea what you are in for." She pouted her lips and gave him a snarky sympathetic look.

He swallowed hard for a second in anticipation of her hot threat. "Neither do you, baby," he threatened aggressively but gave her a kiss so soft and tender it left her wanting more. She appeared slightly disorientated. He smiled at his victory and walked away.

When he arrived next to his car he received a phone call. Standing on the pavement he took the call as he distractedly walked down the sidewalk past some shops. A supplier was on the other end and informed him in detail of a supply problem.

Taber listened intently, but became very distracted suddenly. Could that be Silka? What was she doing? Where was she going?

"I'll call you back," Taber hung up on the supplier. He ran to his car and told the driver to follow Silka. She drove out of town towards Soweto. He followed her into the township, which consisted of brick mansions and tin shacks all mixed up in one. She continued past the shacks, shops and houses to the outskirts of Soweto until she reached a school in the middle of Dobsonville. Taber made the driver turn around a few minutes later after they passed her. *What the hell was she doing here?* Silka stood talking to some women when he walked into the school.

"It's good to be back. We have a lot of work to do!" she said to the ladies.

"Silka?" he called to get her attention.

She turned around in shock. "Tay, what are you doing here? Did you follow me?" she asked exasperatedly, clearly annoyed by his presence.

"What is this?" he asked. Just when he thought he knew her, she sprung another surprise on him.

The look Silka saw reminded her of the night in Moscow when they had entered her hotel room. The same look of confusion, fear and disconcertment was in his face. Silka stepped forward, but he stepped back.

"I can explain," she said calmly.

"Explain what?" He shook his head in disbelief. Millions of questions raced through his head. She had lied about the kind of work she had done in Nigeria. That had almost got her killed. After everything they had been through, why would she keep this from him? Working at a school was not a big deal, yet she had lied to him about it. Why would she lie about working at a school? What was she doing here if she worked for the USAID? What was she doing in town everyday if she worked all the way out here? Maybe she was stalking him. Who the hell was this stranger?

"Tay, please?" Her voice was shaky.

He was dazed and confused. After all the killing he had done for her. After putting him through hell when he thought he had lost her. After saving her life and nursing her back to health. After all the trouble he had gone through to bring her out of the darkness and now this? He was tired of being lied to and being treated like a mushroom. He did not deserve it. He shook his head and stormed off.

Silka tried to run after him, but it was too late. He was gone.

Chapter 16

Silka decided to let Taber cool down after their fight and carried on with her work. She knew some good people in Nigeria. She had made friends with locals she did not help interrogate. The majority of people in the country were good, hard-working people who just tried to make a living under horrible circumstances. She reached out to them to try and find out more about the team's actions and their whereabouts. Two guys called Benji and Zola actually offered to help her and set off on fishing expeditions of their own.

Benji and Zola worked as administrators at a local orphanage and also volunteered at the local clinic. They were not highly educated but they spoke English very well and helped the Red Cross and UN with whatever they could.

They learned through some women who knew Team BARF, that Brett had plans to retire to an island. Ferdy was going to live like a rock star and look after his family, while Alex had plans to travel the world in style. Ricardo was going to blow his money on fast cars and easy women. Like his dad always said - if you are not in bed by ten, go home. He had always lived by that motto when it came to women.

"Hey Baby Twos!" Benji exclaimed when he called her a few days later.

"Hi Benji," she giggled. He always called her baby twos and she still had no clue why. She didn't mind it, even if she was thirty four years old.

"Z and I were thinking," he said.

"That sounds dangerous," Silka interrupted with a joke.

"You are not far off," he added, "My brother is a member of the infamous B.H. organization. He told me that the Basel's are still looking for their diamonds. They are headed your way."

"If they are looking for their diamonds, they are heading the wrong way. I don't have them, Brett and his cohorts have them," she said annoyed.

"Well, that's where we thought we could help you," he sounded cheerful.

"Ooh, now you have my undivided attention!" she said, sounding excited.

"Let's send the terrorists after Brett and the team?" he suggested.

"Can you do that?" She was surprised at their genius plan, but not sure how they could accomplish a feat of that magnitude. The entire terrorist organization was after her. How could they make them change track?

"Sure, my brother can do that." He didn't say how, but Silka believed him.

"You guys are amazing. Thank you very much. That is a great plan!" She was happy with the idea.

"I just don't see how they can track them down, when the entire US intelligence community can't find them," she added, feeling slightly despondent.

"They couldn't find Osama Bin *'Hiding'* for ages either!" he told her.

"It takes bad guys to find bad guys and trust me they will have snitches everywhere," he consoled her.

"That's true." She laughed at his proclamation and hung up after they said their goodbyes.

Benji called his brother and explained the whole story. The syndicate had people imbedded in every criminal activity of the world. They knew every black market player, bad guy and emotionally corrupt person in their circle of friends. As soon as these guys came out of hiding they would hear about it and be on them like ticks and fleas.

Joshua and Bill could help by informing everyone in the intelligence and communications community that more help was on the lookout for team BARF.

"Hi, Josh," Silka greeted him.

"Hello Silka," he was not surprised to hear from her so soon. It had only been a few days since she had gone back home.

Silka told him about Benji and their plan.

Joshua was impressed with the plan. He had a plan of his own. "What do you say we track the terrorists and trap them along with the team?" he suggested.

"No, I don't want Benji's brother to get caught," she insisted.

It was the least she could do for him after he had taken the Basel Hakims guys off her back.

"We will warn him before we strike," he consoled her, but he had made up his mind.

"Keep me updated on their progress to find the team and then we will set the wheels in motion to trap the lot. In the meantime we will keep our eyes and ears open for your team as well," he instructed her.

Silka had the distinct impression this was not a discussion. He was wearing his government cap. The one that would make the good old U.S. of A look good. Every world organization would jump on the band wagon to trap these cockroaches and rid the world of terrorists, with the Yanks in the forefront, leading the charge and coming out shiny and smelling of Armani. Ambitious and patriotic to the bone, that was Joshua Stonewall. He was even more stubborn than his surname suggested.

Silka didn't know if she should tell Benji about this plan. She decided to hold off until the last minute. His brother might get cold feet at the possibility that he would be unemployed if he knew this now. She had other things to attend to that were far more important while she left the dirty work to other people. It had become somewhat of a personality trait over the last six years. *Oh what the hell,* she thought. Better leaving the dirty work to others than doing it herself, hey?

She spent the rest of her time trying to reach Taber, but had no response.

Chapter 17

---*T*ABER---

It had been two days since Taber had last seen Silka. He had left her at the school, not knowing what was going on. The rest of week, Taber had not taken her calls at his home, office or mobile phone. She wrote him emails explaining it all. Explained how the USAID had started this school, but decided after five years to phase out their long term program in Education. They used the funding to spend on other problems in South Africa like sustainable farming to curb poverty. She explained that this school was going to be closed down and the children would be forced to take unsafe, expensive minivan taxis or even walk to schools miles and miles away. Mildred, her mother's patient housekeeper, had begged for her to help, because she had four children in this school. Silka had filtered funds from the USAID sustainability mission which she now worked with and put it into this school to keep them afloat, ergo the reason for the secrecy. No one could know that she was keeping this school going with unauthorized funding.

---*S*ilka---

Endless emails and phone messages to Taber, along with many tears later, Silka finally gave up. It was over for her too. In the weeks to follow she emptied her office in town after officially completing her notice period with the USAID. She could focus all her energies on raising funds for the school without 'borrowing' from the USAID missions. She set up numerous appointments with companies to gain corporate sponsorships and scholarships for the kids. She even made amends with the USAID by paying back every cent into the sustainability missions from her trust fund. Thanks to Joshua, no charges were pressed by them. She was never going to hear the end of it from her mother, but she was prepared to live with it. She had atoned for everything. She even sold her car, because she was driving the school's car that was donated by the USAID when they had first opened the school. It was the very car Taber had followed her in. She took the money from the sale of her car and put it into the school as well.

She thought about Taber every minute of every day. She could understand how he did not want to see her anymore. A corporate thief was not exactly the kind of woman that a man like him should be with. She resigned herself to a life alone. She still didn't trust other men as far as she could throw them. She was never going to trust anyone again - anyone but Taber. It hurt so awfully to be without him - it hurt more than the torture she had endured.

---

*T*aber was lost. Devastated, hurt and confused he threw himself into work and gym. He made no effort or time to think. He just could not think. If he did, it would be about Silka. He listened to her voicemails. He read her emails over and over again. He couldn't believe that she still did things behind everyone's back. What was next? He needed to trust someone just as much as she did, but how could he trust her? He had been right all along. She was Dangerous with a Capital D.

People who love each other should not keep secrets from each other. For a relationship to work, both parties needed to be open, honest and as transparent as Clingfilm. That much he knew.

---*S*ilka---

When Silka arranged a fund raiser for the school on a Thursday night, naturally she did not invite her mother. Silka made a point not to join her mother at any social engagements, just in case Tabitha dragged Taber with. Her mother never went to events without her favorite accessory called Tabitha. She had made her peace with God, USAID and Taber. She had not seen him in a month and was not going to see him ever again.

The night ran smoothly. All the rich and famous people she had grown up with were there, with the exception of Lucelia and Tabitha with Tay in tow. The venue in Sandton's Michelangelo hotel was perfect. The set menu was diverse and the courses were delicious. The

Master of Ceremonies was brilliant and kept the jokes coming with every announcement. He had managed for them to open their wallets with huge success. She had raised a fortune for the school. A lot of computers, interactive whiteboards, stationary, books, toiletries, educational toys and maintenance equipment could be bought. She even received news of an anonymous donation for a million bucks. The school could easily afford all their utility bills and keep going for another decade on that alone. She could even add more classrooms and teachers. Silka was over the moon. After everything she had been through, her life was finally starting over. She was doing something she was passionate about. She had found herself in the process and lived a good life in every aspect. Her happy ever after had arrived - ever after alone.

She drove home that night mentally content but emotionally depressed. Her heart felt empty and heavy. A lump burned at the base of her throat. She wished nothing more than to be able to tell Taber how sorry she was and how much she appreciated everything he had done for her. She wanted nothing more than to tell him that she still missed him and loved him, even though they could not be together. That much she had already accepted.

The next day she gave the school the good news. She decided to take all the teachers out that night to celebrate. They went to a nice restaurant in Soweto where they were entertained by an African drum band and traditional dancers. Her teachers, who were all African, joined in the dancing. Silka immersed herself in the culture and danced too. She loved it. They all partied up a storm. She left early because the Saturday she had to join her mother for an unwilling shopping spree.

Her mother left after breakfast and met Silka at her loft. The usual exchanges about interior decorators ensued and they eventually set off for a day of shopping. Silka had known physical torture, but she was sure the US government could use her mother for emotional and mental torture. The woman was relentless. After a full day of shopping, lunch and more shopping, Silka had had enough. She was at her wit's end, but endured for her mother's sake. *Moan-moan, swipe, babble-babble!*

They finally arrived at her mother's house just before dinner. Her mother was upstairs unpacking her loot and telling her father all about their day.

Silka stood in the reception room looking outside the window. A strange feeling arose. She sensed *him*. She didn't want to turn around and look. *What fool would believe that?* She mentally slapped herself out of her delusion. She turned her head to her shoulder to look with her peripheral vision. At least then she'd know she was wrong. She smiled. *Stupid cow...there's nobody there,* she shook her head in disbelief of her gullibility.

"Hey," Taber's soft voice filled the silence.

202

Silka gave herself another moment and turned around slowly. Taber was right behind her.

"Hi," she said wispily. Her voice was shaky and sad. She had moved on. She was over him. Though seeing him there snapped that incorrect assumption out of her. She was sad because she missed him and she was excited to see him at the same time. Her feelings were compounded by the uncertainty of what he was doing here.

He looked clean-shaven, tidy and knock-knee gorgeous. He was wearing denim jeans and an expensive long-sleeved shirt.

"I was angry that you had hidden something from me. Relationships work when there is trust, loyalty, respect, love and friendship. Each partner has to be transparent, forthcoming and honest to gain the other's trust." He spoke slowly and softly.

Silka listened silently and braced herself for an epic lecture after a long day with her mother.

"I'm sorry Silka. I hid something from you too."

Huh? What? She was really confused but kept quiet and maintained her composure.

"My ninja moves," he laughed a little and then continued, "Paul and I were in the army together when it was still compulsory for eighteen year olds to do a two year service in the South African military. It was before the end of apartheid. The army trained us and eventually put us into divisions. Paul and I were put into

Intelligence and Reconnaissance. They trained me in sleuth assault, sniping and various assassination techniques over and above normal combat. We were sent to the border to fight against the Cubans and the Angolans. Once we left there, they put us in the townships. There was a lot of unrest, riots and political uproar over the Apartheid regime. In the 'bush' we knew our enemies, but there, everyone was shooting at us. Anybody and everybody was the enemy." He looked haunted and embarrassed.

"We did a lot for our then government that we are not proud of, which is why we kept it a secret from everyone. Since then I have been working as a hired 'problem solver' to help good people in need to atone for what I did. Working at my dad's company is just a front and part of my cover," he said softly.

Silka was so floored you could use her as a mop. *What the hell am I meant to say to all that?*

"So we both did things we believed were right at the time. We both believed people knew right from wrong and trusted them. We both made mistakes and have regrets. We both hid things from each other," he said quietly.

"So we're even. Where does that leave us?" she stated, still uncertain about the reason for this conversation.

"Right here, right now?" he asked softly as he moved towards her. He took Silka in his arms.

"Room for this," he inhaled sharply and he kissed her. Right then her mother entered the room.

"Taber Blake! I shall not have that behavior in my house. Unhand my daughter this instant!" she exclaimed, raising her commanding voice.

Taber and Silka both jumped back like two naughty kids who were caught playing doctor-doctor.

Chapter 18

Her father stood there with a smirk on his face. He was happy that they found each other. He knew his parents and knew Taber was a responsible, successful man and that they would make a great union of the two houses, so to speak.

Her mother liked Taber and thought they would make a good match, but in her eyes, the public display of affection was deplorable. She had to put an end to this un-chivalrous and provocative behavior in her house.

"Are you staying for dinner?" enquired Ted.

Taber looked at Silka. "I regrettably have a reservation already. I was just about to ask Silka to join me." He gave her the 'kid at Christmas' look, as his heart frantically held on for her response.

"I'd love to." Silka smiled at her Hero. *Anywhere but here!* She went upstairs to change into an outfit she had bought earlier. Once she was camera-ready, she went downstairs.

---

*T*aber stood staring like someone had pressed the pause button. She had a white, tight-fitting dress on that made her tan stand out. Every curve was accentuated. Her cleavage was adorned with a necklace that had a think, long diamond pendant, which covered her scar. The dress ended just above her knees. Her tanned, toned legs glowed all the way down to strapped diamante stilettos. On her tanned feet they sparkled like real diamonds.

"You look beautiful," he said in an appraising tone.

They said goodbye to her parents and climbed into his silver Austin Martin Lagonda.

"Where are we going?" Silka asked as she realized they were not going into town.

"I know this great restaurant. It has a world class chef. They are open twenty four seven and serve anything you want no matter what time of day it is," he smiled secretly.

"Even Crème Brûlée for breakfast and Beef Bourguignon for brunch?" she teased.

"Anything you want – three sixty-five," he smiled back.

---**S**ilka---

They reached a suburb. Most businesses were run from previously owned residences, so Silka thought nothing of it. The particular affluent area they were in had many businesses and homes mixed together. All of them in perfectly landscaped gardens and multiple storey properties. The estates were so big, you felt the distance from the one to the next property. This was the area code of the rich and famous in Johannesburg. New money as her mother would call it.

They turned into one of the driveways. It had massive black security gates. They opened as they approached. Taber drove in past massive Cycads and Palm trees. The whole area looked colorful and tropical, but well maintained as well. The gardens were so lush you could not see the house from the street. Silka could see other cars parked in front of two beautifully carved double garage doors in front of them. The garage looked big enough to hold a fleet of cars.

They turned towards an incredible triple storey house. It looked like an English Castle in a pale sandstone color. As they stepped out of his car, a man approached to greet them.

"Good Evening, Mr. Blake," he said as he took the car keys from Taber.

Tay greeted him. He introduced Silka to James. *Regular?*

They walked towards the castle and through the front door.

"Welcome home, Sir," a young woman in a uniform greeted him. *Home?* Silka looked surprised. The housekeeper took his jacket and handed him two glasses of wine. He introduced Silka to Gladys. While they drank their wine, Tay gave her the tour.

Nothing was open plan. The exquisitely decorated rooms where separate from one another. The inside was modern and held every modern accessory known to mankind. The TV's, heating, cooling, lights and fireplaces, waterfalls from the walls, music and everything electrical or electronic ran off a central panel on the wall and on his iPad.

The lowest level had an entrance way to a modern lounge the size of a small house. It had a fireplace on one side and water wall on the other. Behind the door of an adjoining room to the left was a games room with pool tables, Xbox consoles with huge HD LED televisions. Another room held a ten-seater movie theatre with reclining ox leather chairs complete with cup holders. The room was nestled next to a bowling alley and snack bar. There was a space big enough for a dance floor in front of them. On the other side of the lounge was a door to the kitchen, scullery and store room that led to the garages.

The lounge was separated by glass electric swivel doors that made a seamless transition to the covered outdoor limestone terrace. There was a lush pool and Jacuzzi area outside with a tall waterfall flowing into it at the end. It boasted modern architectural details with British Columbian furniture, fireplace, bar, dining area, kitchen and various kinds of chaises, chic weatherproof couches and loungers which gave the entertainment area an inviting resort feel.

The middle floor had the formal lounge, a living room, a huge dining room, library, study and some guest rooms. The formal lounge had a balcony that overlooked the back garden.

The third floor had an enormous brown and black master bedroom with a balcony half the size leading off it. Inside the master bedroom was a lounge, massive four poster bed, humungous flat screen TV and a fireplace. On the right were walk-in closets, which led to a room with mirrors and enough shelves to run a shoe store and sell accessories. Next to the walk-in closet was a bathroom that was the size of a decent bedroom.

The en-suite bathroom had his and hers sinks and toilets. The spa bath could fit four people comfortably. The shower had a large square shower head built into the roof. There were two more bedrooms upstairs all with balconies on the other side of the passage. It looked like a modern five star hotel's penthouse suite.

Taber arranged for dinner to be set up on the balcony outside his bedroom. As night fell small LED lights appeared from the roof like little stars. The one corner of the balcony held a two-seater swing chair with a table at each end. Soft music played in the background. There was an outdoor lounge suite in the middle of the balcony with pot plants and coffee tables. A soft furry throw covered the back rest of the one couch. The other corner had a small round dinner table set up illuminated by soft candle light. The gardens below were lit up by spotlights, including the pool and waterfall. There were round lights set along a pathway. Above, the stars glittered in the night sky. It was the most romantic place Silka had ever been in.

The butler came upstairs to take their orders and went away again.

"You have a beautiful home," Silka complimented him. They were facing each other as they stood with their hands holding the balcony railing.

"Thank you," he said softly and continued, "About earlier, what you did for those kids at the school was kind and caring. I heard that you resigned and made things right. I am sorry about everything I said and the way things ended," he added.

"I'm sorry I wasn't honest with you from the start, Tay. You have done more for me than you'll ever know. If it weren't for you, I'd be cut up in pieces or in jail for murder right now." She smiled although she didn't think it was funny.

He said nothing for a while. Silka wasn't sure where they were going from here or where they stood at the moment. It felt like they had made peace again, but more than that she didn't know. The kiss they had shared at her home left her reeling with questions. Would he want her back? She didn't think so.

---*T*aber---

Silka was exceptionally quiet. Taber was at a loss for words. He apologized, she apologized. Now what? They had kissed at her mom's house, but that *something* was missing.

He had never been in this situation before. It was the most awkward experience he had ever had. All he knew

211

was that he wanted her back. He had intended to fetch her and bring her here to chat in private and win her back. Right now things seemed different than what he had anticipated. She didn't seem like she wanted him back. He wouldn't blame her after the way he had treated her. He wished he could read her mind.

"At least we don't have secrets anymore," she broke the ice in a joking manner.

"Yeah!" he nodded and smiled. "I hate surprises, by the way."

"I hate blue cheese, overly spicy food and awkward silences," she informed him accordingly.

He laughed. She had started a conversation. That was promising.

"I shall remind my chef. I hate the whole pumpkin family and awkward silences too," he reciprocated.

"Good to know," she smiled that sexy, seductive smile that made his legs wobble.

"I love Thai food, chocolate, New York and Crème Brûlée," she continued with some antonyms.

"I love Thailand, chocolate, Xbox and technology," he added. With the awkwardness broken, they continued on the topic of technology.

The butler brought their food and more wine. Taber held her chair out for her. As they sat chatting through dinner, the friendship connection they'd had before things had ended was restored. They chatted like old friends again.

"That sounded like a lot of fun," Taber laughed when she told him about the night out in Soweto.

"It was!" Silka said, laughing.

She seemed more relaxed and Taber seemed more at ease as well. When they started dessert there was an air of hope.

"I'm glad we're friends again," Silka acknowledged after dessert.

"Do you want to be more than just friends again?" Taber leaned forward and bit the tip of his thumb. He wanted to pick up where they had left off at the coffee shop and needed to know if he stood a chance in hell.

"If it's still on the cards, yes," she answered without hesitation. *What the hell, they were adults after all.*

Taber was speechless. There was no way he would have bet on a yes.

"So do I," he said after a while and looked pleased. Silka's joy showed in the smile she gave him. The butler interrupted.

"Excuse me sir, your mother is on the line." Taber excused himself and went into the bedroom.

Silka stood up and leaned against the balcony railing as she stared out into the garden. They had made peace and established that they wanted to be more than friends. They had come so close to making love so many times and now the opportunity seemed perfect. The timing seemed perfect. The place was perfect. *Now or never!*

213

"Thank you for that delicious dinner. Your chef is phenomenal. I almost feel compelled to try his breakfast in the morning," she said mysteriously when he joined her on the balcony.

"Hey," he said softly and turned her to face him. "I didn't bring you here to force you to do anything you don't want to," he said softly.

She looked into his eyes. "That's a relief, because I rarely eat breakfast." Her husky, sexy tone implied she wanted anything but breakfast.

She knew his threshold for self control was being tested.

"You should, it's the most important meal of the day." The slow and low tone of his sexy voice, teased every muscle in her body to life. He moved closer to her until their bodies touched. Their individual fragrances wafted together to deliver the ultimate aphrodisiac.

"Oh, I prefer to do other things than eat breakfast," she oozed out the lust she felt at that moment. She put her arms around his neck.

"Really, what would that be?" he teased in his sexy tone. He wrapped his arms around her waist.

"A relentless, vigorous workout, followed by a rejuvenating shower," she implied everything in her tone.

--- *T*aber---

He decided to play a little longer and drag out the suspense.

"Is this vigorous workout limited to only one person?" He bit his lip while pulling her hard against him. The heat of their hard, tight bodies increased as they swayed slowly.

"It's much more preferable and fun with two," she said as she slowly licked her top lip and then bit her bottom lip.

"We'll give it a try in the morning," he teased. He was milking this for all it was worth.

She kissed him hard. She had finally broken his resistance and hers. They kissed each other until they were panting.

In that moment, they knew that they were each other's soul mates.

Chapter 19

---SILKA---

They lay there breathless after round three in the early hours one morning. She had spent more time at Taber's house in the last three months than at her own place. She only went home once a day to shower and change clothes. While Taber was at work she would do chores at home like laundry or plan fundraisers before waiting for him back at his house in the afternoon. On weekends they couldn't get enough of each other and spent every possible moment together, mostly naked. They might as well have moved in together, but she wasn't ready for that yet. She liked knowing that she had a place of her own where she could go to in case she needed space. For now, she enjoyed going home every other night and not being under the staff's feet all day. Silka didn't think she'd ever get enough of him inside her, on her, under her or over her. All that might change should she move in with him.

"Let's work on your beauty sleep," he suggested and pulled her into a spooning position.

She smacked his hand when his arms snaked around her as punishment for his last remark.

"Sleep tight ugly," she teased.

"Sleep tight Silly," he quipped.

As Silka lay there, she wondered about her life. Right then she was doing a lot of fundraising for the school, but that wasn't something that could keep her busy on a full time basis. She needed to find another job. She wasn't going back to the USAID due to their policy. Her experience had been limited to PA stuff, Admin and a lot of physically exhausting missions. She was not one to stay at home like her mother. She would need the human interaction and the mental stimulation one got at work. She would start finding something Monday. *Cue the Classifieds!*

"Hello, Sleepyhead!" His soft voice woke her up later that morning. At least it was daylight outside this time.

"Good morning," she smiled. Taber wasn't dressed yet. He was sitting next to her stark naked.

"Thought we'd grab that rejuvenating shower after all the exercise we did up to two am this morning," he hinted.

"Sorry honey, but I have to go home," she gave him a sympathetic smile.

"Why?" he asked. "It's Sunday? I wanted you to spend the day with me." His tone was almost sulking.

"I would love to, but I need a change of clothes and to catch up on house chores and laundry," she told him.

"Very well," Taber smiled. "When can I see you again?" He gave her the 'shy guy' look and bit his lip.

"Oh, I think sooner than you think." Her sexy smile reduced him to a slobbering mess as she pulled him onto her again.

A knock at the door startled them both. Henry, the butler, stood behind the closed door. As soon as Taber got off the bed, she knew there was a problem.

"Forgive me, Sir," he spoke softly through the closed door. "There's someone here to see you."

"Give me a minute," Taber quickly jumped into the shower and got dressed.

Silka slipped on her dress from the night before, minus the underwear. She tossed it in his sock drawer as a memento for him.

After putting on her shoes she stood up to leave.

"Don't go now. Stay until you've at least had breakfast?" he asked.

"I have to, besides you have company," she reminded him. "I will be back tonight," she promised.

"Drive home safely," he said softly. He somehow seemed disappointed.

They walked downstairs together while holding hands. Taber went with Silka to fetch her bag.

*What the…*in the entrance to the formal living room stood Amber.

"You freaking asshole!" she screamed at him.

"What are you doing here Amber?" He looked shocked.

"I came to find you because you wouldn't take my calls. Now I know why." She gave Silka a look that would make killer whales cower.

"I have to go," Silka said in the calmest voice she could muster. She decided it was best to leave. She somehow knew she did not want to be in the middle of that conversation.

She walked out the door.

Taber ran after her. "What's wrong?" he asked.

"You have some unfinished business and I have chores to do," she shut the car door in his face.

Taber stood in the driveway watching her leave.

She had never been insecure. She never took a man's shit. Until she had fallen in love with Taber, that is. Yet again that little voice inside her screamed for her to run. She was getting sick of hearing the damn thing go off like a siren. Taber was the only man whose shit she would be happy to put up with. He had proven himself worthy. She loved him too much. She was not going to run.

She got home, took a shower and dressed for a day of chores.

She was sure that she would hear from Taber eventually. She wasn't sure about what to say to him. She began sounding like a broken The Clash record. *Should I stay or should I go?*

Her insecurities broke through and were now singing in harmony with that little voice that sang "run". *Would you shut up already?*

Had he really broken up with Amber or not. Why was she so upset? What was going on? She had never loved a man like this. What if she got hurt? What if he was cheating on Amber with her? They would both be made fools of.

Her chores were over quickly as she pondered on all of this. She had one last load of washing in the tumble dryer. She didn't know what time it was, but it seemed late. No word from Taber. *Please let him be OK from Psycho Barbie aka Amber.*

Her last load of washing was packed away. She contemplated dinner. The fridge was empty because she always ate with Taber. She never managed to do her shopping or much of anything with him in her life!

She dressed in jeans and a T-Shirt and decided to go and buy some take-out.

When she arrived back home there was still no call from Taber.

She ate her dinner and went to the kitchen to do her dishes. There was a knock at her door.

Almost excited, she ran to open it. James had driven her home sometimes and must have given Taber her address, she thought. It dawned on her that they had yet to christen her place as well as the majority of his palatial home.

When she opened the door her surprise could not have been more evident. It wasn't Taber. It was his mother.

"Hi, Silka. May I come in?" she asked.

Stunned, Silka opened the door to let her in. She couldn't say a word. She didn't know what to think of the situation. Was Taber OK? She was on the brink of panic.

"I'm sorry to arrive uninvited and unannounced," Tabitha said.

"It's all right," Silka stated calmly. "Would you like anything to drink?" she offered.

"No thanks, darling. I just came to apologize," she stated simply.

Apologize? What is going on here! Silka was slightly irritated but kept her decorum above it all.

"I sent Amber to see Tay, even though I knew you were there with him," Tabitha said after Silka remained too silent for her liking. "I gave her his home address, I am sorry."

"What did Amber need to tell Tay?" Silka could not contain her curiosity. Tabitha would not have given her Taber's address unless it was important.

"I think it's better if he tells you himself, dear. I am not sure what is going on. Amber just sounded very urgent," she apologized.

"Sorry, I didn't mean to pry and make you uncomfortable," Silka responded.

"Not a problem. Have you heard from Tay?" she enquired.

"No, not at all." Silka's concern was glaringly obvious.

"I shall tell him to phone you if I hear from him first," Tabitha convinced her. "I'd better be going," she continued, as she moved towards the door.

Silka gave Tabitha a hug and kiss goodbye and let her out. That little voice inside her was hoarse from screaming for her to run.

Dreadful thoughts popped into her head. What if Amber was pregnant? Taber would want to do right by his baby and marry Amber just to be a devoted father. There would be no way they could be together then.

What if they talked and he realized that he'd rather be with a twenty-two year old blonde than some scarred, mid-thirties brunette. The thought made her sad, then angry and highly irritable. *Shallow prick!!* Her mind was still racing when there was another knock at the door. *Great! Does the whole country know where I live?* She flung it open without thinking.

Taber was leaning against the doorframe. His head was bowed down and he looked worried.

Oh! Please don't let Amber be pregnant, she begged silently.

"Hi" he said softly.

"Tay?" Silka looked confused. She hadn't expected him to arrive after his mother's visit.

"Please come in," she said, happier now that at least she knew he was still alive.

"I'm sorry I haven't phoned or anything. You looked so pissed off this morning, I thought I'd give you some time," he said.

"I was going to send a search party in the morning… with guns," she joked.

---

*T*aber laughed. It reminded him of the last time he was shit scared of her. Devastatingly dazzling and disturbing with Capital D's, he remembered.

"Have a seat, would you like something to drink?" she asked politely.

"No thanks," he smiled. He went to the back of the loft where her living room was. Silka followed him and went to sit next to him.

"Nice place," he complimented her.

---

*S*ilka was about to jump out of her skin. *Screw the politeness and get on with it*, she begged silently.

"I have something to tell you," Taber started. The look on his face was filled with fear, concern and disappointment at the same time. She never thought she'd see a combination like that on anyone's face, but there it was!

"Hey," she said softly. "Just tell me, OK?" The kindness in her voice didn't match the fear she felt.

"Amber," he started saying, "she has no idea how it happened or how long ago, but she is HIV positive."

Why couldn't Amber just be pregnant! she wished after hearing the news.

"J.Z, Tay. Are you telling me you could be too?" She was shell-shocked.

"I went for a PCR test today, so I won't know the results for a few weeks," he said softly.

"It's OK. We'll get through it. There are antiretroviral drugs, plenty of possible cures being tested and..." she said, trying to be positive.

"You might have it too, Silka. You should get yourself tested tomorrow," Taber interrupted.

They'd had sex - a lot of sex. Incredible, out-of-body-experience kind of sex, two, three times every night to be exact, but all unprotected. *Shit! Crap! Well, this story just got more interesting,* she thought. Silka was lost for words, speechless, dumb-struck and everything-struck after that little tit bit she hadn't even thought about. She could have HIV and then AIDS. Taber could afford all the treatments, but she didn't even have a job.

Run! Where to? she considered.

Chapter 20

---SILKA---

The next day Silka went to a day clinic. Taber offered to go with her, but she needed some space. After he had told her the news and left last night, she needed a lot of space. She wanted to run away. Everything was too much.

Inside the day clinic it was clean and modern. She sat in the waiting room and filled out the mountain of paperwork. Once she handed the clipboard over, she sat there looking at the laminated flooring and the art work on the walls.

She had spent this year being chased by bad guys and recovering from them. Three more weeks was spent coming home, and sorting out her life after Taber had broken up with her. They finally found their way back together and had three glorious months of peace and now this.

Silka tried to do the maths of when exactly Taber had broken up with Amber. It must have been a week or so after she returned from Nigeria. HIV took two to four weeks after exposure to show symptoms in 40% to 90%

of people, sometimes longer. Not everyone showed symptoms and those that initially did could go into a latency phase and feel fine again for up to ten years. She knew the *HIV for Dummies* version from what she had learned at school and from the USAID. There was a lot more she really didn't know. Last night she had Googled the crap out of this subject. She couldn't afford the drugs, further testing for other STD's and infectious diseases or the counseling. If she was HIV positive and her CD4 cell count dropped to two hundred cells per cubic millimeter, it would mean she had AIDS and was going to die.

Her now meager trust fund would be depleted in no time and no one would hire her. Even if she was HIV negative, she couldn't afford the continued tests every three months which she would have to have anyway.

Silka couldn't help think about how she had gone from life threatening torture to a life threatening disease. She would laugh at the irony, if it hadn't been so scary. Her life seemed threatened all the time. She was more scared now than ever before.

She couldn't afford the extensive, very expensive PCR test which took longer to get the results, but detected the HIV virus directly rather than just assessed antibody counts. Instead she opted for the quick and cheap test, known as the Rapid test. It was just as accurate, but further tests would be required if you were HIV positive, whereas with a detailed PCR test you would not require further tests.

The nurse took her to a small room where she had her sit down for a series of questions. She was counseled on her risky behavior (which felt more like a lecture from her mother) and two drops of blood later from her finger, she sat in the waiting room again.

Twenty agonizing minutes later her tests came back. It was a negative. Silka felt so happy and relieved she could have French kissed that woman.

She would have to go back in another three months time while still dealing with team BARF.

Now all they had to wait for was for Taber's result. He was probably busy at work.

---

*T*aber sat in his office, overlooking Nelson Mandela Square, working on his laptop. His PA knocked on the door and let herself in.

"There is a lady here to see you, Sir. She does not have an appointment," she informed him.

"Let her in please," Taber said, hoping it wasn't Amber.

After she had told him she was HIV positive yesterday, he had thanked her for her honesty but told her to stay away from him. He knew exactly how she had contracted the disease and it did not involve any good hearted blood transfusions. That girl had been around the block more than a kid with a new bike. She was the 'Taj-ma-whore' of Jo'burg. The Friday after they had broken up, she had tried to worm her way into his best friend's pants. It hadn't mattered that it had been at a party full of people or that his wife had been present. She was to him, and Star Trek fans, something referred to as a 'Cling-on'.

The door opened. Silka smiled as she walked to him.

"Hello Mr. Blake," she greeted him politely.

"Silka, Hi! Good to see you, please sit down," he stood up. He was happy to see her and very relieved. She looked elated.

"I cannot stay long, I just thought I'd tell you the good news," she said and remained standing. Taber walked around his desk eager to hear her news.

"I'm negative!" she exhaled a deep breath of relief as she said it.

"Oh thank God!" Taber was so relieved he lifted her up high and hugged her so tight, her internal organs hurt. He released his tight grip and continued to hold her. His head was rested against her breast.

She was still floating in mid air, partly because he was holding her there, but also because it felt *that* good to be in his arms.

"I am so glad you are OK!" His happiness was written all over his face. He put her down, but his arms remained around her waist.

"I'm sure you will be too," she assured him.

"Am I going to see you tonight?" she asked as she prepared him for her departure.

"Yes. I shall pick you up at seven," he said. "I have a surprise planned for you."

"Careful not to spoil me too much, I might never leave you," she winked and warned him jokingly.

"That's the idea," he said in a serious tone, but with a genuine smile.

"Some commitment-phobe you are," she teased him. Silka leaned forward to kiss him. He pulled back.

"We still don't know my HIV status," he explained.

"There's a little thing called Wikipedia. You might want to give it a bash. Turns out you cannot get HIV from kissing or sharing utensils," she stated kindly.

"I shall see what I can do about my ignorance," he admitted playfully and kissed her.

Silka left him and went back to her apartment. She sat on her couch with her laptop firmly secured on her lap. Job hunting wasn't something she'd ever had to do, but she decided to register her CV online and look for work. The job market looked dismal. Unemployment in South Africa was endemic at the best times, ergo the crime rate. Unlike other countries, though, the criminals in South Africa didn't value the meaning of life. You were very lucky if you got robbed or hi-jacked and lived to tell the tale. Despite the crime, it was still her favorite country in the world. She had been all over the world and had seen how the other half lived. South Africa had snow covered mountains, hot arid desserts, beautiful, soft sandy beaches, enormous wild animal parks and rainforests. Even in winter the days were warm enough to sit outside and entertain. The general cost of living was much lower than in Asia and Europe. You could get bigger properties for far less than there. Crime along with the cost and bother of private security companies was a small price to pay for the quality of life you received - provided you had a job of course.

She also decided to help the school plan an outing for the kids with the help of some sponsors. She wasn't going to spend the fundraising money on something so frivolous.

With the day almost over Silka prepared for her date with Taber.

Taber picked Silka up from her loft. She was wearing a purple mini dress with a zipper from top to bottom and a pair of black heels. Her diamond necklace still covered her scar. Her hair was up and her makeup soft.

Thank God for daddy's trust fund, she cogitated, because the look on Taber's face spoke volumes.

Dress – eight hundred bucks. Shoes – four hundred of her hard earned dough. Look on Tay's face – priceless!!

"Hey, beautiful," he smiled but his twinkling eyes already made plans for that zipper. He walked her to his car and opened the door for her.

They drove into town to a well-known restaurant. Tay pulled out her chair for her. They sat down and ordered some wine.

"This is my second favorite restaurant," Silka conceded.

"Oh, really?" Taber was curious.

"Which is your first?" he asked.

"Oh, I'm not good with names," she jibed playfully. "But the chef makes everything and anything you want, no matter what time of day." She flashed the hint at him.

Her come-hither smile rocked more than his world right then. Taber laughed. *Man, he enjoyed this woman.* Her wit and sex appeal kept him on his toes.

"You are sensational," he said, shaking his head.

They looked at the menus and shortly afterwards placed their orders.

Silka smiled as she stared at the striking, stunning man in a suit.

"What did you do today?' He decided to make conversation before he lost the battle with Tay junior in his pants.

"Job hunting mostly and I made plans for an outing for the kids," she said. "It isn't a necessity, but these kids have a lot to deal with. More than normal kids do. I want to take them away from it all just for one day. One day where they didn't have to worry about food. They didn't have to think about their bed on the floor and doing homework next to a paraffin lamp. One day where they didn't have to worry about money or their parents never being home to look after them or their siblings."

"I can sponsor a trip to the zoo." Taber smiled shyly.

Silka loved his idea and his thoughtfulness, but felt uncomfortable with the idea of him paying for it.

"It's good social ethics and it is the social responsibility of companies to do charitable things. My company does it all the time," he convinced her.

"Very well. Thank you, Tay," she said politely.

"On one condition," he added.

Oh Boy! This ought to be good.

"That I may join you that day," he continued.

"That would be lovely." Silka smiled, very pleased to have a day with Taber in the great outdoors.

"When shall I plan this for?" Taber asked.

"Any Friday that's convenient for you," she offered.

"Excellent. This Friday it is, then," he affirmed. She smiled and shook her head.

"Tay?" she said after a little while.

"Yes, baby," he responded. He could tell she was curious about something.

"How did Amber not know where you lived?" she asked.

"I always took my girlfriends to my mom's boat house after dates so they wouldn't overstay their welcome and spend the night, after you know…" he reluctantly replied.

"Clever, I should've thought about that. No guy would have wanted to spend the night if they had met my mother," she joked. She was impressed. He had commitment phobia down to an art back in the day.

Most women would have been jealous or angry, but not her.

Taber was equally impressed with her. "You don't think it was a bit harsh?"

"No. I once excused myself to go to the ladies and walked out of a restaurant to get away from a guy who had become too much," she confessed. "It took 500 bucks in taxi fares, but it was worth it," she gloated.

"You are so not going to the ladies room tonight," Taber joked, with a fake expression. Silka gave him her familiar sexy smile that made him twitch.

Thankfully, their food arrived and they sat eating and talking about their delectable meals.

After dinner, Taber settled the bill and walked with Silka to his car. He decided to drive Silka home instead of going back to his place. As much as it killed him, he thought abstinence was prudent in these uncertain times. They were in the middle of a quiet suburban road when his car started slowing down.

Taber stopped. He had plenty of fuel in the car. His first instinct was to check under the hood. Everything was fine and nothing was out of place. As he walked back to his door, he noticed the flat. His tyre's rim was practically on the road. Fortunately the car came with the world's best anti-flat technology that had enabled him to drive this far without losing control of the car. They must have driven over something sharp enough to cause the huge gash in it. He enjoyed the fact that you could not feel anything in this car, let alone the speed you were doing, but at times like this, it annoyed him. He set about changing the flat. Thankfully the suburb they were in had plenty of well-lit street lights. As soon as it was done he closed the boot where he had placed the damaged wheel and looked towards Silka's door to see if she was all right. It was then that he noticed the scratch. *Perfect!*

Very much incensed by then he got back in the car and drove Silka home.

"What is the matter?' Silka asked as they drove through the streets.

"Someone at the restaurant scratched my car and now I have to replace the wheel too. It's just not my day! I really love this car. It's infuriating to know I won't be able to drive it every evening while it's in for repairs," he was sulking like a three year-old by then.

---Silka---

"It is outlandish that someone who could afford to dine at that very affluent restaurant that we had just been to, would resort to such childishness," she stated with empathy. The parking lot was filled with Bentleys, Aston Martins and Porches. *Boys and their toys?*

"Good night," she said softly and smiled as he pulled to a stop at her loft.

"I'll walk you to your door," Taber offered.

"No, it's quite all right. I think she needs your protection," Silka tapped the dashboard and smiled at him.

Taber laughed. "You haven't asked me about your surprise," he hinted.

"I thought it was that you knew my second favorite restaurant," she joked.

"Come here," he said and pulled her into a kiss.

The kiss was almost spiritual. It was soft, tender and slow. When he pulled away from her, she could not bear the separation. She kept her eyes closed just to commit that kiss to her memory.

"Open your eyes," he commanded gently.

Chapter 21

---*TABER*---

She opened her eyes. In his hands was his iPad, which was on some app she didn't recognize.

"Move in with me?"

He asked so sweetly that she could pinch his cheeks and hers.

"Tay," she was shocked. "This is so soon," she shook her head.

"I know you are a commitment-phobe. I am too, but the thought of not coming home to you is unbearable," he said with a frown. Last night when they had spent the night apart, had given him a lot to think about. He realized that he was hopelessly attached to her and had become used to her presence in his home.

"I'm under contract to give thirty days notice on my lease, Tay," she looked conflicted.

"Then give notice tomorrow and move in with me in thirty days time?" he said, offering a logical solution.

At least she would have time to mentally prepare herself for this huge change.

"Yes, OK," she nodded and smiled.

"Put your thumb on the red square," he commanded, in a soft voice.

"What's this?" she asked.

"The key to our home…you need fingerprints to get in, not keys," he explained almost laughing at her inability to the grasp the technology.

Silka did as she was told. "There," she said once the system registered her fingerprint.

Taber touched a few things on the screen. "Done. Welcome home, baby," he smiled and kissed her again. They sat making out in the car like a couple of teenagers. He felt almost guilty and expected her mother to appear any minute.

"I'll see you tomorrow night," he said.

"I'll meet you at your place."

He knew she thought it best that he wasn't reminded of the injustice tomorrow night.

"Seven?" he asked.

"Seven. Thank you for dinner. Good night," she said and left.

The next day, Silka and Taber went about their business as usual. Tay was at his office. He missed morning coffee with Silka. His days seemed 'off' without it. He decided to give HR a call and find out about their job openings. Nothing would please him more than to live with her, have morning coffee and drive to work and back home together. *You've really lost it!* He thought to himself. Not so long ago, the thought of spending twenty-four-seven with a woman would have made him run off a short pier with an anchor around his ankles. *This was insane!* Tay decided to put that call on ice for the time being.

Silka's day was uneventful. She gave notice to her landlord. He was very understanding and told her she could leave at the end of the month instead of thirty days. That was two weeks away! *OK.* By then they would also know Taber's HIV status. Regardless of what the outcome, she was going to endure it with him. She was certifiably out of her mind in love with this man. There was no way any other man could have convinced her to give up her home for them. Let alone a man who might have HIV.

Afterwards, she spent the morning pottering around the house and looked for jobs on the internet. That afternoon she decided to do some grocery shopping.

On her way back, a red sedan with tinted windows almost ran her off the road. The experience shook her. Silka had never really gotten over the trauma in Moscow and New York. She knew that Stan and a great number of his henchmen were dead, but a part of her always wondered if anyone else might be after her. She often didn't feel like that saga was behind her. What if his 2IC decided to come after her? What if the terrorists decided to still hunt her while they were looking for her team? Sometimes she felt like she was being watched, but that little voice inside her seemed to have found the mute button.

She arrived at her loft and unpacked her groceries. Once that was done she showered and prepared to go and visit Taber. She packed an overnight bag just in case, but right now she didn't want to push Taber, considering the drama surrounding his former slut and her predicament.

When she arrived at his house, he was waiting for her in the driveway. *This must be serious,* she thought.

He waited for her to gather her purse and opened her car door for her.

"Hi honey," Silka greeted him.

"Hey, babes!" He was all smiles and hugged her tight.

"Any reason for the welcome committee?" she quipped.

"Come here," he smiled and led her to the front door.

"Put your thumb on the keypad," he instructed her excitedly.

She did as she was told and heard the door click open.

"You're quick," she smiled, very impressed that he had programmed his house before she had even moved in.

"Just part of my mojo," he teased. *Boy! Did he have to mention that word?*

He already had given her a taste of that and now she was addicted to it. She was addicted to Taber's love.

She gave Taber a smile that flared up his hormones like a teenager with a bad case of acne. He positively could not wait to get her naked again. The fitted black pants and tight blouse she wore made it even more difficult.

They went to his living room where she stood waiting for him to pour her some wine.

"It's such a beautiful evening I thought we'd picnic by the waterfall," he recommended.

"That sounds beautiful," she smiled.

He looked down and smiled as he poured her some wine and took the bottle with them.

Alongside the pool was a jungle garden with a well-lit path all the way to the side of the waterfall that flowed into the pool. They sat next to the waterfall where there was a patch of grass. She could hear frogs and crickets, along with the water tinkling softly into the pool. It sounded like gentle rain. The pool had a LED light that subtly changed its color from blue to green, red, purple and yellow. The dim lights that emitted from the orbs planted along the garden path set a romantic and peaceful tone.

They sat on the lush green grass that smelled freshly cut. She loved the feel of the grass underneath her fingers. The blades were soft and squishy. There was a basket with buttered bruschetta bread and baguettes, a selection of imported cheeses, fig preserve, pomegranate preserve, cream cheeses and some luxurious Kobe beef, pastrami and caviar.

They sat talking with ease for a while, about their day and the weather, until they decided to eat.

Taber looked relaxed and casual in jeans and a golf T-shirt. The look suited him well, as if he was a real athlete. He helped himself to cream cheese and caviar.

---**S**ilka---

She never cared for caviar, so instead made herself a Pastrami and cheese snack.

They sat there eating and listened to the sounds of nature. Silka did not like awkward silences, but this was not awkward at all. This was comfortable and peaceful. The level of contentment they felt could've tamed a wild animal.

When they finished, Taber helped her up and they strolled hand in hand through his massive garden. Part of her wished it was daylight so she could see it all in its natural beauty. All the time she had spent with him so far had involved 'indoor activities'.

"I have a function I need to attend tomorrow evening," Taber mentioned. "Would you care to join me?"

"Sounds lovely, what kind of function?" Silka needed to plan her attire for the dress code.

"Nothing big, just a movie premiere followed by an after party," he said.

"Oh, which movie?"

"Some new James Bond one," Taber stated simply.

"Great. What time shall I meet you here?" she offered, just in case he was still upset about his favorite toy.

"My driver and I will pick you up at five thirty," he said, catching her drift and smiling at her sweet gesture.

They walked and talked and sat in his entertainment area for the rest of the night, chatting away. When it was time for her to leave, they stood in his driveway kissing next to her car.

She could feel him against her tightly coiled stomach. She was all knots and loops. That energy, electricity and spark was there in full force and could kick-start a jumbo jet.

The sound of a car horn brought them out of their enchanted state. It was never polite to sound your horn at this time of night in a suburb, but some people had the etiquette of a fruit fly.

They said their goodbyes and Silka drove off.

The following evening, Taber picked her up. James, his driver, was in the front seat of a limo. Silka could yawn at the Prom reference this made. At their age it would have been in the capacity of chaperones or as the stars of the High School Musical twentieth reunion show.

They arrived at the movie theatre, walked the red carpet and once inside were greeted by a very eager young woman. She must have been in her mid twenties and she hovered, fussed and glued herself to Taber like a little lap dog. *Does she roll over and play dead too?* Silka wondered, especially about the play dead part. The kid was irritating.

Taber paid no attention to her and introduced Silka to Belinda, the company PR Representative. *Nice!*

Silka greeted her with the utmost composure and decorum, like her mother would, to make a good first impression. Channelling her mother's conduct was a sign. It was not good! The little voice inside her wanted to tell her to calm down, but decided to find the eject button instead.

As far as Taber was concerned, she liked the PR Rep and was not irritated by her presence in the least.

As they met some of the cast and chatted to new acquaintances, Silka relaxed more. Taber was the perfect partner. He was attentive, never excluded her from conversations or never made her feel like anyone else was more important than she was.

At the after-party in some swanky nightclub, they danced together like two teenagers auditioning for an episode in Glee.

Her black gown and his black suit matched perfectly in the devil-may-care display they created for each other. Each dance was followed by a laugh and a hug. Then they teased and taunted with their moves again. By the end of the night, Silka's feet were killing her.

They walked to the limo laughing about the funny things they had done, while he carried her shoes. Inside the limo on the way home, Taber massaged her feet while they chatted and laughed some more. Once they reached her loft, Taber walked Silka to her door. In front of it was a brown box.

"Were you expecting a delivery?" Tay asked innocently.

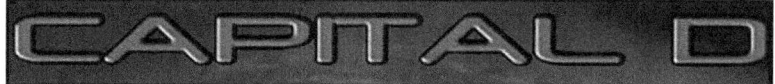

Chapter 22

---*T*ABER---

"No," Silka opened her door, picked up the box and went inside. Taber followed.

With Taber still there, she decided to open it. Inside was a huge plastic Ziploc bag with a dozen or so dead rats. The smell made Silka run to the bathroom and throw up. By the time she had brushed her teeth and re-emerged, Taber had disposed of them outside.

"What was that about?" she asked, visibly and deeply troubled. The look on Taber's face mirrored hers.

"What's wrong?" she asked.

"Do you have something to tell me, Silka?" he asked bluntly.

"What is that supposed to mean?"

He could see her emotions run rampant, as they tilted towards anger at his insinuation.

"You will pay for what you have done," he read from the note he had taken out of the box and threw it at her.

What could she possibly have done to warrant death threats? "Tay, I swear I have no idea what this is about!" she insisted and picked up the note to study it.

He turned his back on her. It must have been something she had done again, Taber thought. *What the hell was wrong with this woman!*

Silka picked up the phone and called the police. After she hung up, she walked over to Taber.

"Tay," she said softly. "I haven't worked in ages. I haven't dealt with people since the Fundraiser for the school. Please believe me? I have no idea what this is about," she said, with slow conviction.

---*S*ilka---

When he kept quiet, Silka wanted to cry out of pure frustration. She really had no idea why something like this was happening.

"The cops are on their way, I think it's safe enough. You should go home." Her voice was a broken whisper, but her confidence commanded him to follow her instruction. The lump in her throat was starting to hurt.

---*T*aber---

"I'm staying until the cops leave!" he insisted. Regardless of how she had dug herself into another mess, he was more concerned that these people knew where she lived. He needed to protect her.

"Fine," she muttered abruptly and sat down on the couch with her arms and legs crossed.

They sat in silence until a knock at the door broke through the silence.

"Good evening, I'm Sergeant Mbanda and this is Sergeant Scott," said a neat and handsome police officer.

246

"Good evening, please come in?" Silka opened the door for them to enter.

Sergeant Mbanda shot straight to the point and Silka filled him in on the box and the note. He told Sgt. Scott to retrieve the box from outside and Taber went to show him the way.

By the time they had brought the box back, Sgt Mbanda had finished taking her personal details to open a docket. He proceeded to ask questions regarding the box while Taber and Sgt Scott stood there.

"I do not know who it was from. I have no idea why. I have no enemies." *Not ones that were alive or in the country anyway,* she thought. Every answer Silka gave was a no until the next question.

"Has anything out of the ordinary happened to you recently?" he asked, in a routine tone which matched his routine question.

"Yes," Silka answered.

Taber shot her a look of surprise.

"Yesterday a red sedan with tinted windows tried to run me off the road," she said.

"Flipping hell, Silka! Why didn't you tell me?" His uncertainty about her role in this turned into major concern.

He sat down next to her.

Silka ignored him and continued, "I thought it was a random road-rage incident at the time. It was almost rush hour and people get crazy on the way home," she explained, looking at the police officers.

"Where and how exactly did this happen?" Sgt Mbanda asked.

"It was two blocks away from here, on my way home from grocery shopping. The car came out of nowhere and raced past me. It suddenly swerved into my lane and slammed on brakes. I swerved to the right lane and it tried doing the exact same stunt again, except this time I was prepared for it and switched lanes to the left. The car had slammed on brakes again and tried to swerve into my driver side door but I turned left into a side road off the main road. It kept driving and I never saw it again," she completed her statement.

Taber was running his hands through his hair and then down his face. He was beyond worried. He looked like he was waiting for the results of a paternity test.

Taber asked, "Can..."

"We will ask the questions, Mr. Blake," said Sgt. Mbanda.

Taber nodded and allowed them to proceed.

"Can you remember the model of car or the license plate number?" Sgt Scott asked the question this time.

"No, I am sorry. It happened so fast and like I said, I thought it was a road-rage incident," she stated.

"Miss, even those have to be reported," Sgt Mbanda informed her.

"I'll remember that," she confirmed, like a naughty school girl caught with her skirt too short.

"We'll phone you with a case number and take the evidence with us," said Sgt Mbanda, giving her a break.

---*S*ilka---

"Thank you," she smiled and let them out. When she closed the door behind them, she wished Tay had left with them.

She needed space again. *Lots and lots of space!*

"Pack your things, you're coming home with me," he ordered her.

OH, Zooey Descha-hell no!!! She thought. Bossy Taber could fly off! She'd had a hard day.

"I'm fine right here. Thank you for your concern," she blurted out, with anything but appreciation for his gesture. She proceeded to put chairs back in their place like a waitress closing up for the night.

Taber blew out a deep breath. "I am staying here or you are coming with me. You pick," he said.

"Ooh, I get a choice? That is sooo kind of you!" Her sarcasm could cut through glass.

"I'm sorry Silks, OK?" he apologized sheepishly. Neither of them was sure what exactly he was apologizing for, but it seemed the only way to make peace.

"Fine," she said, in the universal tone women used when everything was anything but fine.

They were silent for a moment. Silka pretended to clean her counter.

He stared at her like she had a UFO hovering above her head. "I'll tell James to bring me some work clothes for tomorrow morning," Taber decided for her.

---

*T*aber left and by the time he re-entered her loft, the mood in the room had lifted slightly. The reason mainly was that she wasn't in the room. Taber went looking for her in her bedroom. She wasn't there either.

It was then that he heard the shower turn on. *Right Miss Fontein, let's give you a real apology then, shall we?* He undressed and went to her bathroom.

---

*S*ilka had decided to get some space and have a shower. She turned on the water and disrobed. Once she stepped into the shower, once again she noticed her scar. With Taber's reaction to the note and the cops there, she hadn't had time to process the meaning behind the dead rats. Events of the night she got the scar flashed through her mind as she wet her hair. She saw them pull at her pants while she struggled. She saw him smear her blood all over her upper body. She heard her own screams. She saw the scissors and knives. She heard his voice. She felt the pain. She saw him there. *The dead bad guys were there. They were alive. Either that or the terrorists had found me. They had killed and sent me dead animals!* She could never escape them. Once again she felt the words - powerless, helpless, small. So very, very small.

Taber opened the door and stood behind her. She had obviously not registered he was in the shower with her. Her body twitched when he touched her shoulders.

"It's OK baby," he whispered, calming her. "We'll get through this and sort it out." His tone implied that he believed her and that he was no longer perturbed by the episode.

The nightmare that was the last few months, yesterday and tonight, exacerbated by their recent health scare, threw Silka into a stunned, frozen and scared state.

She just stood there like an ice sculpture.

---

*T*aber took the soap from the shelf and started washing her. Each touch was met with a jerk or a shudder. The water was warm but as he washed her legs she started trembling. Taber felt like a total asshole, as if he was violating her in some way. He put the soap down and turned off the shower. He grabbed a towel, wrapped her in it and carried her to bed. He sat her on the edge of the bed. After drying himself and putting on his boxers, he proceeded to dry her hair and body.

---*S*ilka---

The entire time Silka sat there shaking at the thought that the bad guys were after her again. The syndicate's torture would be like a beach party compared to what the

251

terrorists were capable of. She had seen their handiwork first hand in Nigeria when they had killed snitches.

"Stay with me baby?" Taber begged her softly to come back. He went to the kitchen and came back with a glass of sugar water.

They were coming to finish what they started, she heard in her mind.

"Drink, babes. It will help you," he encouraged her softly.

Silka just sat there staring vacantly into space.

---*T*aber---

This was bad. Her catatonic state almost sent him into a panic. How was he going to get her out of this?

He looked up, inwardly prayed for help and exhaled a deep breath. He kneeled in front of her. He stared at her. Her eyes were big and she didn't blink. Her breaths were stunted and short as if she was hyperventilating noiselessly.

"I'm not going to let you out my sight. You hear me? I will not let anything happen to you." His voice was loud and clear. He touched her face as he spoke those words. He spoke the last sentence over and over again until she registered.

Silka looked at him. She blinked a few times and swallowed hard.

"They're here. They've come back for me," she whispered in short breaths.

"No baby," Taber shook his head. "They are not back and I will find whoever is doing this," he promised.

"K," she barely whispered the word and nodded slowly as she said it.

She looked around helpless and then looked down.

Taber lightly touched her face with his fingers and made her look at him.

"I will not let anything happen to you!" He held her arms and commanded her trust and belief.

She nodded, still shocked and dazed about everything. Taber stood up.

"Don't go!" she whispered, almost panicking, as fear gripped her again.

"I told you, I am not leaving you," he smiled gently. "I am getting ready to put you into bed," he explained softly.

He took her hand, kissed it and helped her into bed. He climbed in beside her and spooned her into his arms. They lay there as she stared into the darkness in the deafening silence.

He had certain skills that required very little effort when it came to making people pay. By Jove! Whoever was behind this was going to pay. Finding that person was his new Directive with a capital D.

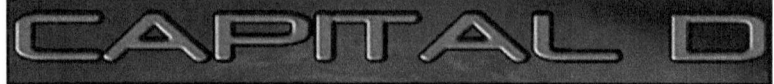

Chapter 23

---*Silka*---

The next morning, Silka was remarkably quiet. She dressed herself but refused to eat. Taber called James while she packed her bags. He helped carry her bags to the car. They sat in silence as they drove to his house. On the way there, he arranged for his security company to send cars with armed guards to protect the property around the clock.

She wondered about team BARF.

Brett Sheffield was playing with the diamonds in his hand. He was deep in thought. He remembered how he and the rest of the team had heard that the crime syndicate was tied to the terrorist organization. The only problem was that no one would tell them anything about the major players in the crime syndicate.

They had learnt that General Stan Shuman was one of the 'middle management' members in the organization. He called himself a General, but he had never been one.

He was really a big fat nobody. He handled 'employees' all over the world that filled his coffers and that of the syndicate. In Nigeria, he kept a low profile and had a fortified, secret hideaway, where he kept the fortune that he skimmed off the deliveries to his bosses over the years.

Brett and his men had had no idea where it was or how to get their hands on some of his treasure. They had been in Nigeria for several years. They were tired of going to 'backward' countries and facing danger, while living in poverty like the rest of the natives. They had decided to do something about it. They constantly fished for information and were getting closer and closer by the day.

The perfect solution to their problems came, the day they discovered Silka was a South African. South Africans had a bad reputation in the world due to Apartheid and the crime in their country. From the politicians to the sports personalities, all had tarnished reputations. The whole country had a bad name. They always played bad guys in the movies. This South African could be the perfect bait and perfect scapegoat. If they were going to steal from the General, the bad South African would take the fall.

The entire year that they had been training Silka to gain her trust, they had also fished for information. They needed to know where Stan was. They needed to get to him. They decided to spread the rumor that a South

African woman was looking for him. She had assembled a dangerous team with great skills and was coming after Stan. The rumor included that Silka was a spy for the South African government and was looking for something. They told her to start off asking the questions. If she felt like she wasn't getting through to the person, she was to leave the room and leave the rest of the questioning to them. She followed orders like a superstar.

The naive little South African thought they were there to get Intel on a General of a terrorist army. *Stupid cow!* It was the original objective of their mission, but their rumor made everyone else think she was after the General of the syndicate.

Ricardo always stayed with Silka outside while Brett, Ferdy and Alex tortured people inside each and every village, and every shop or home. After they were done, Ricardo would go in and tell them he wanted to get in touch with Stan to help him get rid of their vicious female leader. He would say that she had made the other three guys on his team hurt them. All they needed to do was get the General to contact him or tell him where to find the General.

The good cop, bad cop routine of the team, was very effective on these 'third world barbarians'. They'd had a regular laugh about the stupidity and gullibility of the people in the villages. Little did they know it was their killing and barbaric torture that made people cooperate out of fear.

Their plan worked like a bomb. The more damage they did after Silka 'interrogated' people in villages, the closer they got to Stan. He finally made contact with the 'friendly and concerned' Ricardo who in turn, told him of her 'scheme' but that he knew nothing about what she was after. After numerous meetings due to the escalation of 'Silka's rampage' on his people, he finally told Ricardo about the diamonds worth eight million American Dollars that he had stolen during decades of smuggling operations.

The dumbass just assumed that was what she had been after. The bad news was that by the time they had what they needed, Silka's contract would expire in a week. They needed to get this done and frame her. With renewed conviction and persuasion, Ricardo planted a seed that she was close.

Stan refused to cooperate and tell them where his secret stash was. He insisted it was safe. He was about to leave the country as well, so that she could not find him. *Time to play hardball!* During their meeting the next day, they planted a tracking device in his car. Afterwards, they followed him and bombed the first place he stopped at with a 'borrowed' RPG. It happened to be the home of a friend and business partner he was meeting with.

Having been persuaded that she was closing in on him, Stan arranged a meeting with Ricardo. He convinced Stupid Stan to move the diamonds to another location and also follow through with his plan to leave the country, but on the Friday night. Coincidentally, it was the night before she would leave the country.

Things could not have worked out better. With the info on which road his men would be taking so they could help secure the transport route, their plan was set in motion.

To Stan's knowledge, they would set up look-out points on the road to make sure the car wasn't followed and arrived safely at its new destination while he flew somewhere safe.

Instead, the four of them had followed the car, blown its tires and removed the case from the wreckage. It was a huge silver metal suitcase, big enough to carry the luggage of a family of six for a long vacation. It was filled to the brim with diamond stones. It took all four of them to carry it with a huge effort.

Once they moved it to their own little hide-out, they divided it up among themselves and waited. The next morning at the crack of dawn, they called Stan to tell him what had happened. He had been so secure in the knowledge that the road was safe and the case was guarded, that he had never bothered to find out if it made it to its new location. The worst part was that he wasn't in Nigeria anymore. His arrogance, stupidity and cockiness worked to their advantage.

He was told that Silka had recruited other people to help her steal the case under their noses by using a 'blind spot' where there was no lookout and escaping in the exact same car as the one that crashed. *Dumb luck!* Now she had left the country with his case and they had no way to trace her. Damn shame with a Capital D.

With Stan and Silka out of the country, they took their time over the next few days to plan their escapes. They each made their own shipping and transport arrangements for their respective plans. Within days they quit their jobs and scattered to different parts of the world. Each would try to find a buyer for their goods.

Unfortunately, their jobs had never afforded any of them to deal with rich people interested in diamonds. Their jobs had always entailed fighting in politics, religion and war. They were the ones who used to eliminate the diamond smugglers and bad guys, not get into bed with them.

Still, they knew a few other bad guys they had met along the way and decided to give them a call as soon as the dust had settled. They needed to keep lower profiles than Al Qaeda members at that stage. They agreed to hold off any transactions for a few months. They knew that if the Nigerians searched for Silka, which they would, they would figure it out and come after them.

They just needed to survive for three or four months max. Each of them thought at the time that it was doable, but Karma is like a boomerang

He, Ricardo, Alex and Ferdy had lived like paupers for years, a few months would not make much difference. They switched their mobile phones on only when necessary and made sure not to give anyone their numbers or details. No one could track them using the built-in GPS in their phones. He was going to sell his stash off bit by bit in different parts of the world as and when he needed the cash. He knew better than to attract too much attention by selling all of it in one go. Besides, you did not need a lot of money to live in a beach hut in the Maldives. At that moment, he was in Malawi. The people were nice and the country was beautiful. He stayed with friends.

Ferdy also had a plan. He would sell half of the diamonds and put the rest in a safety deposit box until he needed more. His first priority was to settle in Malaysia and give his mother in Detroit some money and buy her a house. He just needed a couple of hundred K to start off with. You didn't need much to buy a foreclosed property in a hoity-toity area. His mama could live in style while he lived like a rock star. He hadn't decided where yet. He would do the rolling stone thing for a while and see where he'd end up.

Ricardo was in LA. He was already worming himself into the lifestyle of someone rich and famous. He didn't have the fast car yet, but he got his fair share of easy women when he threw enough money around.

Alex wanted to travel around the world in pure first class fashion. He went to Dubai to see how the other half lived and quite enjoyed putting on a facade that he was one of them. For now their life savings saw them through.

Brett thought about Silka and wondered if they had caught her yet.

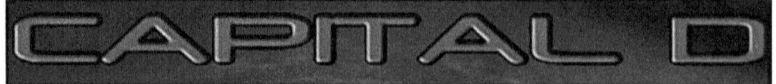

Chapter 24

---*TABER*---

In his car en route to his home, Silka stared blankly out the window. She was in deep contemplation. As it was a Thursday, Taber decided to call the office and take the day off.

"So, what do you want to do?" he asked chirpily. Silka kept quiet.

"We could do some skydiving, shark fishing or lion hunting," he joked.

Silka gave a slight smile.

"Come on, since we live dangerously anyway, we might as well do a good job of it," he said, cracking another one.

Silka smiled. "Stop it. I'd never be interested in any of those activities," she admonished him playfully.

"Really, not even skydiving?" he asked.

"Not today," she said, trying to hide a smile.

"Well, I'm not leaving you out of my sight, so you'd better think of something for us to do," he goaded trying to get a reaction from her.

"I want to find who is after me," she said simply.

"How do you intend on doing that?" he asked, his curiosity shaded the hope that she wasn't thinking what he thought she was thinking. The Silka he knew would become rattled by something but given enough time would turn into an evil Tasmanian She-devil bent on destruction and revenge. *Please God, let this woman just think straight?* he begged.

"By going out in public and luring them." Her tone was soft and playful but he knew she was as serious as a Buddha statue.

He held his breath and counted to ten. *Well, at least she was talking now*, he thought.

"How are you going to use yourself as bait?" he asked, as calmly as he could muster. Inside, he was fuming and ready to go Hulk-smash on her ass, just to hit the stupidity out of her. He had never hit a woman in his life but this lady was asking for a hiding.

"Whoever is after me knows where I live and probably follows me everywhere. My best odds are to carry on with my life and wait them out. Sooner or later they will make an appearance," she said in a voice devoid of any emotion.

---Silka---

She expected Tay to hit the roof right then. He was quiet. Too quiet!

"You are right," he said softly after a while. "But we will do this together. You will not go anywhere without me and I will be there to help you catch them." His voice was calm, controlled and commanding.

"We'll start tomorrow at the zoo." He laid down the law on that one.

When they arrived at his house, armed security guards were there already. Taber instructed them on his requirements, while James and Henry helped Silka carry her bags to his bedroom. Gladys offered her some tea.

Silka went to sit on a beach lounger next to the pool. They were exactly like the ones on cruise ships, with adjustable canopies and backs. She loved the waterfall. The flow of soft and feathery water cascaded down into the pool. The white water in the sun contrasted with light grey water in the shade. It was as beautiful as the hot sunny day. It was so calm she could almost fall asleep.

Taber joined her moments later. "Do you want anything?" he asked sweetly.

"Not right now, thank you." She smiled. Her demeanor was still dark from concern and fear.

"Swim with me then, please?" he asked so beautifully. He was trying to get her out of her dark mood.

Aw!!! How could she deny him when he asked so nicely? Silka smiled sullenly. It was Hot-az-Hel and not the place in the Northern Cape.

"This is not the playboy grotto, but OK," she quipped.

Taber smiled. Silka went upstairs to change. She came downstairs to find him already doing some laps in the crystal blue pool. He had plugged his iPod into a docking station built-in at the side of the pool which resounded music around them.

She sat down inside the water on the second step with her feet resting on the step below. Her body was submerged up to her ribs. She rested on her arms and watched him swim from the steps to the waterfall and back again. His body was a tanned powerhouse that cut through the water like a karate chop through air. *Blimey! He was magnificent, spectacular and striking.*

Taber startled her out of her daydream when he lifted himself out of the water. He was raised half way out the water, holding himself up on his hands which rested on the step between her legs.

"Hey beautiful," he smiled, glistening from his head to his lower body. "Thought you said you're going to swim?" he teased.

"I'm just getting used to the temperature," she said, but the water wasn't that cold.

"That's not the way to do it." He shook his head slowly. He deliberately licked the corner of his mouth to half way up his upper lip. The tip of his magical tongue was exposed in the process. He looked her up and down like a hungry wolf.

Damn her, if her entire deceitful body didn't decide right then to respond. He knew from experience how to get her out of the darkness. He pushed all the right buttons to distract her.

---

*T*aber saw when her eyes had brightened, her lips parted and her breathing altered. He pushed the final button when he licked and bit his lower lip. *Come on, baby,* he willed her in his mind.

"Gosh I love you!" she breathed, before she made her move.

She used her arms to push herself away from the step and in the process lifted her hips against him, then wrapped her legs around him. He caught her in his arms and took her off the steps into the water with him.

They kissed as their bodies pressed together. He moved them to the deep end of the pool, where he stood with her coiled around him. Their arms splashed water as they touched and frantically ran their hands down, under, out and over each other's bodies.

It had been four tortured days since they had made love. Their bodies pined for each other. They were pushing the envelope into dangerous territory. Somehow, right then, it didn't matter. Wet, slick bodies groped and pushed together out of pure raw desire for one another. With their kiss, they were lost in their deepest darkest needs which pulled them into another dimension, in an alternate universe far away from this one.

The inevitable reality sank in when they realized their hands had touched each other's naked genitals under the water. They both understood the consequences of the next move. Neither was willing to face it.

"I think you have magic fairies in this pool," she joked at their incomprehension of how exactly the bottom halves had been partially removed.

"I shall find and dispose of them at once," he joked. His giggle made her laugh.

Silka let go of him and tied the strings of her bikini bottoms again on either side, while he held her wrapped around him. When she was done she held onto him, while he pulled up his swimming briefs.

He smiled solemnly. He was sad that though she needed him and wanted him, his poor decisions had forced them into this. She smiled back.

They held each other for a while, smiling into one another's contented faces. When his tent had deflated, Taber took her with him to the shallow end and lowered her to stand. They held hands as they walked out the pool and rested on the beach loungers next to each other in silence for a while.

"What are you thinking about?" he asked her.

"Not much. Just how lucky I am to have you," she smiled.

"You're joking right?" he snorted and frowned.

"No. I assure you I am perfectly serious," she said dead straight. "Why?"

"You are with a stupid man you cannot make love to because he slept with a stupid girl," he said, shaking his head.

"In my book, that is anything but lucky," he stated.

She sat up and leaned forward. When she turned to face him, she looked troubled.

"If those guys had raped me without the added extras on the table, would you still have wanted me and made love to me?" she asked softly.

"Absolutely," he said without hesitation and sat up to face her. "It wouldn't have mattered. It would not have changed how I feel about you and how much I need to be with you. It also wouldn't have been your fault," he said honestly.

"That's how I feel about this situation and you," she explained. "Even if you were HIV positive and we had to use condoms now or for the rest of our lives, it would not change how I feel about you or how much I want you." She ended her words with a comforting smile.

Taber looked disturbed and lost.

"I know we can use condoms, but we can't…the last thing I want is to take chances when we don't know for sure," he said and looked down.

"Then we wait for your results and take it from there," she suggested.

They were interrupted by Gladys bringing lunch. They ate in silence after which Silka left to get changed.

Taber considered what she had said. This woman was so remarkable and unlike any woman he had ever been with. He wanted her so badly in every way possible. He couldn't wait for this to be all over.

He decided to get dressed. He went upstairs to his room. Silka was sitting on the bed dressed in jeans and a top.

"Hey, you OK?" he asked.

"Yeah, just admiring the view," she said.

"I have to go run an errand, I'll be right back, OK?" he asked.

"Sure, I'll be here," she reassured him.

Taber dressed in his walk-in closet and entered the bedroom again. Silka was still there.

"Bye, babes, see you in a bit," he said and kissed her tenderly.

"Bye," she smiled.

As he arrived downstairs he picked up his mobile phone and made a call as he headed out the door.

"Jocelyn it's me," he said, "I'm coming over."

Chapter 25

Silka sat in his bedroom. She had grown distracted after she had changed her clothes. The view of the colorful garden was spectacular. She sat on the bed thinking about her life. So much had happened. She fell back onto the bed and closed her eyes. Before long she fell asleep.

When she woke, it was nearly dinner time and almost dark. She walked through the house. Taber was nowhere to be found.

She went and sat on the well-lit grass patch next to the waterfall. Once again she thought about her life. She was finally living with Taber. He had practically moved her into his home already. Her mind still had two weeks to prepare until the sudden change of plans. Now that she was there living with him, it actually felt pretty nice and normal. She realized that she would do anything for him. She would die for him. She didn't care about the danger she was in. Part of her was excited to take the kids to the zoo the next day, but another part was scared that something would happen to Taber. She knew from experience that nothing was going to make him stay away. Somehow the thought made her happy. *At least one good thing had come out of everything*, she mused.

She heard Taber's voice calling her. She stood up and walked along the path back inside again.

"There you are!" he said relieved and hugged her tightly.

"I was out by the waterfall," she comforted him.

"I came back and the house was dark and empty. You scared me," he said, as he brushed her hair from her face.

"Oh, honey," she calmed him down with her tone and smile. "I hadn't realized that I had been out there that long."

"It's okay. Dinner is ready. Let's eat," he shook his head and gave a quick smile.

They sat talking about the trip to the zoo with the kids the next day.

"Brace yourself for a lot of screaming and talking," she warned him.

"I kind of like kids, it won't bother me," he assured her.

"Wait, Taber Blake likes kids?" She sounded amused.

"Where are news crews when you need them," she teased.

"I always wanted kids. It's no big deal," he said as he took a bite.

"Let me get this straight. You never wanted commitment but you want kids?" Now she was confused. The two kind of went hand in hand.

"Single dad," he pointed to himself in a joking manner while he ate.

"That ought to be good. I hope I'm around for that," she joked.

"Me too," he said softly. "What about you?" he asked.

"I never thought about it before," she frowned as she realized she had really never given it much thought. "I wouldn't be helping a school if I didn't like kids, I guess," she confirmed.

---

*T*aber smiled and shook his head. He had plans for this woman, but she wasn't making things easy for him.

---*S*ilka---

After dinner they went bowling. Silka was impressed with the bowling alley in his house and his bowling skills. He beat her by far. Her competitive nature didn't like it much, but she ceded defeat with grace and poise. It was hard. Normally she would have thrown a John McEnroe, but first impressions and all that...

---

*T*aber was impressed that she had outgrown her childhood, competitive streak. She used to blow up when she was defeated as a child.

The hardest part came when it was time for bed. Taber had plenty other bedrooms in the house, but he refused to let her sleep in them.

Part of her was grateful because she still had nightmares
sometimes. Silka showered and dressed in her ugliest,
longest sleepwear just to go easy on him. She climbed
into his bed. She was dying inside. *Please let it be over soon!*

Taber showered and climbed into bed next to her.
They said their goodnights and spooned in silence.

"Hey, Silka," Taber's soft voice sounded in the dark.

"Yes?" she responded.

"I'm glad you are here with me."

"I'm glad I'm here with me too," she joked.

"Sleep tight, Silly," he joked back.

She giggled as quietly as possible.

Across the ocean Alex was scheming. He was the
youngest of the four. He was nearly broke and had
grown impatient. He had been in too many corrupt
countries and had met many black market dealers. He
reached out to them now. A scumbag he knew would
take all his diamonds off his hands. He arranged for
Scumbag to meet him in Dubai where he was living off
his last bit of savings in absolute opulence. One of the
cells of the terrorists received word of it through the
channels of communication with ex-cons. Not to miss an
opportunity, they headed for Dubai as well.

---**S**ilka---

The next day Benji called Silka. She had been sleeping. Before she picked up her phone she noticed Taber was not in the room.

"Hi, Benji." Silka tried to sound awake and lively.

"Baby twos!" he exclaimed. "Just thought I'd let you know that they have found the guy called Alex."

"Brilliant!" Silka was ecstatic.

"Tell me everything?" she asked excitedly.

"He's in Dubai. There is a cell headed his way to intersect the sale he is going to make," he said and gave her the address.

"Great. Is your brother going to be there?" she asked.

"No." He laughed. "He doesn't do the travelling thing."

"Oh, that's good!" Silka was relieved, knowing that he wouldn't be caught.

"Thank you Benji." She said goodbye and hung up to call Joshua.

"I have good news and bad news," Silka said after he picked up.

"There always is, let's hear it," Joshua sounded amused.

"The good news is that we can take down the whole team without Benji's brother getting caught," she started.

"The bad news is that only Alex had decided to have a yard sale," she spoke despondently.

"We did not expect this to be easy and to catch all of them at once," Joshua smirked. "Don't worry, we will take down Alex and the other guys one at a time if need be," he consoled her.

"I know, but even catching them one at a time will be a huge problem. The poor scumbag and Alex had decided to hold their meeting in a very busy shopping mall. Scumbag and Alex are clearly very distrustful and stupid."

Silka filled him in on the deal.

"The devil's in the details," he muttered. "We will make a plan."

"Please keep me informed?" she requested.

"Will do," Josh said, intending to keep his promise. Silka deserved to know everything, even if she didn't work for the company anymore.

Joshua contacted one of his connections in SOG. They sent a small army of guys of the same caliber as team BARF to set up the trap.

Taber brought Silka breakfast in bed. He looked like centrefold material in Levi jeans and a T-shirt. He greeted her with a kiss. Day 1 of officially living with Taber Blake. Somehow it felt like a weird dream, but a comfortable and content one.

"I know you are not a breakfast fan, but we have a big day so you'd better eat up," he tickled her memory of their last breakfast discussion.

Not a dream!

"Fur you I kill da bull," she joked in a Spanish accent. Taber laughed so hard his tummy hurt. "What are we going to do with you?" he asked, grinning from ear to ear and shaking his head.

"Same thing we always do, Pinky. Try to trap the world!" she raised her fork and tried to look serious.

Taber laughed again. "You are in a good mood, aren't you?" he smiled.

"I slept well and I am ready to take on thousands of kids," she smiled. Silka filled him in on what Benji had told her as well. "We are finally getting somewhere with this," she said.

"That's a start! Eat up. I'll be downstairs in my study when you're ready to leave," he stood up and kissed her forehead before he left.

"Yes, dear," she mimicked her father's famous response, but happily ate her breakfast.

When she was ready she went downstairs to meet up with Taber. She wore a conservative denim mini-skirt and a white T-shirt that covered her scar.

The day was bright and so was she. Hopefully, by the end of today, Alex and the terrorists would be caught.

Taber had arranged two big busses to take the kids and teachers to the zoo. The noise was deafening, but Taber and Silka didn't mind. They sat chatting and laughing all the way to the zoo. When they arrived, they helped the teachers help the kids out of the busses. After they had lined them up, they entered the zoo. It was enormous with natural habitats as enclosures for the animals. They walked behind the teachers and kids the whole time, looking at the animals and holding hands. Taber bought the kids' hot dogs, fries and cold drinks for lunch. In between meals he spoiled them with ice-creams. Silka was taken by his generosity and the way he interacted with them. He was a natural and had remained calm, in control, patient and completely engaged with them. It made more than her biological clock start ticking.

"Last one to the bus is a rotten egg!" Taber screamed, as they set off towards the busses.

The kids stormed through the gates to the awaiting busses in front.

One by one they embarked on their journey back to school. From there, their parents or taxis would take them back home.

When they arrived at the school, Taber and Silka disembarked from the leading bus. They assisted once again to herd the kids out of the busses. They said goodbye by high-fiving the boys and hugging the girls.

By the time they had reached his home, clouds had moved overhead to cool the hot day they'd had. Instead of taking Silka into the house, Taber led her to his front garden. They walked on stepping stones through huge trees, leafy shrubs, ferns and huge Philodendron leaves that they had to push out the way to walk past. It had the feel of a real forest except for the splashes of color on the ground covers and seedlings that grew beneath the colossal canopy of nature. They arrived at a huge grass patch in the middle of the garden surrounded by the forest. There was a large Koi pond with a rock water feature. Taber led them to a bench covered in soft cushions where they sat holding each other.

"I like to come here to get away from it all, you know, when things get too hectic," he explained.

"It's even more peaceful than your pool area." She closed her eyes, as her head rested on his shoulder.

"I had fun today ... and you?" he asked.

"Yes, very much, but it's nice to be home," she said without thinking.

"You have no idea how happy it makes me to hear you call this home," he smiled.

She looked at him and smiled, not once breaking eye contact. Taber leaned in to kiss her. His eyes searched hers and his smile faded as his lips neared hers. They both stopped briefly. She blinked slowly again and gave a bigger smile. His lips touched hers. She opened her mouth wider and slowly darted her tongue towards his. Their tongues gently touched.

Suddenly, it started raining cats and dogs. They were soaking wet in seconds. Taber grabbed her hand and ran towards the house ducking plants and pushing through the forest. They were laughing like little children by the time they had made it into the house.

"This way," Taber led her away from the stairs on the left of the entrance hall and into the kitchen.

"An elevator?" she gasped, as he pressed the button and the doors opened.

"You didn't think I'd let my staff walk up three floors, did you?" He smiled and let her walk in first.

"Oh, so the staff don't have to walk, but I do?" she teased.

He laughed.

"Are you trying to tell me something, Mr. Blake," she asked coyly and winked at him.

"Just keeping you fit for a rainy day." His tone hinted that one day soon they would make love again.

Silka shook her head and lowered her eyes. Her smile faded. *Yeah, clearly not this rainy day.*

--- Taber ---

Almost as soon as they had ascended, the elevator stopped. Taber held her hand all the way to his bedroom. They were sopping wet. Her white T-shirt clung to her breasts and her small dark nipples showed through. This turned Taber on. His T-shirt and jeans clung to him as if he'd been vacuum-sealed in it.

"I'll grab some towels," he said. He went into his walk-in closet and took off his clothes. He decided right then and there to finish what they had started in the garden. He wrapped a towel around him and grabbed another one for Silka.

She had taken off her white t-shirt and was bent over finger drying her wet hair. He walked over to her and handed her the towel.

--- **S**ilka ---

"Thank you," she smiled. When she finished she stood upright and proceeded to dry her face and hair. He stood there with his perfect upper body fully exposed, while the white towel around his thin waist accentuated his tan and shape. She stared at his gorgeous figure and then noticed he was staring at her scar. She covered it quickly with the towel in her hands.

"Don't," he said softly in a low voice. He stepped towards her.

"Don't." He leisurely pushed her hands down.

She looked away. *Fine, stare away if you must*, she thought resentfully.

He touched her scar.

"Does it hurt?" he asked, when she jerked slightly at his initial contact.

"No," she said, but preferred to look at the rain outside.

"Does this?" he lowered himself and kissed her scar.

She stiffened a little but said nothing. She watched him, to see his reaction to her hideous scar.

He kept his eyes open and licked the length of her scar and kissed it with such gentleness as if she was a burn victim and he the soothing ointment. He traced the scar with the tip of his tongue, followed by a gentle rub of his lips over them.

The tenderness and endearment he had for her scars seemed unnatural, yet she saw it with every touch and kiss. She could not deny it. It was baffling that something so hideous to her, that turned her off and that she would not want to touch, he seemed to love so much. She had no idea how it was possible. She could never imagine not being a little grossed out and put off by another person's scars. Yet he seemed to be very much in his element around hers and every kiss and touch was that of adoration and even admiration. In that moment she felt more tolerant of her scars, but still would feel a little self conscious about her body for a while. Especially in public!

He continued his kisses as she succumbed to his touch. Every ounce of her yearned to be touched, but in her mind she felt disheartened.

"We should stop," she whispered.

"Okay baby," he relented and moved away.

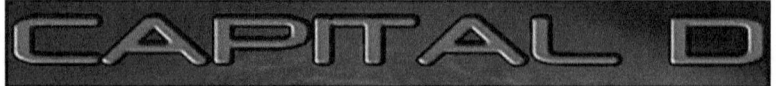

Chapter 26

A few days later, the time had arrived for the long-awaited meeting. Dressed in plain clothes and armed with communication devices, the teams of Special Forces men positioned themselves in various areas of the grand mall.

Alex and Scumbag met at a small café in the food court. Each had a duffel bag with them and put it on the chair next to them.

"You've got my money?" Alex asked.

"Right here, it's all good," Scumbag said, in a heavy accent and smiled. His skin was so dark all you could see was eyes and teeth. He opened his bag and sat back.

Alex leaned over to check inside. He didn't touch the money, but could see the hundred dollar bills filled to the top. He closed the bag. All in all they had agreed to sell the diamonds for two and a half million dollars. He opened his smaller bag.

Scumbag inconspicuously took a diamond and pulled a small mirror out of his pocket. On his lap he casually tested it to see if it was real. *Yep, all good.* He smiled from ear to ear.

"Pleasure doing business with you," Alex stated and got up to leave. He took the bigger duffel bag with the money inside it.

As he left, Scumbag stood up to leave as well.

Two men in plain clothes stood behind him.

"Make a move and you're dead!" the one threatened in a low voice.

He had a strange accent which Scumbag could not place.

They took the bag from him and dragged him by his arm to the parking lot.

As Alex approached his car in the outdoor parking area and opened his rear passenger door to put the bag inside, two men approached and one attacked him from behind. He knocked Alex's head against the roof of the car. Though in pain and slightly dizzy he pulled himself together. His instincts kicked in and he turned around to fight. He was met with an injection to the neck by the other man. Instinctively, he punched the first attacker in his throat while simultaneously kicking the second who stood by his side. The one he kicked stumbled backwards and landed on his behind next to the rear wheel of Alex's hired car. It took the man he punched in the throat a moment but when he saw his comrade was man-down, he attacked Alex again. Alex struggled with him and fought him as long as he could. When he started losing consciousness, he continued to wriggle as both men by then struggled to grip him. When the drugs eventually took effect, he slumped unconsciously into their grasp. A car pulled up and someone else helped the attackers drag him into it. They collected the bag and drove to the parking lot.

They met up with the Scumbag and his party of two there. They had already decided to take both men and their bags with them. The terrorist bosses wanted to get more information from Alex about the others' whereabouts. Scumbag was collateral damage, and would eventually die as they did not leave witnesses behind. They drugged Scumbag too and dragged them to an unmarked van with two occupants.

All hell broke loose. Armed men in plain clothes from every direction surrounded them and screamed orders in perfect American accents. The van sped off with two of the terrorists and the rest dropped Alex and his accomplice and dove for cover. The van was intersected by a car, from which two men opened fire on the driver and passenger, killing them instantly. Two of the terrorists who took cover behind cars decided to take their chances and opened fire on the Special Forces guys. Since they were surrounded, they didn't live long to tell the tale. Short bursts of fire delivered precise and accurate head shots. The Special Forces men moved into position, clearing every corner of the immediate vicinity. They found the other two terrorists cowering behind a car on the other side. They surrendered without a fight. More vans and cars pulled up. The men got out and picked up Alex and Scumbag. They dragged them to one of the cars while the terrorists were placed in the van. With Alex and all the survivors in their custody, the Special Forces guys took them to a holding facility. They would be held there until the rest the team was found.

Silka woke up. Her phone was ringing. She rose to check the time and answered it.

Josh told her the whole story about Alex. She thanked him and hung up. She heard a stir behind her. Taber had woken up too.

"Hey," he said sleepily. "What time is it?" he asked, as he stretched himself out onto the bed.

"It's almost noon," she smiled and filled him in on the latest development. They had spent another night in sleepless passion.

"What do you say we finally have that shower and get some food?" he suggested.

"A man with a plan. I like it!" she quipped.

He stood up and tossed the condoms, while she headed for the bathroom.

Taber followed her in and opened the shower door for her.

"How do you turn this thing on?" she asked, before she stepped in. There were no taps or fittings anywhere.

"By doing this," he smiled and gently pushed her into the middle of the shower, in front of the motion sensor. Warm water rained down from the large square panel in the ceiling down to every corner of the shower. *Anorexic friendly!*

He got in and smiled at her distress when the water covered her from head to toe, pushing her wet hair into her face. She looked like the cutest drowned puppy he had ever seen.

"Let me," he laughed as he helped her get hair out of her face.

"I think I still prefer the baths we've had so far," she joked.

"Fine with me," he giggled.

---

*T*aber took soap from a built-in shelf inside the wall and started washing her. His hands washed her everywhere, including her scar. It was the first time he had touched her there that Silka didn't tense up. It made him smile.

---**S**ilka---

"Hi mom."

She heard him greet his mother from the bedroom. She decided to get out the shower.

"Thank you, we'd love to," he responded and paused to listen. "Love you too, bye." He hung up and put his phone down again.

Taber went back to the bathroom where Silka was already drying herself. They dried their bodies and wrapped towels around themselves. Silka went to get dressed immediately. She was very pleased with herself. She enjoyed the payback she had given him.

Once they were dressed, they went downstairs to eat.

"My mom is having a dinner party in two weeks with some friends, including your parents," he finally told her.

"And you want to go," she completed his sentence.

"Well, yes. I think we should break the news that we are officially a couple and living together." His logic was not what she wanted to hear.

"Fine," she said, and then went on, "But my mother will have a cadenza if she finds out along with other people. She has to be the first to know her own daughter has shacked up, or else you will suffer her wrath." She smiled. "Why don't you go to the dinner and I will join you with my parents, once I have broken the news to my mom at her house first?" Silka offered as a solution.

"No! I am not letting you drive there by yourself. It is too dangerous with those nut cases out there," he refuted.

"Then drop me off there?" she countered.

"Don't you want me to be with you when you break the news?" he asked.

"Of course I do, but trust me, after she caught us kissing in her house ... you do not want to hear a lecture from my mother," she said with a weary sigh. "It's better if I smooth talk her first so she'll leave you alone," Silka convinced him.

"Very well," Taber consented, glad that Silka would take a bullet for him in this regard.

They ate and watched a movie in his theatre. They weren't so much watching as making out like a couple of back row teens.

Ricardo was already in Los Angeles where he craved the lifestyle of the rich and famous. While they had travelled the world on missions, they had lived off Uncle Sam's dime. Lodging, food and all their basics had been provided. Therefore their entire salary could support their families, had they had any. Instead they had saved their money. Each one of the team had enough money to live off for a year if they wanted to.

Unfortunately for Ricardo, L.A and his party lifestyle was not cheap. He had made a lot of new friends and his entertainment budget was running on empty. He decided to go against the agreement and sent out his feelers for buyers. He was lucky, because L.A had many underground criminal activities. He found a buyer in no time and a meeting was set up.

---*S*ilka---

Benji phoned Silka and told her they'd found the next member of the team.

"Josh!" Silka said hurriedly as he picked up the phone. She couldn't wait to tell him the good news.

"Hi there, Silka, what's up?" he answered.

"You will not believe what I just heard!" She could've jumped out of her skin. "Ricardo came out of hiding. He set up a meeting next week with the L.A clan of the very same crime syndicate he screwed over," she said, laughing, because the irony was just too much.

Joshua laughed too and said, "Well his stupidity just hit a new low. Someone didn't do their research."

"Luckily for us patience doesn't seem to be the teams' forte. With any luck we'll have all four soon," Josh added.

Silka told him that the meeting was going to take place in a bad part of town, where gangs and drugs were rife. Ricardo and Dumbass buyer were clueless that they were somehow linked. He had no idea he was trying to sell them their own property. The terrorists thought of telling their bosses, but decided to keep it to themselves. They were going to get the diamonds and money, so in the end, they would score a freebie and it would not matter.

The terrorists decided to leave their guys alone and just take Ricardo. Since no one had heard from the first set of terrorists who went after Alex, they were pressured to get information and fast. They went to a park in the slums of L.A late one night. Apart from a street light in the distance, near a block of apartment buildings, there were no other lights. Ricardo showed up first. He lit a cigarette as he waited in the cover of darkness.

Dumbass buyer got there a few minutes later. He saw Ricardo standing in the dark near a tree.

Ricardo noticed a figure approaching him from a distance. He pulled a last drag from his cigarette and tossed it to the ground.

"Ready to do this?" Ricardo asked.

"Where are my rocks, Hombre?" Dumbass buyer asked.
Ricardo tossed him the bag he was holding.

"It's all there. You have my money?" he questioned the dark figure that stood in front of him.

The man reached into his jacket pocket, but instead pulled his gun out his shoulder holster. He shot Ricardo twice. As he fell to the ground four terrorists moved in and threw dumbass against the tree.

"You dumb dick!" the one shouted at him. "Why did you do that?" he asked, as he held him against the tree.

"Get off me!" Dumbass buyer shouted at them. "What the hell is this?"

"Your bosses sent us to bring this man to them. They wanted him alive!" he said. "Why did you kill him?" he asked again.

"That Loco Papi wanted two million bucks in cash ... you think we have that kind of dough lying around?" Dumbass responded.

"Nobody move! Get down on the ground with your hands above your heads!" someone shouted.

The terrorists were startled to see bright red dots appear on each other's clothing from every direction.

More Special Ops guys moved in from behind trees and obscured corners, shining red lights in their direction. The terrorists decided that escape was their best alternative. They shot in every direction the red lights appeared, while they dove for cover. The terrorists were shot first in two short burst of meticulous muted gunfire. Even though he did not shoot at them, the fact that he still held his gun firmly resulted in Dumbass being taken out too. The Special Forces guys pulled the bodies into their vans and disposed of them in an abandoned crypt by the Evergreen Cemetery crematorium.

---Silka---

Josh called Silka the next day. The snag they had hit was a devastating blow. Things were not looking too good in the retribution department.

Silka kept Taber in the loop, and therefore told him about this new development as well. It took Taber all day to cheer her up. That morning, he took her out for a magical hot air balloon ride in the Magaliesburg Mountains and forced her to leave her phone at home. They sipped champagne as they watched the view below and around them from the air.

Taber kept cracking jokes, "I'm going to throw you overboard if you don't cheer up soon!"

It worked and pretty soon their exciting adventure turned romantic, as he held her close and fed her strawberries and cream.

By lunchtime their balloon ride was over. Taber continued their date by treating her to a delicious lunch in a quaint countryside village.

By the time they had driven home, Silka had cheered up a lot. When they arrived back home she went to check her phone for messages. Perhaps Josh had found the other two in the time Taber had banned her from electronics.

She had several missed calls, but all were from an unknown number. She listened to her voicemail. Each time she heard a person's voice, but she could not make out what they were saying. She gave the phone to Taber for him to listen. Perhaps he could understand Mumbling Moron, because her ability to speak it, let alone understand it was nonexistent.

Taber frowned and hung up the phone. "I lost my ability to understand Moron the day I stopped drinking beer many years ago."

They thought nothing of it for the rest of the night and enjoyed a romantic night in the Jacuzzi. She had invested in a sexy, full body polo neck costume, with no sides for occasions like this. It was worth every penny it cost importing it.

The morning of Tabitha's party, Silka and Taber spent lounging at home. Taber played some Xbox while Silka sat in the garden reading.

By late afternoon they had enjoyed lunch, a long walk around his entire property and an afternoon swim. Silka slid into the purple mini dress with the long zip she had worn previously. This time her hair was down and her makeup a little more daring. *All part of the plan!* she muttered to herself. She knew she looked hot when she saw Taber's expression as she appeared out the bathroom.

His sparkling grey eyes slightly narrowed and softened. His mouth was agape as he stared at her. She was tempted to lift his chin to stop him drooling.

Taber was dressed in a suit. He looked so finger-licking good she could use him as a drive-thru all night long.

They suppressed their urges and left so he could drop her off at her mother's. Once they arrived at her mother's house, he got out with her and walked her to the door.

"Good luck," Taber said, as he kissed her goodbye at the door, before he went on to his mother's colossal home.

"Thanks, I need it!" she smiled. She waited for him to walk to his car and waved as he drove off.

"Silka, darling!" her mother was at least happy to see her. They had been waiting for her in the reception room.

"Hello, Mother," she smiled.

"Hello, love," her father joined them and gave her a long hug.

"Hi, Daddy!" Silka returned his hug and gave him a kiss hello.

"I am so pleased you decided to join us for Tabitha's dinner tonight," Lucelia said.

"Yes, about that, Mother… " Silka paused and looked at both her parents. "I wanted you guys to be the first to know. I shall not be at the dinner unescorted. I am meeting Taber, the man I love and the man I live with," she said slowly.

Lucelia stood there in shock.

"Well, which one of the three must we sit with?" her father joked.

"Don't be incongruous, Theodore!" Lucelia chirped.

"Sweetie, darling," she continued and then paused.

Oh gosh! There it was, Silka thought, but she let her mother carry on anyway.

"You know we are very fond of Taber, but indubitably this is far too soon?" she said.

"Mother, I have known Tay almost all my life," Silka responded calmly.

"I know, dear, but… in love?" Lucelia questioned.

"We had coffee every morning before work after I moved back and we reconnected our friendship and fell in love," Silka explained simply and patiently.

"How long have you been living together?" her father asked.

"Only a short while," she reassured them.

"What are his intentions?" her father blurted out.

"For now…just to make me happy, Daddy. Please can we not get ahead of ourselves before Taber and I even get started?" she grinned, like a monkey on LSD.

"Silka, darling," Lucelia took over. "You know your happiness is my foremost concern. I do want you to be happy darling."

BUT…Silka waited for that word. *Wait for it….Wait for it…. HUH?*

"The same goes for me," her father smiled.

"I shall endeavor to give the young Mr. Blake my best propriety," Lucelia smiled. "I wish you both well."

"Thank you, Mom!" Silka smiled and hugged her.

Lucelia couldn't remember the last time she had been referred to as 'mom' or shown affection by her daughter. She was almost emotional.

"Aw! Come here!" her father pulled them both into a hug which made them laugh.

"I wish you both the best as well. Taber is a fine young man and you'd do well with a man of his caliber," her father added.

Silka gave him and her mom a big hug and kiss. "Thank you. Shall we?" Silka asked, eager to get to Taber to give him the good news. *Phew!!!*

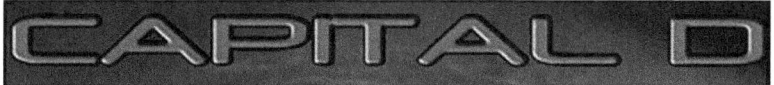

Chapter 27

*T*aber was the first person to arrive at his mother's estate. He greeted his parents warmly and after they had chatted for a while, he went to get a drink. He greeted more people that entered, as he made his way to the patio.

He stood with his drink in his one hand and the other hand in his pocket. He watched the lake and hoped Silka was managing all right with her parents. His mother's home was soon abuzz with movement and people.

"Hello Taber," a small voice said from behind him.

"Amber?" he turned around and leaned on the railing. He greeted her coldly and frowned. *What the hell was she doing there!*

"I came with your friend, Timothy, who was invited," she explained.

"He's not a friend of mine, and neither is someone going around infecting people with HIV!" Taber responded, hard and cold as steel. He removed his hand from his pocket and crossed his arms over his chest.

"Taber, I didn't mean what I said. I wanted you back and when I discovered you had a place of your own and saw her there…" she started explaining before he interrupted her.

"You freaking lied to me about being HIV positive?" he hissed every single word slowly, as he felt his rage build. He was Hulk mad…

"You have to understand…" she said almost in tears.

"You – immature – freaking – psycho – slut!" he screamed every word, as he threw his glass against the wall behind her. He didn't notice that the whole place had gone quiet and was staring at them.

"You don't lie about something like that!" he screamed. "You put me through HELL!!" he continued his rampage.

"I'm sorry…" she cried and whimpered.

"Sorry! After what you put Silka and me through. You are *sorry*?" he screamed.

"I knew she had stolen you from me. I had to make her pay!" she cried some more.

"Oh – My – Gosh! It was *YOU!*"

You could've used him in a detergent advert - he had gone *that white* when he realized she had sent the dead rats to Silka. He looked as if he had just had the wind knocked out of him. He bent forward and breathed deeply as if he'd just finished a Triathlon. He had blamed Silka all this time, when in fact it was this cow. He was so livid he could have used his special skills and killed her. *Shit! Not here.*

Amber stopped crying. "I was so angry with you at first. I keyed your car and slashed your tyre. I followed you everywhere and hooted to stop you when you kissed her. But then I realized it was her fault. I knew she was trouble when I first met her. I had to get rid of her. I tried running her off the road in my brother's car. I sent her the rats to scare her off and left the death threats on her phone." She paused and stepped a little closer to him.

"Baby, I just wanted you back and now that she's not with you anymore, we can be together," she said in a squeaky voice.

Taber felt like he was about to black out from pure anger. His hands on his knees where shaking from crazed wrath. He was seconds away from launching himself at her and killing her.

"That's not going to happen, little girl."

Silka's calm and collected voice blurred through his fury. He looked up.

She walked over to him with a huge smile on her face and stood beside him.

"We are still very much together," she said, looking at Amber as he rose up. Her one arm reached behind his back and gently stroked him, as she stood with her body facing Amber.

The rage inside him was simmering down. Her confident, sexy smile, her soothing touch and calm voice was slowly bringing him out of the darkness. They looked into each other's eyes.

Silka was still smiling. He knew the meeting with her parents had gone well, at least. He smiled back.

---*S*ilka---

The little voice inside her melted away even though it wanted to warn her - Bang! Bang!!

Amber lost it completely. Tears streamed down her face as she shot Silka in the stomach without as much as a word.

Silka and Taber had been so busy staring at each other that they hadn't noticed that she had pulled a gun out of her bag. In slow motion, Taber saw Silka fall to the ground with her eyes still open.

"You cow! Just piss off and die already!" Amber screamed, as she was about to pull the trigger again.

When she saw Taber step towards her, she hesitated for a second. In one swift, split second move, Taber took one step and killed her.

As her eyes closed, Silka saw how, with just one hand, he had tilted Amber's wrist forcing the gun up under her chin as the shot went off. It was over in a second. Amber dropped to the floor.

---

*T*ay turned to Silka and fell on his knees beside her. Her eyes were still closed. A swarm of people had collected around them.

Silka's mother was hysterical and kneeled down opposite Tay. Her father was next to her mother on his knees crying and screaming.

Tabitha stood behind them and was crying as Don held her while he cried. Everyone else stood around, shocked and crying.

Tay took off his jacket. He felt for a pulse. She had one but it was weak and fading. He used his jacket to stop the bleeding and screamed for someone to call an ambulance.

"Don't leave me, baby girl!" he begged.

"Stay with me, please, Silka!" he pleaded.

"I love you baby. Please! Don't go!" he cried.

---

*S*ilka didn't feel any pain. It was the strangest thing. She heard the gun go off. She felt a pain the one minute, but the next minute, it was gone.
She saw Tay kill Amber. She felt her head hit the railing before it touched the ground. She closed her eyes upon impact.

She lay there, grateful that she had finally made a connection with her mom. She could hear her crying.

Mom... a word she had seldom used in her life. She was grateful that she had said that word to her that day and had kissed and hugged her. She was grateful for one last hug and kiss from her daddy. Silka could hear him screaming her name. She heard Taber beg and plead. His tears were falling on her face and were warm. She was grateful that at least she had made love to Tay one final time the night before. Mostly, she was grateful for the few days they'd gotten to spend together at home.

Home was such a wonderful place. She would miss home so much. She would miss her mom and her adoring daddy.

She would miss Taber most of all. Silka wanted to tell him that it was okay. If she could've, she would've reassured him, comforted him and held him with all her might.

By then she started gargling blood, as her punctured lung struggled for oxygen. She heard Taber scream.

"God, no! Silka!"

She felt sleepy right then and drifted off.

The funeral was that Thursday afternoon. Not many people showed up. It did not matter. Not to Taber. He wasn't going to show up either. They'd only dated for a short while, but he knew her parents well. He couldn't face them. Nothing else mattered...

Chapter 28

---*T*ABER---

After the ambulance arrived, Taber followed as they took Silka away to the hospital. Shortly afterwards, he was remanded into custody and taken away by the cops. He spent several hours in jail, waiting for the murder charges to be filed. The cops were still interviewing guests from the dinner party and investigating the events of that day, before they decided to file charges against him for murdering Amber. At that moment they were holding him on suspicion.

The charges were never filed and Taber was released. The guests at the party all knew the families and loved both Taber and Silka. They'd heard the entire sick, twisted confession Amber had made. They'd seen how she had shot Silka. In the end, they all decided that Amber had wanted to commit suicide and Tay had tried to stop her. The gun had gone off at the exact moment Taber had tried to pull it away from underneath her chin. It was tragic - they all told the police investigators. Naturally the police believed them. These were the City of Gold's elite. They had nothing to gain by lying.

Taber spent his days working himself to death and distraction. At night he would go visit Silka in a coma in ICU. He would tell her about his day and how much he missed her. He would beg her to come back to him and sometimes cry. He would go home and sit in the dark.

Ferdy had thought the time was right. He kept to the agreement and waited for the Nigerians to track Silka. He had a woman in Nigeria that had heard via the grapevine in that country that Silka had been captured. What he wasn't told was that she had been rescued and had escaped. He gave a few corrupt officials around the world a call. With the money they could make from the diamonds these power-hungry men could stage a small coup. He got lucky when a power-hungry business man from Zambia and corrupt politician from Sierra Leone returned his call. They'd had an election coming up and would need the money to either stay or get into power.

Ferdy decided to go with the Zambian for now. Later when he needed more money, he would approach the corrupt politician. He arranged to go to Zambia to meet with him. He couldn't give two hoots what he was going to use the diamonds or money for.

The terrorists heard through one of their dealers about the Zambian shindig.

--- *T*aber---

Silka's cell phone rang. Taber answered it and told Benji what had happened. He was very upset, but in the end told Taber about Ferdy. Taber called Joshua and set up the sting.

"Hey, Joshua," Taber said.

"Hi, Taber, how are you?" Josh asked. He had heard about Silka and was still in shock about the way things had turned out. Who would have known that after everything she had been through, some jealous chick would ultimately do the most damage.

"Hanging in here, but at least I received word today on the third guy of the team. Ferdy has decided to stick his toes in the water and set up a meeting with a Zambian," he said.

"It's about time we got one of the instigators. Ferdy will know for sure where Brett is," Joshua said, sounding more upbeat.

"I will send out a hunting party as soon as possible, but the CIA has sent their men to Kabul on another mission," he explained.

"How long before they can be wheels up and on Zambian soil?" Taber asked.

"A day or so at the most ...after they've concluded their soirée. They won't want to miss shaking the tree," Joshua assured him.

They said their adieus. Taber hung up the phone. This was the first thing in ages that Taber had shown any interest in. He felt alive again. He wanted to go to Zambia and be part of the action, but decided to stay out of it. Joshua and the authorities could handle matters well on their own.

He phoned Blane, an old friend. In case the special ops guys weren't in time, his good friend could track the terrorists. The last thing he wanted was for Blane to go one-armed-bandit against the lot of them.

"Blane, hi, it's Blake," he said.

"Well hello to you sir!" He was greeted with Blane's friendly British accent. "Whatever it is, the answer is yes!" he said immediately.

Taber and he had a long standing arrangement of doing favors. They couldn't remember who had started it first, but no one was keeping score either. They had been the light sabers to each other's Jedi, since the day they met in Istanbul eight years ago and saved a UN ambassador.

"Thanks, brother. I'll text you the details shortly," Taber said, and hung up.

Ferdy arrived in Lusaka without incident. He hired a car and programmed the coordinates of his meeting location into the GPS. He arrived at a dilapidated house on a huge piece of land. As soon as he stepped out of his car, a man came out of the house wearing dark sunglasses.

"Freddy?" the man asked.

"Ferdy," he corrected and removed his bag from the back. They went inside and sat at the kitchen table.

"Is this all?" the Zambian asked in his heavy accent, as he took a handful of stones out the bag.

"Yes, there are more diamonds in there than what you are paying me for, my friend," he assured him.

"That sounds like a good deal to me," he replied, as he let the diamonds slip through his fingers like desert sand and fall back into the bag.

"I know a lot about diamonds," the Zambian continued, "I can tell these are real and very high quality."

"They should be," Ferdy quipped. "It took me a great deal of effort to get them."

"Good, then here is your money." The Zambian pulled a duffel bag from underneath the table.

"You may take your money, but know that if I find out you screwed me, you are a dead man!" he threatened Ferdy.

"Same here, pal!" Ferdy threatened back.

He took his dollars and left the abandoned farm house. On the long drive back to the airport, he noticed that the road was quite busy but contemplated his spending spree instead. He eventually arrived back at the airport and booked himself on the first flight out. It wasn't on a commercial flight, but he didn't care. The Dakota airplane was flying out the country, which was all that mattered. God forbid the buyer changed his mind. It was also safer travelling on a smaller flight with one million gorillas in your carry-on bag. He would make travel arrangements from Abuja.

It was only when they landed in Nigeria that he realized he'd walked straight into a trap. The plane belonged to the terrorists and was packed with them. They quickly overpowered and subdued him, and took him to their hide-out. They'd managed to get one of the thieves before the Special Ops guys could. They celebrated in style that night.

Fortunately, Blane had arrived in Lusaka in time to track Ferdy down. As soon as the meeting was concluded, he followed him. At the airport, he ran into a slight problem. The Dakota Ferdy was departing on was fully booked. He opted for Plan B. He sat down next to Ferdy where he was waiting to board. While Ferdy was reading a paper, Blane bent down pretended to tie his shoe, and planted a bug in Ferdy's jacket, which was folded over his bag.

Ferdy was taken to the compound of the terrorist organization. The who's who of Global destruction was based there. The main building was immaculate but the brick buildings at the back were dilapidated. They kept him there, in a barren room, where he sat on a cold concrete floor while they partied up a storm.

Blane honed in on Ferdy's signal and told Taber where he was located.

Taber once again kept the loop going. "Hi, Josh," Taber greeted him. "We have Ferdy's location."

"Excellent!" Joshua replied. "Taber," he said, pausing for a bit. "We still have no idea where Brett is. I think we should let the terrorists hang on to Ferdy for a while. If they can trace Brett we can move in, arrest him and then take down the whole Basel Hakims dot org when we go in for Ferdy."

Taber contemplated this for a while.

"Sweet," he said.

The man had a good plan. There was no point in taking out the terrorist organization when Brett was still on the lam. They needed them around still.

"Glad you agree," Josh said solemnly. This was not his best plan ever, but under the circumstances, it needed to be done. They hung up and waited for more word from Benji and Z.

A few days later Taber received a call while he was at work. He was reluctant to take the call when he saw Lucelia's name on his caller ID.

"Hello, Mrs. Fontein," he greeted her respectfully and listened to what she had to say. He was expecting the worst.

"Thank God! I shall be right there!" He hung up the phone and flew out his office.

He drove like a bat out of hell. When he arrived, he stopped the car and ran as fast as he could and almost fell as he skidded to a halt at the door.

"Hey, Speedy Gonzales," Silka teased.

Lucelia, Ted, Tabitha and Don were all staring at him as if he'd escaped from an insane asylum. Seriously, he needn't be so dramatic, they all thought.

"Hey babes!" he smiled, as he walked up to Silka lying in the hospital bed.

The small twenty-two caliber bullet from Amber's hand gun had penetrated her lower left lung, but no other vital organs or major arteries. Silka's biggest enemy had been blood loss, lack of oxygen and shock.

The paramedic had immediately stopped the bleeding, inserted an ET tube, and put her on an IV at the house. When she was taken to hospital they'd pushed her straight into surgery. Afterwards they'd put her on life support. They'd finally taken her off life support and the ET tube a day later and she'd breathed on her own. She'd been in a coma since she'd fallen and lost consciousness. Things had been dicey for a while but every day after that she had recovered a little more. Today she came out of her coma. She was disoriented and very weak, but she was alive.

Everyone else decided to leave the room to give Taber and Silka some time alone.

"Gosh, I missed you!" he said the minute they all left. He leaned over and planted little kisses on her forehead, nose, cheeks, chin and everywhere he could.

"I missed you too," she said, laughing at his puppy dog affection.

Taber stopped and looked down at her. *She was alive!* he thought once more, before he kissed her lips.

Silka closed her eyes and kissed him back with as much warmth and tenderness as he was displaying.

"How are you feeling?" he asked after they broke their kiss. He sat down in the chair and waited for her response.

"OK," she nodded and smiled. "The doctors say I might be out by the end of the week."

"Just know it will take a few months of rest before you are completely recovered," he informed her from personal experience.

"Yes, sir!" she smiled, when he narrowed his eyes at her.

"You are already in hospital. I can easily break your legs so you won't have a choice but to rest," he joked, winking at her. "The doctors are right here, they'll fix you immediately."

Silka laughed and then started coughing. Her pain was evident.

"I shall leave you to rest and return tonight, okay?" promised Taber, as he stood up to leave.

"Okay," she said. "I love you, Taber."

"I love you," he said back and gave her a lingering kiss.

---**S**ilka---

Taber visited Silka every morning before work after that. He would bring her the coffee she used to have with him

311

in town. They'd sit drinking coffee and chatting away until visiting hours were over.

At night, he would go back and visit while her family and his parents where there too. The men all made jokes about her bullet catching abilities, much to Lucelia's horror. She had no sense of humor on the best of days, let alone then.

That Friday, Taber took the day off. Silka was coming home. He had brought her a change of clothes and had helped her get dressed. The trip took a lot out of her weak body, so he carried her in his arms into the elevator and their bedroom.

She slept until the late afternoon. He played Xbox for a while but later went back to sit with her. When she finally woke up, they chatted about what had happened to him after he had killed Amber.

Her parents came over to check up on her.

Lucelia could not grasp the modern home. To her it looked too much like a bachelor version of Disneyland. He needed a feminine touch in there. She appreciated the fact that Taber showed her to the elevator rather than make her walk up all those flights of stairs to the top floor where Silka was.

Ted loved the house.

They sat next to her on the balcony overlooking the pool and waterfall. Silka's overbearing mother continued to ask questions about every little detail of her health, life and her stay there.

"You only need to call should you require anything," she reassured Silka several times.

"Thanks mom, but I have everything I need here," Silka would say several times more. *Deep breaths!!!* She warned herself.

Eventually, her parents left.

They had dinner in bed that night and afterwards, sat watching TV until they fell asleep.

In the weeks to follow, Tay spent his days at work, while Silka stayed home and wrote a book about her experiences. It was something she would never have contemplated due to her love for privacy, but Taber made her feel like anything was possible. She received daily calls from her parents, Josh and Taber while she was at home. Every night, they'd sit blissfully together in each other's presence. She still hadn't recovered enough to make love, so talking and kissing was about all they did in those first few weeks.

Brett hadn't heard from Ferdy in a long time. He knew something was wrong. The time had come for him to disappear. He knew of some guy in the Bratva which was part of the Russian mafia. They'd only met twice but he knew this guy had a lot of money and the whole supply-slash-demand setup going for him. He started searching for the man to set up a meeting with Mobster.

The terrorists had no affiliation with the Russian crime organization, but fortunately they overheard the chatter in the form of a bona-fide Russian diamond dealer that was recruited to verify the authenticity of the stones before the sale could take place. The guy was as discreet as a killer ant.

---Silka---

Their evenings outside in the entertainment area moved to the front of the fireplace as winter neared. It had been three months since she had been shot. Silka had made a remarkable recovery. Her lungs and wound had healed perfectly.

"Baby twos!!" Benji screamed out of joy, when Silka answered her phone. He was over the moon that she had bitten a bullet and spat it right out.

"Hello, Benji. How are you?" she exclaimed and was equally happy to hear from him. They had a long, meaningful chat about life, the universe and demented exes. They exchanged stories for a while and chatted away about everything from the weather to current affairs. The most current affair of all was that Brett had crawled out of the woodwork.

Silka was deeply concerned. Brett was experienced and not stupid, unlike the others. They were in for the fight of their lives to take him down.

"Benji, I cannot tell you how happy I am to hear that!" She pretended that she was tickled pink for his sake.

"Slight problem," he said, interrupting her thoughts. "They didn't fill the diamond dealer in on where the meeting would take place or when. All he knew was that they would text him the location of the pickup point. From there he would be taken to the diamonds. The Bratva have HQ's in Kiev, Moscow and St. Petersburg. It could be anywhere," Benji said, almost admiring the Bratva for their suspicious setups and trust issues. "The Basel Hakims guys are sending people to Kiev, Moscow and St. Petersburg in search of Brett, but I don't know if they will find him in time," he concluded.

Silka knew time was of the essence. They discussed their problem a while longer before she phoned Josh to tell him the news. *Go time!*

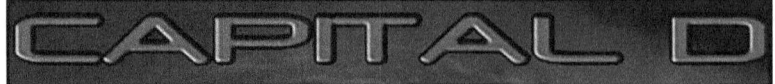

Chapter 29

---SILKA---

The real kicker was that the Bratva had numerous places in the Ukraine and Russia where they liked to conduct meetings, plus no one but them knew where. This much Joshua knew when she relayed the news to him.

The dealer could inspect the diamonds anywhere in the world and the sale could take place in a totally different location.

"Fudge balls!!" Joshua exclaimed. "Wish I had an Ouija board to contact Geo. He would know for sure where the Russian mafia hung out."

"What's happened to your search for a new Geo?" she asked.

"Not much. We were referred to a guy in Amsterdam, but he's practically still in diapers. I doubt he'd be able to be of any help," Joshua responded.

"Our luck just gets better and better, doesn't it?" she joked.

"We'll send in every company we can, I promise," he tried to assure Silka. "The CIA, UN, NSA, FBI, DHS and DOD along with everyone else would have a finger in this pie." Joshua knew how much they all wanted credit for taking down these men.

"I know, but in fear of sounding like a three-year-old whiney, how can we get to them when we don't have a place or time like before?" she asked despondently.

"Silka, we have people running every database and going through every avenue looking for him. So far GPS tracking on his mobile phone came up empty. He doesn't switch it on much," Josh informed her. "To catch them, our best option is to rally as many boots as possible and take every location by storm if needs be," he said. "We really could use Taber and his men on this one too," he added, but he knew she would not want that.

The truth was that the other men did not have independence. They were all bound to superiors who made decisions for them and dished out orders. Taber and his 'Robin Dudes' could come in handy when the red tape came out.

"No! He's staying with me. I am not going to let him traipse through Eastern Europe after the Russian mob, Nigerian terrorists and a guy like Brett Sheffield," she promised in her tone.

"Fine. If that's how you want it, but at least let his friends come out and play?" he mocked her, knowing she would eventually see reason.

"I'll talk to him about that. But I can't promise anything." She smiled slightly at the way he made her sound like a mother hen. They hung up.

When Taber arrived home that evening, Silka braced herself for the conversation they were about to have. She wore a short long-sleeved dress that showed off her legs, but not her scars. They sat down for dinner after he removed his suit jacket and tie.

It could possibly be their ugliest and longest fight since they had been twelve years old. Her little voice inside her told her to wait until after dinner.

"So," she started on the topic. "Brett's come up for fresh air," she said and took a sip from her wine.

"Finally! What is Joshua's plan?" his excitement was evident.

"He's going to send in a substantial international team, but since no one knows when or where the meeting will take place, they are calling all pockets," she said, making a billiards reference. "That includes Bulldog and his team's services too." She put it out there. This was about to get interesting.

"Seems like they can do with all the help they can get this time," Taber said, stating the obvious.

"Not all the help," she smiled and pointed a finger at him, but her tone warned him not to go there.

"I've been a gun for hire in much worse situations," he assured her with a smile, as if he was privy to an inside joke.

"Taber, not like this. There's the Bratva, Nigerians and Brett. The worst of the worst are going up against each other," she frowned.

318

"And so will the best of the best to catch them," he seemed excited to become one of them.

"I don't want you to go." She pursed her lips, as the bitter taste of him out there in the line of fire filled her. Her concern ran deeper than just the immediate danger. *What if he got killed?*

"Silks, they need me. You want Brett to be caught before he pulls another Houdini again, don't you?" he asked with a frown. He started rubbing his hand against his thigh in agitation and grasped his wine glass tighter.

"Yes, but let other people do it!" she commanded, sternly.

"No way. Not my style," he said calmly and lifted his hand and planted his fist gently on the table.

"Taber, don't do this!" she yelled. His calm resolve was scaring her.

"What you fail to understand is that I will not send Paul or any other guy into a situation I'm not willing to go into myself," his voice raised an octave. "These guys will be going there to help, Silka. I can't just stay at home while they do this on their own!"

"They won't be on their own. The entire world's organizations and peace keeping forces will be there!" she corrected him.

"Exactly! So I am going!" he yelled to make his point.

"What about us. What about me!" she shouted. "You're willing to leave me to go play 'Die Hard' with your buddies?"

"I'm willing to leave you to make sure you are safe for the rest of your life!" he screamed.

"I will be safer with you here!" she shouted, stood up and started to walk away.

Taber stood up and followed her.

"For how long?" he yelled after her. "Those fools won't rest until all of you are dead! How long exactly will you be safe?"

His anger was blatantly displayed on his face.

"I don't care!" she screamed louder and hurried upstairs. She got to the second flight of stairs before she realized how out of breath she was. She wanted to storm to her bedroom, but that was another two flights of stairs. Instead, she walked to the formal lounge on the second floor.

"You got yourself and everybody else into this mess and YOU don't care?" Taber yelled disgusted and grabbed her arm. He had been right behind her the whole time.

"That is not true and you know it!" She pulled her arm away.

"It might not have been your idea, but you fell for their bullshit and helped people get tortured and killed." He regretted saying it the minute it was out there.

She gave a huge gasp as if he'd just slapped her. She had thought they had been protecting people's lives.

"That's a low blow!" she said, her voice was low and dark. She knew the deaths of good Nigerians and Geo

320

was on her conscience. *Her kitty could scratch!* If it weren't for Brett being out there and time being so crucial, she would have dumped him right then. She was about to bite back twice as hard and he was about to apologize, but instead she stormed off. The less she had to say to that prick the better. Taber didn't follow her.

She went and sat all the way at the back of the garden, way in the jungle in front of their tennis court. It had a lot of privacy and she would not be found there for a while. She needed time to think.

---

*T*aber went to the balcony and watched her as he rang up Paul.

"Howzit, Paul," he said.

"Hello, Tay. What's up?" Paul asked.

"The business with the Nigerians has been extended. Care to join me at the Conference?" he asked.

"Sure, I rather enjoyed our last meeting," Paul joked.

"Thank you. I'll send you the agenda," he said. "You might want to get Riley and Herman to sidekick this trip."

"They'll be there," Paul smiled and promised.

They hung up and Taber went upstairs.

---*S*ilka---

When it was almost midnight, Silka took a leisurely stroll back to their bedroom. With any luck the asshole would be asleep and she could grab her nightgown and sleep in one of the other rooms.

321

She opened the bedroom door. The bedside table lamps were on, but the room was so big, the light paled in comparison. She could make out that the bed was still made. He was probably downstairs somewhere. For a house that looked like a castle, it could sure use a dungeon. She would have had fun banning him there during times like these. She went to her side of the walk-in closet doors and opened it to grab her sleepwear. She decided to dress in the other bedroom and turned to leave. As she closed her closet door, she saw that Taber was in front of her.

She got a fright but didn't say anything. She took a breath and walked past him.

"I didn't mean what I said," he said softly. She turned to look at him as he turned too. He put his one hand on his hip and ran his hand through his hair with the other. "I'm sorry, baby." He looked away briefly, still holding the back of his neck. They stood there in silence for a while.

"You will be. I'm going with you."

Taber was shocked at her blasé, calm statement. *There was that Buddha statue again.*

"Yeah, that's so not going to happen!" he smirked.

"I have as much ownership in this as they have. I need to make things right ... so damn straight, I'm going to chase them down as well," she snarled.

"How? You have the lung capacity of a freaking toothpick!" He stopped himself from laughing at her absurdity.

"I know Brett inside out. I will stay out the way but I can help you track him and anticipate his every move," she said.

---

*T*aber shook his head, but said nothing.

"I need to do this, just like you," she said, nodding her head and folding her arms.

She looked like his mother did when she put her foot down. She knew exactly how he felt and what buttons to push. It came as no surprise to him, after all the time they'd spent together. Still, what the hell would she do among elite task forces and highly trained men? She would either get in the way or need rescuing again.

"Tay, I almost died twice! I'm not going to go there to test the third time charm theory," she promised. "But I also don't need your permission to go."

She'd made her intentions clear. He knew her flight had already been mentally booked.

"Man, you are an impossible woman," he said, flabbergasted.

"Oh, honey, you have no idea," she shook her head and smiled.

Taber went and sat down on the balcony. He spent a good while contemplating her suggestion. She sat down next to him. The last thing he wanted was for her to get hurt again. In the end he made his decision.

"Fine. But you won't be anywhere near the action. As sure as God made little green apples, none of those guys will even know you are there. Not the good guys, bad guys and especially not the rotten to the core guys. Understood?" he commanded.

"Aye-aye, captain!" she saluted and spoke in a Scottish accent. "I will be as invisible as a Ho in church," she joked.

He laughed and threw her down on the couch. She giggled as he hovered above her.

"God help me, you will be the end of me one day," he smiled and kissed her hard.

---**Silka**---

Instead of romantically kissing and making up like a normal couple, they went at it like rabbits. It had been three excruciating months since they'd last made love. Taber hiked up her dress over her head and ripped off her underwear. Gentleness was not his forte at that moment, which made her feel wanted like never before.

In the last couple of months, her figure had become more rounded from the lack of exercise. The scars from her torture and surgery had turned her upper body into a road map. She'd felt very conscious about the ten kilograms she'd gained, until that very moment. Taber had the power to take her from the blackness into the sun and from disliking her body to thinking she had the

324

perfect skin and figure. He had the ability to turn her into what she had been like before, by just the way he looked at her and touched her.

Chapter 30

---*T*ABER---

Within two days Taber had arranged for Bulldog, Eagle Eye and Flash to gear up and head off to Russia. They arrived in St. Petersburg and stayed in a posh hotel, courtesy of Taber.

Joshua was there too and had kept close tabs on the members from every church. Since the USAID was not invited to the party, he couldn't join in the festivities. It was a bummer but he flew under the radar undetected and saddled himself in a nice cozy position far away from the bonfire. In fact, it was so cozy it was in Moscow to be exact. Ram-brandt, aka the Netherlands version of Geo had flown there too at the request of Joshua. He decided to give the kid a chance and test-drive his skills. He looked like a surfer dude with his long blond hair and thin frame. Naturally, Silka joined them.

Taber had taken them from the hotel where they met, to Geo's old command centre at his house. That was where he had all the gizmos and gadgets at his disposal. With the help of Ram-brandt, they had over-ridden all the access codes and security systems. Taber had opened the door using some finesse with his boot. The house was spacious and open plan. It held a lot of old looking furniture but at least it was tidy. Down the hallway was a command centre in a reinforced steel room. They were going to settle in there to play in a game of real life dungeons and dragons after breakfast.

Taber left them and took a train from Moscow to meet up with Team Awesome.

"Miss me?" he asked the guys, when he walked into Bulldog's hotel room later that day. They were all there.

"Like a mosquito bite!" Flash aka Herman smiled and shook his hand.

Taber just laughed. "Thank you for showing up anyway," Taber told him.

"We couldn't resist the temptation to scratch where the Nigerians had an itch," Eagle Eye Riley snapped jokingly and laughed as he shook Taber's hand as well.

"You should see a doctor about that," Taber smiled broadly.

"Good to see you, old friend." Bulldog stepped in and hugged him.

"You too Paul," Taber replied. "What's the news so far?"

"Nothing," Paul sounded bored. "We are waiting for your friend Josh to point us in some direction."

"Yeah!" Eagle Eye chirped in. "We just need a whiff and we'll be on their scent like bloodhounds in the hunting season."

"At least you will be less worried about your looks this time," Taber joked. They ordered room service and watched TV.

---*S*ilka---

Josh, Silka and Ram-brandt settled in well at Geo's house. She was keen to play Star Wars in the high-tech room and find Brett, but Josh suggested they eat breakfast first. She learned that Ram-brandt's real name was Hans Wentzel. He was a twenty year old student at university, but his parents had no idea he was actually a very rich, world-class hacker. His name was derived from the famous Dutch painter, Rembrandt Van Rijn and his first love, computers…ergo the name Ram-brandt.

"I could do more damage on my laptop before breakfast than a terrorist in his whole lifetime," he said, seemingly proud.

Josh shot Silka a dubious look. They would have to wait and see if big-mouth's horn blew as hard as he made it out to.

After breakfast they entered the dark room. The room looked like one giant plasma screen. Everywhere had monitor screens, consoles and electronics.

Ram-brandt sat in front of a large set of computers and consoles in the corner. Joshua sat close to the phones and wireless communication devices so he could direct the men. Silka settled in front of the monitors between the two.

Ram-brandt pressed a few buttons and the whole place lit up. Bleeping noises and various other electronic sounds filled the room as every gadget and piece of equipment came to life. Thankfully, an air conditioner also circulated the stuffy air out.

"Nice one!" Silka congratulated Ram-brandt.

"I used to help Geo when his work load became too much or if he was on a tight deadline. He gave me all his program source codes and commands," Ram-brandt said simply.

"Right junior! What do you say we get this rally kick-started?" Joshua was eager to see his skills.

"Showtime boy," Silka instructed him.

Ram-brandt wasted no time. He tapped ferociously on the keyboard and had his own laptop hooked up to the AIO server. He had another rubber keyboard he rolled open in front of another computer screen. Every consol and monitor was used.

"The FBI and other local authorities have the Integrated Automated Fingerprint System (IAFIS) and Combined DNA Index system (CODIS). The Department of Defense had Scattered Castles which was the Intelligence community security clearance repository. The DOD also used the Automated Biometric ID systems (ABIS). The NCC had TIDE - Terrorist Identification Data mart Environment. The US

Department of State had the Consular Consolidated Database (CCD) and the DHS had IDENT which was their Biometric Identity system. NSAC and the NGA had various GEOINT systems which allowed them access to satellites, aerial pictures and mapping data. These alphabet agencies could only use the specific program they have. I can use them all thanks to Geo," Ram-brandt bragged as he typed away ferociously.

Along with the facial recognition software and suspicious activity reporting programs, he also made a 'firecall' and gained access to the other security and intelligence agencies in the Ukraine, Russia and other countries.

He ran TIDE, NSAC, IDENT and every program he had access to and set up a crowd-sourcing process and went about geo-fencing his attention in Kiev, Moscow and St. Petersburg using the Russian Satellite, GLONASS. This was similar to the standard stuff Geo had done while he was still alive.

Josh was not impressed until Ram-brandt did something unexpected. He set up a website with Brett's details and called it GetThetr8r.com and sent the URL hyperlink to social media networks and various mailing lists he had created. He entered various terrorist websites and blogs and set up an algorithm to alert buzz words involving Brett, the Nigerians and the Russians. He also hacked the mainframe of the Bratva and had a teraflop of operations running simultaneously.

The three of them watched every monitor and screen for hits. Joshua called some airline authorities and placed Brett on the VIP list of people to watch out for. He called the teams to get status updates. Kiev, Moscow and St. Petersburg so far had no sign of the Bratva, Nigerians or Brett. The searches were uneventful and disappointing.

Brett was already in Kiev. He'd arrived a few days earlier, just to suss out the place and set up a plan B if the shit hit the fan, so to speak. He was far more patient and experienced than his team mates. He was many other things, but unprepared was not one of them either.

Mobster set up a meeting with Brett and told him to meet him in Troyeschchyna in the raion of Desnianskyi or Dresna. There weren't many businesses in Dresna, and it was largely a poor neighborhood with lots of appalling apartment buildings and a small industrial site. This was where Brett would meet Mobster late that night.

"We have a lot of chatter!" Ram-brandt exclaimed. The social networks and internet buzzed with talks and community forums on Brett and hinted that he was in Kiev. The websites the terrorists normally used for planning, coordination, fundraising, recruitment, information sharing, networking, mobilization, data mining and propaganda. Today, however, they were pinging with information about a huge operation in St.

Petersburg. The Bratva's Facebook page and Zetaboard forums had deals going down in Moscow and St. Petersburg.

"We should get some Strats and Tats." Silka implied they needed strategies and tactics to formulate a game plan.

"Cool, where can I download one of those?" the clueless geek asked.

Joshua smiled and shook his head. "Not yet, we need more Intel," Joshua proclaimed. He turned to Rambrandt.

"How difficult is it to infiltrate the terrorists and mob online?" he asked.

Ram-brandt smiled. "For you, very difficult," he said. "For me," he paused and typed furiously, "not so much." He pointed to the screen. Ram-brandt had a profile, complete with a picture and a summary, of a grade A scumbag. He created an alter ego of someone every bad guy would want on their team. He hacked his way into their version of personnel records and was officially part of Solntsevskaya and the Yusuf Islamic brotherhood.

"Excellent. Time to crank up the volume." Joshua winked and smiled. For a moment, Ram-brandt looked at him in such a way that Josh hoped Ram-brandt wasn't gay.

"You are a very funny man, Mr. Stonewall, but would you mind speaking English?" Ram-brandt asked.

"Just offer your services after you tell them about Brett and see who bites," he instructed.

"Silka, tell our dear friends in the online community about Bret." He waved his hand to the computer.

Silka started typing away. It had been years since she had been Joshua's PA, but she still knew how to type. She smiled at the memories he'd given her. She hoped that her next boss would be as kind, thoughtful, generous and amazing as Joshua was.

Silka gave the whole spiel about Brett's demonic psyche and how the man was responsible for the deaths of their members. She gave all his details and made it clear that no one who had ever crossed his path survived. Whomever was dealing with him, had to know not to do it on his onesie. He would need the help of this specific Alter Ego.

Alter Ego got a hit. The mobster wasn't going to take his buddies with him to meet Brett. His plan was to meet him and take a diamond by train to Moscow to verify. If it was real, he'd set up another meeting, kill Brett and take the diamonds to mobster HQ in St. Petersburg. He moved his business dealings and transactions all the time in order not to be traced or recognized. Since reading about the caliber of man he was going to do business with, he recruited some help in Kiev. His deal with Brett was to become a one-horse rodeo show with lots of clowns. Alter Ego was invited to join the party along with his normal crew.

Joshua sent the word out to the heads of the alphabet agencies and Special Ops men based in Kiev that the meeting was to take place in the industrial area at midnight.

Taber and the guys were to sit tight until they heard about the outcome in Kiev.

With the team prepared and his men in the vicinity, Joshua waited for the go-ahead from the various heads of departments and states. The endless red tape and pussy-footing around could mean that they'd miss the boat if someone didn't step up soon. It was almost time for the curtain call.

Mobster waited around with his crew. Alter Ego was a no show. He decided to deal with him later. They got in their cars and drove to the industrial site called Kulycove. It was dark and almost abandoned, apart from Brett who stood near a car by the side of the building. The guys could do their business in the open, because the whole place was Bratva territory at night and if non-members were found there, they were killed.

The six men got out of their cars and walked to Brett.

"You came alone?" the mobster asked suspiciously. He had a heavy Russian accent.

"Yeah, see you didn't," Brett was very surprised by the unexpected guests.

"You did not think I do my research and know everything about person I do business with?" Mobster said, in broken English. He was very pleased with himself, despite the fact that he had done no research at all. If it hadn't been for Alter Ego, he might have been in danger tonight.

"Remember what you know," Brett threatened in a calm tone.

"Enough about this...how do you Americans say? Chit-chat." Mobster continued, "Where is the diamonds?"

Brett took a small pouch from his pocket and held it up. This was merely a fraction of the diamonds he had. He only needed a start-up fund to live in the Maldives.

"Do you have my fifty thousand US Dollars?" he asked.

"Da, but you seem to think I am a stupid," Mobster said in his broken Russian accent, laying down the terms. "I will take one stone to my comrade to verify. If diamonds are real, I take them and give your money at next meeting"

"I don't have time for this!" screamed Brett.

"It is how I do business. If you do not like it, we can do no business," he stated simply.

"How long do I have to wait?" Brett asked agitated.

"Until tomorrow," the mobster assured him.

"Fine, here!" He took a diamond out the bag and planted it into Mobster's hand.

"Stupid plank!" he swore under his breath, as he walked away.

Chapter 31

They all drove off without incident after the meeting was concluded. Mobster and his crew took a train to Moscow.

The diamond dealer was texted and he met with them in the early hours of the morning. He was picked up and taken to an empty restaurant downstairs from an apartment building along with his gear. Mobster invited him to sit down and he proceeded to take some things out his bag. He could have done the diamond on the mirror trick, but some stones have the ability to mimic real diamonds like moissanite.

Diamond Dealer first laid a newspaper on the table. He then took out a black diamond/moissanite tester, microscope, tweezers, a jewelry scale, UV light, heat probe and a small jeweler's loupe for looking at the diamond. He laid the diamond on the newspaper to see if he could see through it and check its reflective index. The RI was very high and he could not see the writing on the newspaper.

"PokaVse Khorosho - So far so good," Diamond Dealer said in Russian. He picked the diamond up with the tweezers and did the fog test. When he saw the diamond cleared immediately after he blew on it, he proceeded with the heat test. Again the heat dispersed immediately. Once that was done he pretty much knew the diamond was real. He kept quiet to impress the mobster with his array of high-tech equipment. The diamond tester beeped, the UV light reflected blue, and the loupe showed minor imperfections. It reflected shades of grey when he held it up and had no bright orange lights when he held it down under the microscope. After all his tests were completed, he weighed the stone. It was the exact carats he expected it to be.

"Eto real'no - It is real," he told Mobster.

Before Mobster could say anything, a small invasion took place through the front and back door of the restaurant. Ten men with automatic weapons, speaking a strange language, had surrounded Mobster, his crew and Diamond Dealer.

"Where are the rest of the diamonds?" the leader ordered in his strong African accent when he noticed only one diamond on the table.

"Not here. Who are you?" Mobster asked, quite amused.

"The people the diamonds were stolen from," the boss man said, still pointing his weapon at him.

"Then we have problem," said mobster, quite calmly.

In that instant more of Mobster's own men came downstairs. Mobster ducked under the table as the whole lot shot at each other. The diamond dealer was killed in the crossfire along with a few of the other men.

The terrorists and mob guys that were still alive slowly retreated out to the exits whilst firing at each other and also avoiding tripping over dead guys and furniture. Pretty soon the place was empty and loud moans from the dying filled the place.

Mobster crept out from under the table. He walked out of the restaurant and drove off. He thought it was a good idea to change his plan of action seeing as the situation had changed slightly. With the new guys (not known to him as our beloved terrorists) after the diamonds too, things had gotten a little more interesting than he had hoped for.

He sent a text to Brett. *Meet me at St. Petersburg Vitebsk train station tomorrow at midnight. Bring all the diamonds you have. I will find you.*

Brett was still in Kiev. He didn't know if the last sentence was a threat, but he decided he'd had enough of this charade. He booked the overnight train to Moscow and then the express to St. Petersburg that same night. He wasn't going to sell off all his diamonds, but after the way the deal had gone that night, he was less enthusiastic about dealing with scumbags ever again. He would sell all his diamonds and put the money into different off-shore fixed savings accounts and bonds for rainy days.

Silka missed Taber and wondered how he was doing. No one was meant to know that she was there, so she couldn't phone him in case they traced her call or texts.

Mobster went to look for what was left of his crew. Only three guys had survived and were waiting for him at their Moscow hide-out. He needed to recruit more guys for what he was planning in St. Petersburg. His home and base of operations was in the Ukraine. With the influx of refugees there, he made a good living off their desperation. He knew some Bratva brothers in St. Petersburg and Moscow, but they reported to different men, not him. Mobster went online and put the word out there that a big operation was going down and he needed help. He had no idea how the other guys had found him, therefore he wasn't going to take any chances the next time round. The next time they met, they would have a bigger force and all hell would break loose.

---**S**ilka---

Ram-brandt picked up on the SOS from Mobster.

"We need to send everyone to St. Petersburg," he said as he woke Josh and Silka up. They'd fallen asleep in their chairs. The kid had a lot more energy and stamina than they did. It was two o'clock in the morning and he was still as sprightly as a butterfly.

"What's going on?" Joshua sat up and rubbed his face.

Ram-brandt told him that Mobster had a plan to make a very big business deal at the train station in St. Petersburg and needed all the help he could get. All Bratva were called to arms to eliminate the two threats.

Josh spread the word to everyone in the Ukraine and Russia. Team after team descended on St. Petersburg the next day. They had waited through the red tape and clearance was given for the Kiev bust after the meeting between Brett and Mobster had already taken place. *Typical!!!* For all intents and purposes, those orders still stood as far as Josh was concerned. He wasn't going to let bureaucratic bullshit stand in the way of their rendezvous this time.

Silka phoned Benji and told him about the latest development as well. She knew the terrorists had tracked the diamond dealer and that he was not going to be around that night. She had yet to learn that he was not going to be around pretty much anywhere ever again. Benji told his brother and the news of the midnight feast spread like wildfire in their ranks. Every BH terrorist near the scene of the action was going to pitch their tents there later.

---

*T*aber and his guys were at the Vitebsk train station to scope the place out. They arrived at different times and wore normal clothes. Taber went tourist in jeans and a T-shirt with a sports cap and camera. He tried not to get noticed, but the looks he got from women made it difficult. The massive downstairs hall was in a classic Russian Art Nouveau style with light colored walls and gold art with blue trimmings surrounded by arched stained-glass windows under the dome. The railings and lights were made of brass and cast iron. There was a pale blue door on either side of a ceremonial looking staircase in the centre. The massive staircase went up to the bust of V.I. Lenin which stood beneath the stained-glass windows. A bird's crest and a huge clock were above the statue. From there a staircase on either side went up to the second floor halls and through doors to the platforms.

Bulldog and Eagle Eye geared up to look like travelers complete with back packs. All the girls were eager to give them directions to their homes.

Flash disguised himself to look like a run-of-the-mill working man which still did not steer the looks he got from interested ladies.

Taber went upstairs to get a clear idea of the 'land'. The arched stained glass windows blocked the view to the ground floor and could come in handy later.

Bulldog and Eagle Eye tested the doors by the staircase. They were locked but the area was blocked from view which could be beneficial.

Flash walked around to the ornate waiting areas on the ground floor and to the turnstiles and ticket booths on the second floor. They provided perfect cover. They met up a short while later at Bulldog's hotel room to formulate a plan and rest up for the action later.

By eleven they were dressed and looked as if they were doing a casting call for the movie version of Call of Duty Modern Warfare without the cammo wardrobe and make up. They wore bulletproof vests under bulky T-shirts that concealed their weapons. Inside their black cargo pants they carried their necessities. Their bomber jackets housed their communication devices.

"Time to move, ladies," Taber ordered.

"Cool, let's do this!" Flash said excitedly.

"Ready and steady," Eagle Eye acknowledged the order.

"Right behind you, Phantom," Bulldog said.

"Phantom?" Taber laughed.

"Yeah, we thought you needed a new name to match your skills," Eagle Eye informed him.

"And it officially makes you part of the team," Flash interjected.

"Thanks, but don't I get a say when it comes to my nickname?" Taber aka Phantom asked delighted, as he gave them each a pat on the back when they passed him.

"We like Phantom." Bulldog cleared up any misconception that the topic was open for discussion.

Phantom smiled, closed the door behind him and followed his men to the car.

They drove to the Vitebsky train station and got into their planned positions.

The train station was busy, as the last sleeper train for the night was scheduled for departure shortly.

Mobster and his brotherhood took their positions in various parts of the station as well and waited for Brett to arrive.

The SAG, SOG, INTERPOL, UN and local forces sat around on the platforms and the waiting area long before midnight.

The terrorists also made like trees and stood around inconspicuously. They covered the platforms and waited for Brett's train to arrive.

Everyone knew everyone else was there, but with so many people it was hard to tell the groups apart.

---*S*ilka---

Ram-brandt had hacked into the stations security cameras. Joshua, Silka and Ram-brandt watched on the monitors and waited to give them orders.

It was down to the wire. The last call at the bar was about to be made and everyone looked at their watches. All the contestants were there, except for the guest of honor. Brett was late.

"Alpha team, over," Joshua spoke into the receiver.

"Go for Alpha team," Phantom responded holding his ear-piece.

"What's your status," Josh asked about their visual on the subject.

"No sign of the target," Phantom informed him.

"Bravo 2, come in for Bravo 1," Josh called the Special Forces.

"Bravo 1, this is Bravo 2, over," the leader of the agencies' forces responded.

"Keep your eyes open and wait for Alpha team before you make a move," he ordered.

"Copy that, Bravo 1," he acquiesced.

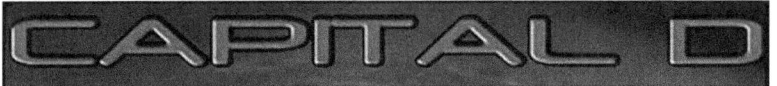

Chapter 32

Brett arrived in St. Petersburg that afternoon. He scoped the place out for possible escape routes and made his own plans. He arrived at the station in disguise a few minutes before the meeting was to take place. He looked around and saw his own kind lurking around. He knew SOG, SAG and other forces when he saw them. They were all hardened and had a certain air of confidence, calm and sadness about them. Their composures made them hard to miss in a crowd. He didn't notice Taber's team scattered all over the place or the terrorists, but seeing his own men there spooked him enough to get the hell out of Dodge.

Brett decided to catch the last sleeper train to wherever it was going.

His distinct walk caught Silka's attention. She knew he had a bad knee and his one leg always stiffened right before it touched the ground. She could also recognize his dark deep set eyes a mile away.

"That's Brett!" She pointed to an elderly man on the screen. He was walking toward the massive staircase.

"Alpha team, over," Josh called.

"Go for Alpha," Phantom responded.

"Target sighted heading due north towards the staircase," Josh informed him. "Elderly man with a brown suitcase."

"We're on it!" Phantom acknowledged his order.

"Time to shine, Bulldog," Phantom calmly gave his order.

Bulldog was standing by the one of the locked blue doors. He left his position as soon as he noticed the old man reach the stairs. He followed him up. When the old man turned right at the landing by Lenin's bust, he turned right as well.

Eagle Eye got into position at the top of the staircase, where the old man was about to make an entrance.

Phantom went and stood on the opposite side of Eagle Eye.

When the old man reached the top, he turned right again and walked towards the ticket stands. He passed large ornate, arched steel structures and shops.

Eagle Eye, Bulldog and Phantom followed him from several angles and at several feet apart from each other. Among the crowds of adults and children, they were not noticed.

The terrorists at that point had become impatient and decided to go look for Brett. They walked from the platforms through the hall doors and towards the ceremonial looking staircase.

When Brett recognized them, he turned around and walked back to where he came from. He had scoped a spiral staircase earlier in the afternoon and decided to go down it.

"He's going out the other exit!" Silka warned them when they didn't turn around like Brett did, but Joshua hadn't opened the communication channels. They couldn't hear her.

"Feel like some company, Flash?" Phantom gave another order.

"Thought you'd forgotten about me," Flash mocked.

Phantom, Eagle Eye and Bulldog noticed the terrorists too and continued walking straight past them.

"He's going to get away!" Silka screamed at Taber, but to no avail. Joshua had promised that no one would know she was there.

Phantom, Eagle Eye and Bulldog carried on walking.

"Taber!" she screamed again. "He is going the other way. You are letting him escape!" Silka was highly agitated.

Joshua smiled at the back seat driver.

Phantom, Eagle Eye and Bulldog reached the luggage elevator. They snuck inside it and went downstairs.

Flash was waiting for Brett at the spiral stairs disguised as a bulky, bearded guard. His black suit and hat along with his Russian came in very handy. He stopped Brett from taking the stairs and offered him another exit, after Brett asked for directions to the parking lot. He followed

Brett as he dragged his suitcase and grabbed him from behind when they reached the parking area outside.

Brett had years of combat experience which enabled him to get out of Flash's snake coil grasp. He punched Flash in his ribs with his elbow and twisted himself around. He did not count on the fact that Flash was even more experienced. Flash grabbed his attacking arm and pushed it down with one hand, while with the other he tazered his neck. He struggled as Flash quickly kicked his bad knee and floored him. Quickly, Flash reached over to get Brett off his knees and vertical.

Instantly Brett fought back by punching Flash in his stomach, which inevitably connected with Flash's bullet proof vest. Flash tazered him again and kicked him so hard in the face that he fell to the floor.

Before he could make another move, Phantom, Eagle Eye and Bulldog appeared with their weapons drawn. Phantom and Bulldog reached to pick him up, but Brett had pulled a knife from his belt. He flung it at Phantom and cut his neck. The other three members immediately subdued the attacker and knocked him out of his disguise and into a new one.

Phantom grabbed for his throat and fell to his knees. He tried to reach into his pants pockets for his small medical kit. Bulldog came to his rescue and forced him to lie down while he checked his vitals and the extent of the damage.

Eagle Eye and Flash tied and gagged Brett in such a way that hardcore BDSM seemed romantic.

---

*S*ilka screamed when she saw what had happened. It was the worst feeling in the world to watch someone you love get hurt and not be able to do anything about it.

"Wimp! It's just nick," Bulldog said to Phantom and proceeded to patch up his neck.

Eagle Eye and Flash came to see for themselves. Their faces went pale and bleak. They paused for a bit. Then they started laughing.

"You won't even need tissue paper to patch that up!" Flash joked and then laughed.

"Tell that to Ryan Gauze-ling over here!" Phantom retorted.

"You should have seen your face, GQ boy!" Eagle Eye burst out laughing. "You'll be fine...little scarred, but fine," he said and held his hand out to help Phantom up.

Bulldog had covered the slice, where Brett's electrocution impaired arm tried to cut him with very little success.

Phantom stood up and the four of them continued with their plan. "Bravo 2 company, come in for Alpha team," he spoke into his receiver.

"Bravo company over," Team leader spoke.

"We have Satan's doppelgänger, proceed with operation Sputnik," Phantom said, instructing them to arrest the Russians and the terrorists.

"Copy that," Team leader acknowledged the order.

They dragged Brett to their van. A familiar sound caught their attention. It was like sixties music. Nobody was really 'there' but everyone knows the music.

They dumped Brett and his suitcase full of clothes and diamonds in the van.

"Sounds like you and Flash have visitors from Mill-Walkie," Phantom instructed Flash and Eagle Eye to take the lead and take out the guys with the walkie-talkies if they were not 'friendlies'.

Just then, gun shots and automatic gun fire could be heard from inside the station. Women screaming and loud banging noises could be heard all the way into the parking lot. The teams were under fire from gangs who refused Bravo team's proposal of handcuffs.

"Flash and I will welcome our guests to Allah…," Eagle Eye held up his one weapon. "BAM-ma," he continued, holding up the other weapon.

"You and Bulldog Delta Force some peace in there," Flash suggested.

Bulldog smiled and shook his head. "Where did I get you walking clichés from?" he laughed.

They all smiled and gave each other good luck fist bumps.

Bulldog took the back and Phantom went in the main entrance. People were running out of the doors past him. Once inside, he noticed people running and some diving for cover among the tracers that flew all over the place. A scared little three year old girl stood in the centre of the hall crying hysterically while her mother stood screaming for her by the square columns, unable to get past the mob of panicked people, as she searched for her daughter.

Silka watched him on the monitor. Phantom holstered his gun and in a split second swooshed the baby girl up in his arms. He ran past the square columns, grabbed the mother and broke into the big, wooden structure behind it. There he hid the little girl and her mother behind the counters, out of the line of fire. Silka's legs went weak from the tenderness and pride she felt.

Bulldog decided to lend assistance to the Special Forces guys that were pinned upstairs in between bad guys shooting at them from every angle including the bottom level. The glass arched windows were shattered and left little cover. Some of the men were badly injured. He sneaked his way from the tracks behind the terrorists. The terrorists had huddled behind the steel arches by the platforms and were shooting willy-nilly at the good guys. Bulldog took them out one by one on his way to the forces.

Phantom did a perimeter check and saw that the Russians and the terrorists were shooting at each other and the good guys on both levels. The train station had become a free-for-all. Most of the civilians had run out, but some had ducked for cover and stayed put, waiting for rescue. Phantom took off his oversized shirt to expose a short-sleeved tight-fitting V-neck and bulletproof vest. He cocked his weapon and took out his trusty steed of a blade. *Battle!!!*

Eagle Eye and Flash took their positions behind their van. They slowly crawled through the parked cars to the noises of the walkie-talkies. Eagle Eye waited behind a car when he heard a guy coming. He pulled the guys legs from under him, so that he fell on his face. He immediately straddled him with his hand over his mouth. Flash came over and searched the guy. He was Russian Bratva, as his tattoo suggested. Flash slit his throat to prevent him for alerting the others.

One by one, Phantom shot Russians and terrorists and when he got close enough he took out the enemy with his knife. He came across some injured good guys along the way and helped them to safety.

Silka watched awe-struck as her Hero moved in between them with the grace and poise of a veteran, but as sleek and fast as a bullet. The shops, stands and offices gave him plenty of cover and perfect locations to snipe away at the bad guys, while rescuing good guys and civilians.

A few more good men had joined Phantom. They helped him get people out of the line of fire and when it was cleared of civilians and injured people, they went for the kill. They took down the bad guys in the waiting area and quickly arrested the ones left alive. Phantom helped a few who had gotten shot in the process to safety too. The other guys made the captives lie face down in a military-style parade. Phantom left them there to babysit.

Eagle Eye and Flash took out the Russian mob guys left, right and centre. They had obviously been stationed outside as security for when the Bratva brotherhood had gotten Brett's diamonds. Their jobs were to surround the front of the building and take out the terrorists, if any lived. Flash and Eagle Eye made quick work to change their job descriptions to coffin-fillers.

Bulldog reached the Special Forces guys and Russian cops that took cover in between some shops. He took out his small medical kit and helped the injured where he could. Some guys had died by that time. Together, they moved in on the rest of the bad guys in front of them at the far side of the hall by a large statue. Slowly they made their way, ducking bullets in between shops and steel. Injured guys were dragged to nearby nooks for protection. They had managed to kill the majority of the guys that were firing at them from behind the walls. They were screaming commands at each other in Russian.

By the time they surrounded the guys, Eagle Eye, Flash and Phantom joined them upstairs. Bratva men realized they had been outclassed very soon after that. The guys that did not surrender and attempted to fire back were killed instantly. Thankfully, the majority were arrested.

The top and bottom levels were silent. The bad guys were either in body bags or in bracelets.

Alpha team and the other teams swept the rest of the station for more bad guys. There were a few cronies still alive in little nooks and crannies. They gave their best shots, literally. It wasn't good enough when it came to coming up against the highly trained forces and cops. They were on them like bees in a hive and arrested the scum of the earth.

They eventually found Mobster, stowed away in a toilet cubicle. He pulled his gun on Phantom, who quickly moved out the way. He put up a hard fight and fired his gun in every direction. In the end, he ran out of options and bullets, when every team outnumbered him. He was also arrested.

Chapter 33

---SILKA---

It had been the longest four hours of Silka's life. Silka sighed with relief as bad guys after bad guys were lead out of the station in cuffs. Emergency services and even the Fire department assisted in helping civilians and injured people outside. The light show from all the official cars illuminated the train station and what was left of its beautiful stained glass windows. In a way, it actually looked pretty cool. Silka thought it might be a good theme for a rave, now that she was such a fan and all.

Phantom, Bulldog, Eagle Eye and Flash went to retrieve Brett. As soon as they handed him over to the authorities, they too left. They went to their hotel rooms for a shower and some sleep.

Silka went to Geo's room and sat on the couch. She left Joshua to sort out the details. She tried to sleep but couldn't.

Joshua had ensured that all the bad guys had been taken to their specially prepared facilities and gave his last orders. He went to Geo's spare room and soon fell asleep.

Ram-brandt had finally crashed and burned on Geo's couch.

It was early morning and the sun had just risen. The night had been quiet and peaceful and yet she still battled to sleep.

She was too worried about Taber's injury. A noise startled her. Taber was in Geo's room watching her.

"How did you get here?" she whispered, so the others would not wake up. She stood up.

---*T*aber---

"Through the front door," he joked. Seeing the look on her face, he explained that he had taken a taxi. There was no way he was going on a train after spending the whole night in a train station. He moved closer to her.

"Are you okay?" She pointed to his neck and went to stand in front of him.

"It's not as bad as it looks. I missed you," he said sweetly, to change the subject.

"Missed you too," she whispered.

Their hands gently touched and they shyly looked into each other's eyes, with huge smiles on their faces for no apparent reason.

Taber leaned forward and kissed her softly. She leaned into him and wrapped her arms around his neck. In their kiss, the relief that the hard part was almost over, deepened.

356

"Wakey, Wa…" Josh stopped as he interrupted their kiss. Silka and Taber stopped kissing and smiled at him.

"Well! Welcome stranger," he greeted Taber warmly.

"Good to see you, my man," Taber said, shaking his hand. "Why are you up so early," he asked. Things had gone well. Too well. It had almost been too easy to catch the bad guys and he expected the bomb to drop at any moment.

"No reason." The smile on Joshua's face turned, as if he was hiding something. "Just thought you'd want to know we got Ferdy." He glowed with pride as if he had just been told he'd fathered a son.

"How the hell did that happen?" Silka asked shocked.

"Blane," Taber said softly and smiled.

"What blame?" she demanded. Taber told her about everything that had happened after she had got shot but had omitted that little nugget.

"I had a friend called Blane track Ferdy. I wasn't sure how things were going to unfold, so I thought it best to keep it on the down low," he said, pronouncing his friend's name properly as he explained.

"So?" she asked, looking at the two men. "What happened?" Her senior citizen moment was still not over.

"After Taber and the teams took down Brett and the other goons, I sent in a lot of teams from Ops and Seals to extract Ferdy and the terrorists," Joshua said, filling in the blanks. "Some heavy fighting took place and it wasn't easy, but their defences eventually caved enough for the

Dream Team to get a foot in the door. They took some heavy fire and casualties, but in the end managed to pull the extraction off. The main team got Ferdy first and then went back for whoever was left. All the other teams provided cover fire and steered the fighting away from them while killing and arresting the small army when they could. It wasn't easy, but the mission impossible theme song wasn't playing at the time," he cracked a joke.

"Did we get some of the big boys?" Taber asked.

"Only the most important ones!" Joshua gloated. "And we got the majority of Basel Hakims, who seemed to be attending a 'shoot first, send flowers later' Expo. Something big was going down," he finished.

"Big?" Taber was intrigued.

"Yeah, we don't know... yet, but whatever it was, as far as we can tell, we stopped it," he said, looking pleased.

"What did Ferdy and the captives have to say?" Silka asked.

"Not even Oprah could get those men to open up!" Joshua shook his head.

"What's going to happen now?" Silka loaded another question.

"International Tribunal," Joshua summed it up. "Silka, you will need to give a statement and testify."

"Of course! When?" Taber needed to know how long this nightmare was still going to go on for.

"You can give a statement today and go back home until the charges have been filed and the court case starts." Joshua was a mind reader.

"Thank you, Josh," she smiled and kissed him.

"Now if you'll excuse me, I need to get to the prisoners. I will see you kids later," Josh said and left them alone.

"Now, where were we?" Taber asked seductively.

"I have the memory of an elephant," she assured him and kissed him hard.

Later that day, they went with Joshua to the local police station where Silka gave her statement to the Head of the CIA. Afterwards, they stood together to say goodbye.

"Take care of her, or else!" Josh gave Taber a playful glare and Taber nodded his head.

"Goodbye, Josh," Silka smiled and kissed him on the cheeks.

Taber and Josh shook hands and gave each other a manly hug.

"Stay in touch," Taber said to Josh, as he took Silka's hand and walked her out the front doors of the police station.

Epilogue

It was finally over. At least that was what she thought. They had slept almost the entire way home, in between becoming honorary members of the mile high club. When they arrived back home two days later, they were truly and thoroughly rested.

The next day, they spent a glorious time driving through the countryside and visiting picturesque little towns. That cold winter's evening, Taber ran them a bath with candles, bath salts, romantic music and wine. They sat talking, as the music played in the background, until the bubbles were gone and the water was cold. They got out of the bath and dried themselves. While she was applying her favorite Isabel Garcia facial products, he set up a romantic atmosphere for them.

Rather than getting dressed, they lay naked in front of the fireplace on a thick, soft, furry blanket. The wood was crackling and the flames danced in tune with the soft music. They had almost finished the bottle of wine. Silka was lying on her tummy and Taber on his back. They talked and joked and laughed for a while longer.

Taber suddenly leaned on his side to face Silka.

"I'm going to ask your father's permission to marry you tomorrow," he said out of the blue.

Silka was too blown away with his sudden decision to respond. She looked into his beautiful, smiling face.

"What makes you think I'll say yes?" she teased.

"Because I'm going to make love to you, repeatedly, over and over again, until you say it to me... starting right now." His slow, sexy threat made her heart boil over from love and lust.

"We'll see about that," she threatened idly.

Their relief that this ordeal was behind them was expressed in their gaze and the smile they gave each other. They were together, happy and content. They had made it through some very trying times. He leaned in to kiss her.

They rested beside each other for a while and waited for their souls that they'd lost somewhere between heaven and earth, to return.

Taber held her as she lay on her side and wrapped her arm and leg over him.

"How's that yes coming along?" Taber asked inquisitively.

She'd screamed many things but not yes. "Seems you have lost your mojo, Mister," she joked, as she turned to him and smiled.

"I'll have to do something about that." He smiled and took her again and again.

He planned to formally propose exactly the way he'd arranged with his event coordinator, Jocelyn. They were destined to be together, with a Capital D.

Two days later, however, his plans were put on hold. But that is another adventure! Another Obstacle with a Capital O!

---THE END---

Author's note

Thank you for reading the first book of the Capital quartet, Capital D. I thoroughly enjoyed the time I spent writing it. It gave me more than I had bargained for. If you would like to follow the rest of Taber and Silka's exciting and passionate life, keep an eye open for the following books:

Book two –   Capital O

Book three – Capital N

Book four – Capital E

Acknowledgements

I would sincerely like to thank the following people for their contribution to my success. Without you this book would not have been possible.

* Substantive Editing – Lisabetta @AllArt Publishing International
* Final Draft Proof Reading – Stephanie Bailey Minton
* Copy Editing, Line Editing & Multiple Proof Reading- Simon Okill (Best Selling Author of the Luna and Phantom Bigfoot series)
* Special thanks to the following Beta Readers or as I call them…Life savers!! Your assistance and support have kept me sane and alive.

- Mette Koustrup (Denmark)
- Jacque Brandt (Florida - USA)
- Simon Okill (South Wales)
- Raquel Rose Young (New Orleans - USA)
- Iain Johnstone (South Africa)

* Cover Art & Website design – Kyle Schrade @ EZ Designs
* A heartfelt thanks and eternal gratitude to Raquel Young Rose for helping with my promotions.
* And last, but not least, my fans who really are like my family! I live each day in awe of my Stoneys and humbly thank you for your time.

About the Author

When Ash Stone (pen name) was born she was a tiny, bouncy, beautiful little baby...and the color blue! Fortunately by the time the journalists arrived to take photos of her, she was no longer blue. She made headlines in the local papers for being the only Christmas baby to be born that day in Aliwal North (South Africa). So started a life of "Merry Christmas...And oh! Happy Birthday too." Before you say, "Aw Shame" and break out the tissues, please know that Ash is a Christmas Diva! She always gets her two presents ...or else!

She is the second eldest of four daughters to a mother who was an accountant. Her father was a high ranking police officer, meaning he sat behind a desk and drank tea all day. They moved around a lot whenever her father was promoted to a bigger desk with better tea. As a result Ash did not have many friends and found her escape in books.

Ash's first writing experience was at the age of 16, when she had to write an essay to Toyota South Africa, in order to be chosen for their Toyota Edulink Program. She wrote a very detailed and motivational essay about how she was going to be the Managing Director of Toyota one day. After they undoubtedly had a good chuckle, Ash was chosen as the only girl to represent all the Afrikaans schools in her province. She went on to be chosen for the Toyota Junior Achievement Programme and became the Managing Director of the company they had set up. The company made a profit and naturally Ash was tickled pink! Ash was chosen to remain in the Toyota Edulink Program for a total of three years. Whilst in her final year at school she also joined another program and studied Journalism and Drama at the Westville University.

After graduating high school at the age of 17, Ash went to study Business and Marketing Management. She was inspired by her father who had left the police force long ago and started his own private company. Being a typical rebel, rather than joining the cut-throat corporate world afterwards, Ash became a vegetarian hippie instead and went into a gardening/ nursery business with her mom. The irony of a vegetarian "plant lover" is still lost on her to this day.

Even though Ash never became the Managing Director of Toyota South Africa, she had enjoyed success in every aspect of her life. She is an award winning Landscape Architect and Horticulturist and won another award for a display when she represented South Africa in the 2000 Amsterdam Hortifair.

Among her many occupations, Ash was more notably the Purchasing Manager for McDonald's Asia, Pacific, Middle East and Africa region. These days she is not a high flying corporate Exec or a vegetarian hippie, but internal sales at a local Mining supplier during the day. At night, she runs her own blog tour company, is an Administator of the Author Association ASMSG, a Guild Reviewer, a book blogger and self confessed Facebook addict.

She lives in Alberton with her childhood-friend-turned-husband and their two gorgeous sons where she enjoys breaking all the rules with her writing. The eternal rebel loves to connect with her fans (or "Stoneys!" as she calls them). So, go on you rebel you!

Twitter: https://twitter.com/newage_author
Blog: http://authorashstone.blogspot.com
My fan page: https://facebook.com/ash-stone101
Rebelmouse: http://www.rebelmouse.com/ashstone
Facebook page: http://www.facebook.com/authorashstone
You Tube Channel Playlist:
https://www.youtube.com/playlist?list=PLtXqSF_cAvnIewyyQAQq12f yBOMC5ed84

www.ingramcontent.com/pod-product-compliance
Lightning Source LLC
Chambersburg PA
CBHW061312170626
46817CB00001B/150

* 9 7 8 0 9 9 2 2 0 7 6 1 8 *